BOOKS B

MW00939924

THAT MAN:
The Wedding Story

THAT
MAN

THE WEDDING STORY

NELLE L'AMOUR

To join my mailing list for new releases, sales, and giveaways, please sign up here:
NEWSLETTER: nellelamour.com/newsletter

NICHOLS CANYON PRESS
Los Angeles, CA USA

THAT MAN WEDDING

Cover by Arijana Karčic, Cover It! Designs
Proofreading by Karen Lawson and Gloria Herrera
Formatting by BB eBooks

THAT

MAN

4

NELLE L'AMOUR

PRAISE FOR THAT MAN 4

"Nelle L'Amour has hit her stride with humorous erotica in the vein of Christina Lauren and Emma Chase. Blake Burns is one of my favorite book boyfriends of 2014."

—*Adriane Leigh, USA Today Bestselling Author of the Wild Series*

"Not only is Blakemeister back, but he's on fire!! ... I cannot believe how even more beyond uniquely quirky, smooth, and honestly in a class of its own L'Amour's writing style is."

—*A is For Alpha, B is for Books Blog*

"THAT MAN, so romantic, so sexy, so passionate...I think I'm addicted to him."

—*Rusty's Reading Room*

"Zinging one-liners, alpha male hotness, steamy scenes and devious bitches!"

—*Fairest of All Reviews*

"Nelle L'Amour's writing is the perfect mixture of sexy dialogue, relatable characters, and laugh out-loud moments. Get ready to fall in love with THAT MAN all over again."

—*Vanessa Booke, Bestselling Author of the Bound to You series*

"Holy Hell! The amazing sex Jen and Blake have is out of this world HOT!...This is one story that will blow your mind."

—*Whispered Thoughts Book Blog*

"Nelle gives you a story worth talking about...A true test of what love can overcome...When you get to the end...you will want more."

—*Love Between the Sheets*

"This installment of the series is just as well written as the first...Laugh out moments and more emotional."

—*My Book Filled Life*

"Nelle L'Amour has a unique writing style...she can make you laugh and cry at the same time describing the ins and outs of the wedding from Hell."

—*As You Like It Reviews*

"Nelle does a great job of mixing comedy, steam, and drama."

—*Book Boyfriend Reviews*

"The THAT MAN series keeps getting better and better, funnier and sexier. Bravo, Nelle! No wonder this series is a runaway success!"

—*Arianne Richmonde, USA Today Bestselling Author of The Pearl trilogy*

**To join my mailing list for new releases, sales, and giveaways, please
sign up here:**
NEWSLETTER: nellelamour.com/newsletter

NICHOLS CANYON PRESS
Los Angeles, CA USA

THAT MAN 4

Cover by Arijana Karčic, Cover It! Designs
Proofreading by Karen Lawson and Gloria Herrera
Formatting by BB eBooks

*To all my Belles who asked for more of
Blake and his tiger.*

This is for you.

Prologue
Jennifer

Paris~Five months earlier

"That *eez* a wrap," shouted our wonderful French director, gurgling the "r" in "wrap" the way I now knew only the French did.

We had just finished production on the first telenovela I'd overseen for MY SIN-TV, the block of programming I'd developed around popular erotic romance novels. *Shades of Pearl,* based on Arianne Richmonde's bestselling series.

The international cast and crew broke out in cheers. Among them were the lovely and beautiful Cameron Diaz, who had played the title character—her first television role ever—and her breathtakingly handsome co-star, Gaspard Ulliel, the French heartthrob, who played her much younger lover, Alexandre. Whoo-hoos mingled with hugs and out of nowhere, bottles of bubbly champagne popped.

I'd invited the author to the final days of shooting. A stunning, statuesque blonde, who looked like she could have easily played the part of forty-year-old Pearl, she was ecstatic. She enthusiastically gave me one of those double-cheek kisses.

"Oh, Jennifer! It's brilliant. Do you think we can win an

Emmy?" she asked in her British accent.

An Emmy? To be honest, I'd never thought about that. All I'd thought about was making the best possible show for my audience. I wanted our viewers to love every sinfully sexy and suspenseful minute of it.

I shrugged my shoulders. "I don't know," I replied, but the fantasy of winning one danced in my head.

With a flute of champagne in her hand, the long-limbed Arianne sauntered off to mingle with the cast and crew. Suddenly, I felt very alone. I missed *that* man I loved terribly—Blake Burns, the head of SIN-TV and my fiancé—and wished I could share this triumphant moment with him. Reaching into my purse, I pulled out my cell phone and speed-dialed his number. It was 4:00 p.m. The time difference between Paris and Los Angeles was nine hours. That meant it was seven o'clock in the morning in LA. Knowing his routine well, he should still be at home.

To my utter disappointment, the call went straight to his voice mail. I left him a message, telling him how well the final shoot went. And for him to call me. My final words: "Oh, Blake, I miss you so much. I can't wait to see you." I was flying home tomorrow.

The cast and crew began to dissipate from the set. Later tonight, there was going to be a big wrap party. To celebrate the completion of production, Conquest Broadcasting, SIN-TV's parent company, had chartered several Bateaux Mouches to cruise around Paris and party. I'd looked forward to the event, but now, missing Blake so much, it just wasn't as exciting.

A chauffeur-driven Peugeot sedan took me back to my hotel. While the stars and director were staying at the Hotel George V where we'd shot some scenes, I was staying at the newly renovated Ritz. It was like out of a fairy tale with its sumptuous décor and impeccable service. I'd never stayed in such luxurious accommodations before. They were so beyond. But what made the hotel even more special for me was this is where Ernest Hemingway, one of my dad's literary heroes, had written his early books. To his delight, I'd e-mailed him a photo of me in The Hemingway Bar and photoshopped the legendary author into the picture.

Wearily, I inserted my key card into the door of my tenth floor suite. Blake had insisted on getting a suite for me, and though I'd protested, trying to save the company money, there was nothing I could do. Being engaged to the head of SIN-TV and the future chairman of Conquest Broadcasting, came with its perks. Most of which I didn't need.

Dropping my shoulder bag on the gilded entryway console, I traipsed to my spacious bedroom with its regal canopy bed and breathtaking view of Paris. My eyes grew wide. Smack in the middle of the thick, fluffy duvet were two exquisitely wrapped boxes...one small, the other large. I recognized the wrapping of the small box immediately. With its signature hot pink heart, it was, of course, from Gloria's Secret. Gloria Zander, the CEO of the renowned lingerie emporium, was sponsoring my block, and she had a popular store right here in Paris on the nearby Champs-Elysées. Though eager to open the big mysterious package, I reached for the smaller one and peeled open the envelope inserted under the bow. A note with handwriting I didn't recognize met my gaze.

Congratulations on your first production! Wear these tonight.

The gift must be from Gloria. How thoughtful of her! With eager fingers, I tore off the wrapping and lifted off the lid.

My breath hitched. Inside beneath layers of delicate pink tissue paper was a magnificent set of pearl white lace lingerie: a demi-cup bra, matching bikini, and a garter. Plus a pair of lace-trimmed sheer silk stockings labeled: Made in France. Little bows embellished with pearls accented the lingerie in all the right places. The undergarments were exquisite enough to wear on my wedding day. I glanced down at the big snowflake diamond ring on my left hand, always awed by its sparkle and size and the memory of that magical night when Blake had proposed to me only a month ago. To my overjoyed mother's chagrin, Blake and I had not yet set a date. We had too much on our plates when it came to work.

Spreading the beautiful lingerie on the bed, I reached for the big package. My fingers anxiously unwrapped it. Inside the tissue-lined box was another envelope. I carefully slit it open with my index finger. Another note with the same unrecognizable handwriting. *And wear these too.* It must be another gift from the generous Gloria, I surmised as I unfolded the delicate paper.

With a gasp, I removed the contents from the large box. First, the strappy silver Jimmy Choos. And then the elegant ivory chiffon dress by my favorite designer and dear friend,

Chaz Clearfield, from his new couture line, which Gloria had helped launch. It had a pearl-encrusted neckline, nipped waist, and full skirt. My size—a four. I'd never owned or worn a dress as stunning as this. Very grown up, it belonged on a movie star. Someone like Cameron Diaz. Or an elegant goddess like Gloria. Not a petite, middle-class, Idaho girl like me.

I padded over to the imposing armoire and stood in front of the mirrored doors, holding the dress up against me. Wow! I was going to look dazzling in it. And then my heart sunk a notch. If only Blake could be here to see me in it.

What a perfect night to cruise along the Seine. The mid May air was mild and the evening sky couldn't be clearer. Chartered buses had taken the *Pearl* cast and crew to the Pont D'Alma along the Rive Gauche from where the glass-enclosed boats were departing. Everyone was decked out to the nines for an evening of sightseeing, fine dining, and pure fun. Numerous partygoers, including Cameron and the very flirtatious Gaspard, came up to congratulate me on the production and commented on how *magnifique* I looked. I was both flattered and humbled. Paparazzi and publicists were snapping pictures at lightning speed. I smiled for the camera. But to be honest, while being Blake's fiancée and my career had launched me into this glitzy, star-studded world, I still wasn't used to so much attention and glamour.

On the quay, everyone was handed tickets, indicating which boat they would be on. I glanced down at mine. Number six...the last one. Carefully, in my new heels, I boarded the vessel and made my way to the upper deck. I leaned against the railing and took in the magical City of Light. The Seine quietly lapped against the side of the boat while my new dress billowed like a sail in the warm Spring breeze. The majestic Grand Palais faced me. All lit up, it resembled a giant jewelry box.

The rumble of motors of the other boats ahead of mine roared in my ears. They were taking off. I guess we were still waiting for more passengers to board this one because I was the sole person on it. Maybe there was another bus of people on the way?

Ten minutes passed. And still not another passenger. The other boats were now well on their way, and they began to fade in the distance. My heart began to race. Shit. Maybe, there was some kind of mistake, and I'd boarded the wrong boat.

"You look beautiful in that dress. Are you also wearing the lingerie I sent you?"

At the sound of that familiar sultry voice, my heart almost leapt into the Seine. I felt my insides melt. And my center grew as wet as the river itself.

I spun around. There he was. Leaning against the banister to the lower deck. *That man.* Who loved me body and soul. And mind. *That* devastating man. Blake Burns.

My mouth dropped. Speechless, I now understood why I hadn't been able to reach him earlier. He'd been flying. Flying to see *me.* And now, every part of me was flying because he was here.

Dressed in one of his impeccably tailored dark suits, he loped up to me. His long-legged gait was as sexy as his smoldering gaze. I sprinted up to him and met him halfway.

"Oh my God, Blake." My heart pounding, I flung my arms around him. "I can't believe—"

He tugged my head back by my ponytail, and then his mouth captured mine, cutting off my word supply. The tongue-driven kiss was fierce, passionate, and oh so delicious. With his hard body and colossal cock pressed against me, the boat began to move.

"Blake, where are we going?" I spluttered, finally breaking the kiss.

"The rest of the cast and crew are going on a tour of Paris. But you, my tiger, are going on a trip to the moon and stars and back."

"Oh," I squeaked.

He tweaked my nipples between his thumb and index fingers. I could feel them harden as he smiled smugly. Heat blossomed between my legs and then his hands slid down my hips.

He hiked up the skirt of my dress and shoved my soaked lace panties aside.

His fingers quickly found something delicate and responsive. My clit.

They circled it. Hard, just the way I loved it. Moaning, I rocked into him as his deft fingers picked up speed.

"Je vais baiser votre cerveau," he whispered in my ear, his accent perfect.

"Parlez-vous français?" I murmured back as a mind-blowing orgasm took hold of me.

"No, I talk dirty."

Blake

If you think I was going to let my little tiger party with that horny French frog, you sure as fuck don't know me by now. *Gaspard-Bastard.* When I'd awoken this morning at the crack of dawn, I'd hopped into the shower, thrown together an overnight case of bare necessities, and driven myself in my trusty high-speed Porsche to LAX. Jennifer had been in France overseeing her first production for over two weeks, and I missed her like crazy. And it wasn't just her tight little pussy I missed that my calloused fingers could attest to. I missed everything about her. Waking up to her in my arms. The taste of her kiss on my lips. Sharing showers. Her adorable giggle. And even the way she knew how to put me in my place. (Jeez. Another pun unintended?) Yes, my cock had a hearty appetite, but she'd shown me my heart hungered too.

Throughout the long eleven-hour flight, my cock had strained against my jeans while my heart beat like a jackhammer. I'd kept the tray table down the whole time except for the departure and landing. I couldn't wait to surprise her and see the expression on her pretty face. And then rid her of the lacy lingerie and that new dress, which I'd sent her with the conspiratorial help of Gloria Zander and her designer pal, Chaz. I was about to line up the three cherries...the right idea, the right person and, with no hitches, the right time. A big win was in store.

Timing, I'd learned, was everything. Without it, everything could fall apart. Even the best laid plans—or plans to get laid.

Luck had it the flight arrived early, and I was able to get to the Bateau Mouche with ease. Little did my tiger know, I'd chartered it out of my own pocket for my own personal use. It was going nowhere until I was on board. And neither was she.

I fucking wish I'd taken a photo of her face when she set eyes on me. Her emerald orbs lit up like two stars in the sky, and her mouth dropped to the deck in a perfect O. An O big enough to accommodate my big ole cock. Damn, she looked hot in that dress. Magically, the river breeze blew the skirt up above her thighs, exposing her frilly garter and stockings and the scrap of lace panties I'd asked her to wear. My rigid dick was itching to get inside them. But first things first. I needed her in my arms. And my mouth needed to consume hers. It felt like years. She melted into me like chocolate, and as my tongue danced with hers, I scrunched up her silky dress. My hand landed between her thighs. Expertly, I maneuvered my fingers under her little lacy panties and found my hidden treasure.

"Oh baby, you're so fucking hot and wet," I moaned into her mouth as I rubbed her nub.

Picking up my pace, I had her panting against me. So ready to come. "Oh God, Blake," she cried out and then she let go.

I felt her shudder around my fingers while she clung to my shoulders so she wouldn't fall down.

My cock was on fire. With my mouth locked back on hers, I walked her backward until she was leaning against the railing. Her harsh breathing mixed with the sound of the soft waves brushing against the boat. I hiked up her dress once more and cupped her sweet ass. And then in one swift move, I tore off her drenched panties and spread her legs.

"Blake, what are you doing?" Her eyes were wide.

Monsieur Dirty Talker wasn't done with her. Do you seriously think I flew half way around the world just to flick her clit? I gnawed at her slender neck and got right to it.

"I'm going to fuck my future wife's brains out."

"But Blake, people on shore will see us."

"Don't worry about it, baby. We're never going to see them again. And when they hear you roar, believe me, they'll wish they were us."

"But, don't you think we should enjoy the cruise? And take in all the monuments?"

"Tiger, there's only one monument in Paris you need to take in and it's right here." I zipped down my fly and out popped my rod. Nine inches of pure pleasure. It deserved a five-star rating on Yelp.

I nudged it against her, and in a hot breath, it was deep inside her. Her muscles clenched around my length. I hissed. I'd almost forgotten how good her tight little pussy felt. On the next breath, I was pounding into her ruthlessly, every thrust taking her closer to the edge. I clamped my hands firmly on her waist so she wouldn't fall overboard. Fuck. That would be bad. Her moans mingled with my grunts as I pummeled her harder and faster. Her face contorted with tortured pleasure, and I kept my eyes open to enjoy the beautiful sight of her. The beauty of Notre Dame, as the boat swung around the Île de la Cité and passed by the famous landmark, paled next to that of *ma belle dame* in my face and in my arms.

"Eyes, tiger," I ordered. I wanted her to enjoy the spectacular view too. On my command, she snapped open her long-lashed lids, and I rewarded her with another all-consuming French kiss—*la pelle* or shovel as some called it in France. In the distance, I heard promenaders along the Seine cheering us on with wolf whistles and applause. *"Allez, allez! A votre santé!"* I waved to them.

"Have you missed me?" I panted out as my cock hammered into her. *Missed this?*

"Oh yes. So much."

Ahead of us, the Eiffel Tower sparkled. At the rate we were moving, it would be at least half an hour until the boat passed it, and headed back to the quay. My own lit up tower of steel wasn't going to last much longer.

"Come with me, baby." An intense tingling sensation surged from my sac to the tip of my shaft. I swear my cock was going to jump out of its skin.

She emitted a ferocious roar you could hear in LA, and then I cried out her name as my own powerful orgasm met her blissful wake.

"Oh, Blake," she murmured, her voice a breathy whisper.

Spent, I nuzzled her neck. "Are you happy I came?" Man, what was with me and these double entendres?

She sunk her head against my chest. "So happy."

With my arms wrapped around her, we stayed in this rest-ing position for several long minutes as we aptly neared the Arc de Triomphe. So maybe we'd missed some of the sites along the Seine, but it didn't matter. I tenderly kissed her silky flesh everywhere I could.

Piano music drifted into the night air. Cole Porter. "I Love Paris."

"...in the springtime," I sang softly against her ear. I'd arranged for a romantic champagne-filled dinner for the two of us on the dining deck below—complete with a pianist and songstress. They were going to perform songs from the play list of *Pearl* to which we'd slow dance. And later fuck some more—I was saving her sweet pussy for dessert.

She sighed dreamily, never lifting her head from my heart.

Yes, I loved Paris in the springtime. There was only one thing I loved more—Paris in the springtime with my tiger. My future wife. I held her tight.

"Oh, Blake, I could make love to you all night."

That was the plan.

Chapter 1
Jennifer

"Happy birthday, tiger."

Groggily, I peeled one eye open after the other. Blake had insisted I take the afternoon off to spend time with my parents. After a whirlwind tour of Hollywood, we were all tired, and I headed home after dropping them off at The Beverly Hills Hotel where they were staying, courtesy of Blake's family. Late afternoon sunlight was streaming into the bedroom where I'd taken a much-needed nap. Through my hazy vision, I could see Blake heading my way. He must have gotten home while I was sleeping. Bare-chested, he was wearing sweats, and his hands were behind his back. I could stare at that glorious chiseled chest all day.

I forced myself to sit up. "Blake, my birthday's not till Monday."

He smiled that cocky smile I loved so much. "Yeah, I know, but I wanted to give you something before our dinner tonight with our parents."

Mom and Dad had flown in for my twenty-fourth birthday. They'd been here since Monday and we'd had a great time. It was their first trip to Los Angeles since I'd started working for Conquest Broadcasting in their adult entertainment division,

SIN-TV. One of the highlights of their trip was coming to my office. My mother, God bless her, kept saying "very lovely" though I knew she was having a mini-coronary each time she passed by a full-frontal nudity poster of one of our pure-porn prime time shows. She was relieved to see that my new executive office was tastefully furnished. Both my parents admired *The Kiss,* the sensuous erotic painting on the wall, and I told them it was a gift from Blake. Having to work, I sent them on a tour of the studio and made sure they got to see some tapings of shows as well as meet a few stars. My mother was in heaven when her idol Denzel Washington gave her an auto-graphed headshot.

Unfortunately for them, they couldn't be here on Monday, the actual day of my birthday, because Dad had to go back to Boise. Though now retired from academic life, the university was making him a Professor Emeritus on the same day. It was a noble achievement and I, like my mom, was so proud of him. Unfortunately for me, my crazy work schedule with a dozen erotic romance telenovelas at various stages of production made it impossible for me to fly back home to share his special day. I was thrilled, however, that they'd decided to come to California to spend some time with me. Tonight, for the first time, they would be going to Blake's parents' house. His mother had insisted on having them over for their weekly Shabbat dinner. I was sure by the time it was over they'd both know a little Yiddish—well, at least, one word. *Shmekel*—that and *shtupping*—thanks to Blake's oversexed eighty-six-year-old grandma. I was sure this dinner was going to be the other highlight of their trip—for better and for worse.

Catapulting me out my mental ramblings, Blake sat down

on the edge of the bed we now shared and handed me a small box. It was shiny red with a small white stick-on bow. "This is for you, tiger. Open it."

My heartbeat sped up. Blake loved buying me presents, and they were always so creative and thoughtful. And sometimes a little naughty. Carefully, I lifted off the lid. Inside was another small box—this one velvet. Removing it, I snapped it open and gasped.

"Oh my God, Blake, they're exquisite," I exclaimed, unable to contain my excitement or tears of joy. Glittering before my eyes was a pair of magnificent earrings—two dangling pink tourmaline hearts, each set with diamonds. They matched the pink tourmaline necklace he'd given me last Christmas. Tourmaline was my birthstone.

Grinning cheek to cheek, Blake planted a kiss on my forehead. "Put them on tiger, and I want you to wear them tonight."

"Oh, Blake!" I gushed, smacking his lips with mine. "I love you so much."

"The same." He watched as I inserted the pierced earrings into my earlobes.

"How do you do that?"

I laughed lightly and then rubbed the dangling earrings between my fingers. "I want to see what they look like on me in a mirror." I made my first attempt to get out of bed, but Blake held me back by the matching necklace I rarely took off.

He smiled at me wickedly. "Not until I give you your other present."

I glanced down and instantly had an idea.

Chapter 2

Blake

Yup, I did have another present for my tiger. But let me tell you, it was hard hiding this one. No pun intended. The tent between my thighs was sizeable, and it was expanding by the second.

The gist of my present was not lost on Jen. She gazed down at my crotch and her brows lifted.

"Oh, and what might that be?" she asked wryly as if she didn't know.

I shoved down my sweats. "This one." Before her stood my big cock, gift wrapped in a big red bow. I suppressed a moan. It was fucking killing me because I'd tied the stupid bow on earlier—just tight enough so it wouldn't fall off—and now my pecker had practically doubled in size. What the fuck had I been thinking? The bow was cutting off my circulation and giving me numb nuts.

Jennifer burst into laughter. She was laughing so hard she was crying. I swear if she didn't take this fucking bow off soon, my dick was going to fall off and I'd be crying tears too.

"Blake, that's the funniest thing I've ever seen," she managed. She was practically howling. "It's like you're God's gift to women."

"Take the fucking bow off," I growled.

Still roaring with laughter, she scooted off the bed so she was standing before me. With her nimble fingers, she undid the bow and tossed it on the duvet. I huffed a sigh of relief. Woof. That felt better. My cock recovered quickly and was ready for action.

"Jen, babe, do you think you could show *Mr. Burns* a little love?" Jen didn't know I reverently called my cock by a proper name (my little secret—that and the fact I also talked to my cock), but she got the idea. My eyes stayed on her as she bent over and kissed the wide crown. I pressed firmly on her head, coaxing her to go down on me. I hissed as that warm wet mouth of hers slid down my shaft, her tongue sliding along the backside. So fucking good. After taking me to the hilt, she came back up, adding welcomed pressure. She knew how I liked it.

That's all I needed, though truthfully, I could never get enough head from her. I was sufficiently lubricated for the next part of this gift. Before she could go down on me again, I gripped her ponytail and yanked up her head. She let out a little yelp that made my cock flex.

"Are you ready for part two of this gift?"

She eyed me suspiciously. "And that would be—"

"The fun part. You get to ride me."

Jen's face lit up like a little kid about to go on one of those coin-operated mechanical horsey rides. Wasting no time, she tore off my boxers she had on and repositioned herself, straddling my lap, knees bent on the bed, with my cock impaled inside her. Gripping her hips, I bucked her hard as she rode me up and down. I hissed. Fuck, yeah! This was good. So fucking good for both of us. Holding on to my shoulders, she got to control the pace while I got to go as deep and as hard as I could. I repeatedly hit her G-spot with each powerful thrust. She shrieked with pleasure again and again.

I gazed at her heated face. Her head tilted back, she looked so impassioned, and I was mesmerized by the way the dangling earrings I'd just given her shook and shimmered. Quivering as if they were having little orgasms of their own. I was tempted to nibble her lobes but worried in my state of lust I might bite off an earring and swallow it whole.

I gripped her hips tighter as she accelerated her pace. The friction and heat of her rubbing against my thick length felt so fucking amazing.

"Do you like your present?"

"Oh God, yes!" she panted out. "I'm so close to coming!"

"Good, baby," I groaned.

On the next deep thrust, she fell apart with a thunderous "yes" and I could feel her throbbing all around my pulsing cock. Her body shook as I grunted out my own explosive climax and met hers full on. Spent and sweaty, we collapsed onto each other, her arms wrapping around me. We stayed in that position for several sweet minutes as we rode our orgasms out.

Five minutes later, we were nestled side by side, her head resting on my chest. We had almost recovered. Now close to five, the sun had begun its disappearing act and cast a mellow amber glow.

Jen traced lazy, ticklish circles on my chest. "Baby, I'll never be able to top that birthday present."

I playfully flicked the tip of her cute upturned nose. "Don't worry, you will."

"Do you have something in mind?"

"Yeah, I do." I was turning the big three-O.

"How 'bout a hint?"

"I want to wake up to my wife."

I felt her jolt against me. "What are you saying, Blake?"

"What I'm saying is I want to marry you on the day before my birthday."

"December twentieth? Gosh, Blake. That's only two months away."

"Jen, we've been engaged for almost six months; it's time to set a date. My mother has been driving me crazy."

Jen giggled. "Mine too. I keep telling her we've just been too busy at work."

Which was true. Except I'd checked our calendars and had come to the conclusion that Saturday, the twentieth would be a perfect time to get married. With Christmas around the corner, most of our SIN-TV productions would be shut down, and our offices would be closed until January third—giving us an opportunity to go on a two-week honeymoon. I explained all this to Jen. She agreed. It made total sense.

She rolled on top of me and gave me a hot spontaneous kiss. "Oh my God, Blake, we're really going to get married!" The excitement in her voice was contagious. I smashed my lips against hers. "Yes, you're going to become Mrs. Blake Burns, and tonight we're going to break the news to our parents."

"My mother is going to be so excited." Jen beamed. "She's been planning our wedding forever."

I didn't know if Jen could feel my heart skip a beat. I quiet-ly gulped. And so had my mother. Instead of letting her know this, I urged her to take a shower with me and get ready for our dinner.

The future Mrs. Blake Burns had another surprise in store.

Chapter 3

Jennifer

"Oh, my good Lord, you have a health club in your house?" Dressed in a demure A-line navy dress and sensible shoes, my mother couldn't contain her astonishment. Her soft gray-blue eyes were as round as marbles. While my dad had chosen to forego the tour of the Bernstein's forty-room Beverly Hills mansion and spend time chatting with Blake and his dad, my mom had taken Blake's mother, Helen, up on her offer. I'd accompanied them.

I didn't know whether to laugh or cringe. Neither my mother nor my father had ever set foot in a house of this magnitude and grandeur. One could easily confuse it with a five-star hotel with its size, amenities, and sumptuous furnishings.

I corrected my mother. "Mom, it's their in-home gym." But the truth, it looked more like a health club, the expansive mirrored room filled with racks of weights and a myriad of state-of-the art workout equipment. There was even an adjacent sauna, massage room, and steam room.

Helen twitched a small smile. She was elegantly dressed in a peach silk sheath and designer heels along with her usual array of mega-sized diamonds. Whippet-thin, the stunning woman, with her upswept platinum hair, towered over my lovely but humble farm girl-raised mother.

"Saul and I work out here every morning with our personal trainers. You and Harold are more than welcome to join us tomorrow morning. And right afterward, our masseuse will be here."

Still in awe, my mother declined politely, letting Helen know that she and my dad would be flying back to Boise in the morning. The week had gone by so fast.

Helen glanced down at her diamond-studded watch. "Come, let's join the others for dinner. Everyone should be here by now."

The Bernsteins' weekly Shabbat dinner was about to begin. I couldn't wait to tell my parents as well as Blake's that we'd finally decided on a wedding date. Having planned for my wedding since the day I was born, my mom was going to be over the moon.

Shabbat dinner at the Bernsteins' house always had a special meaning for me. It was where I got an eyeful of Blake's super-sized cock for the first time. I'd accidentally walked into an unlocked bathroom where he was jerking off. I'd watched him come all over his hand. I was mortified, but now both Blake and I could laugh about it. The unforgettable memory, however, always made me very horny during Shabbat. And the same with Blake, though I wasn't sure if it was for the same reason. Always, in the middle of devouring Grandma's famous matzo soup, he'd reach for my hand, discreetly slip it under the table, and press it on the heated bulge between his legs. Tonight was no different. I could feel it throbbing. With my parents here, I wished for once he'd *"unbig"* himself to use the word he'd invented.

Most of the usual suspects were gathered around the elegantly set dining room table—a daz-zling spectacle of fine china, crystal, and silver. Joining Blake's parents...his feisty sex-crazed Grandma, who I adored, and his older sister, Marcy the gynecologist, who I hadn't gotten to know well. She and Blake were not particularly close. Missing, however, were her seven-year-old twin sons, who were home with strep, and Matt, her husband. Or rather ex-husband. Soon after Blake and I'd returned from France last Spring, a big family scandal had erupted. Marcy had discovered Matt, also a gyno, fucking one of their patients—a voluptuous blond starlet named Kristie who happened to be one of Blake's former hook-ups. Right in the Beverly Hills office the two of them shared. On the examining table, no less. Well, to make a long story short...Marcy got the practice, the house, and custody of the twins, and Matt got Kristie, whom he was planning on marrying. I'd wanted to reach out to Marcy—having gone through a not that dissimilar life-changing break-up with my ex-fiancé, Bradley. But the unspoken estrangement between Blake and his sister made it difficult. I did, however, admire the grace with which Marcy had handled her ex's affair. *The asshat!* And she now seemed more focused on her two children, who also seemed to be handling the break-up remarkably well. However, it did put a little damper on my happiness, and I sometimes felt bad when others in the family gloated over my engagement to Blake when her own marriage had gone down the drain.

As was customary in the Bernstein household, my mother, the female guest of honor, was asked by Blake's father to light the Shabbat candles. My darling Blake helped her do it. More memories of our first night together rushed into my head…his arms around fire-phobic me as I futilely lit one match after another. My mom got it on the first try and welcomed Shabbat into our lives. Shabbat, I had learned, was the symbolic union of man and woman, of God taking his bride. What a perfect time to announce our wedding date, though butterflies fluttered in my stomach. Setting a date made it so real. Blake and I were finally going to get married. I shot him a quick glance, soaking in his handsome profile. I could stare at him forever with that perfect outline of stubble and sexy mop of unkempt hair. He felt my eyes on him and shot back a flirtatious smile. The littlest smile could make desire pour through me like warm honey.

Over Blake's mother's delicious brisket, we made small talk, the Bernsteins mostly asking my parents about their stay in LA. Shortly, their housekeeper Rosa began to clear the table, making room for coffee and dessert.

"Oh, please let me help." My mother leapt out of her chair with her plate and my dad's along with their cutlery in her hands.

"Meg, darling," said Blake's mother coolly. "Please sit down. There's no need."

My mom shot me an awkward glance. I nodded, indicating for her to acquiesce. Rosa immediately took the plates and silverware from her, and my mother hesitantly sat down. Bewilderment flickered in her eyes.

God bless my mom. I loved her so much. She was such a

good soul. Honestly, there wasn't a mean bone in her whole body. While Helen might chair lots of charities and foundations, my mother embodied charitable giving. Or should I say, living? She gave alms to the poor, never missed making meals for the homeless on holidays, and opened her door to anyone in need of a bed. Her whole life was about the needs of others, and foremost, those of my dad and mine. Blake's father was grooming him to one day be the head of Conquest Broadcasting, and I'd have to adjust to that role. In my heart, I wanted to always be like my mom. Humble. Giving. Caring. And genuine. True to my roots. And one day, like her, I wanted to be a great mom.

Blake's grandma hurled me out of my thoughts. "So, *bubala*, *vhen* are you and my Blakela gonna get married?" Always the same question at around glass number three of wine.

I swallowed hard while Blake broke into his dazzling smile. Under the table, he squeezed my hand that was resting on his erection.

"Funny, you should ask, Grandma. Jennifer and I have exciting news."

My heart hammered. My mother's face was already lighting up. Blake continued.

"We've set a wedding date. Saturday, December twentieth."

A rapid-fire chain reaction was set off.

"*Oy!* I should only live so long!" moaned Blake's grandma, pouring glass number four. "*Zei gezunt.*"

"*Mazel tov,*" exclaimed Blake's father at the head of the table, raising his wine glass.

Blake's sister threw her arms up in the air. "Great. The same day as Matt's wedding to bubblehead. Now I have an excuse not to attend."

I didn't appreciate her mouthful of sarcasm, but she was probably hurting. Blake shot her a dirty look.

My mother, oblivious to Marcy's off-color remark, had tears in her eyes. "Oh honey, that's wonderful. I'll call Father Murphy tomorrow to reserve the parish."

Helen's eyes grew as wide as they could. She'd definitely had one too many doses of Botox. Her harrumph silenced everyone.

"Meg, darling, there's no way we can have the wedding in Idaho. Or is it Iowa? I always get those two states mixed up. Regardless, at that time of year, the weather can be atrocious. I can't have our guests flying in those risky conditions."

Shit. I hadn't even thought of the weather factor when I'd agreed to Blake's date. But Helen was right. It could be blizzarding in the Northwest. With the airports shut down. And even the West Coast weather was volatile at that time of the year.

My stunned mother didn't blink an eye while Helen continued. "And as you can imagine, we have a plethora of guests to invite."

"How many?" ventured my father, showing no emotion.

"At least a thousand. Maybe more."

A thousand?

"I see." My pensive father pressed his lips thin while my poor mother gaped in shock. She seemed to be getting smaller and smaller in her chair. There was no way my parents could accommodate or afford a wedding of that magnitude. Why hadn't I thought things through? Her lifelong dream of making me a wedding had just left the planet. The look of defeat on her face was gutting me.

Finally, she built up the courage to say something. "Well, at least, Helen, let me help you plan it. I'm very handy, right Harold?" My mother, always looking for the good in the bad, turned to my father for moral support.

Helen responded before my father could say a word. "Puhlease, Meg. Don't even think about it. With the wedding date so close, we can't afford any mistakes. Enid will handle everything."

"Enid?" I asked meekly.

"My mother's event planner," replied Blake flatly.

"Enid *Shmeenid,*" chimed in tipsy Grandma. "Bubala, you and my Blakela should go to Vegas and elope."

"That's what Matt and I did," said Marcy, getting in her two cents.

Helen pursed her mouth; clearly, Marcy's elopement was a sore subject. She set her fierce gaze on Blake. "Blake, darling, we will have nothing of the sort. This is going to be the wedding of the century."

I hadn't even started to prep for the wedding and I was feeling all stressed out. My chest was tight. I met my mom's sunken eyes and then connected with my dad's. He wore a look of resignation.

Helen called out to the family housekeeper. "Rosa, please get me my phone."

Jumping at her beck and call, the uniformed Rubenesque woman scuttled out of the dining room and returned promptly with Helen's cell phone. Silently, she set it on the table and went back to cleaning up.

My eyes stayed on my future mother-in-law as she picked up the phone with her perfectly manicured hand and tapped the screen with a long red-lacquered nail. Putting it to her diamond-studded ear, she twitched a small smile, indicating her call had gone through.

"Enid, darling, Blake and his fiancée are getting married on December twentieth." She paused briefly, listening to the voice on the other end. "Yes, that would be wonderful if you could get the save the dates out this weekend. And yes, I'll get you the names of the McCoys' guests. I'm sure there won't be too many. And don't forget to book Rabbi Silverstein…and yes, that would be divine if you got the announcement into this Sunday's *New York Times*. MWAH, darling!" And with that, she ended the call.

My parents and I exchanged a nervous glance. I twisted my engagement ring. Reality set in like a crashing meteor. News flash: the wedding of the century had landed.

Chapter 4

Blake

After dropping her hushed parents off at The Beverly Hills Hotel, Jen and I drove back to my condo in tense silence. Following our announcement, the Jewish issue had come up again. Since we'd been engaged, we'd talked about it on and off, never coming to any resolution. Though they were secular Jews, both my parents wanted Jen to consider converting. For the sake of the children being their main bone of contention.

"Jewish *Shmewish,*" my grandma had growled, with a dismissive flick of her wrists. "The only thing she needs to know is the *vay* to a Jewish man's *shmekel* is through his stomach. Learn how to be a good cook," she'd advised Jennifer.

Grandma's words had put a small smile on Jen's face. They had also turned it as red as beet soup. I loved my grandma, and you know what, she was right. Well, at least partially. Yes, I had a hearty appetite. But my cock had an appetite of its own, and my tiger knew damn well how to satisfy that. No one sucked me off better than Jen or could bring me to mind-blowing fulfillment while buried deep inside her ravenous pussy. She knew how to cook my cock to perfection.

I broke the silence. "Jen, we've gone over this. You don't

have to convert if you don't want to. There's really no pressure."

She sucked in a short breath, a sexy sound that always turned me on. "It's not that, baby. It's the wedding."

"It's going to be spectacular."

"It's going to be a spectacle. And it's going to cost a fortune."

I made a sharp turn onto Wilshire Boulevard and picked up speed. I put the top of my Porsche up so we didn't have to shout above the whipping wind.

"Don't worry. My parents are going to pay for everything."

She turned to face me. Her eyes flared. "Blake, you don't understand. My parents were counting on making me a wedding. In their own backyard. Especially my mom. Didn't you see the expression on her face when your mother broke the news about that Enid lady?"

The truth, I wasn't really paying attention. While my mother's best friend Enid had planned all of my mother's philanthropic events and was indeed the most sought after party planner in town, I wasn't that keen on her planning something that was personally mine. Though she'd stayed close to my mother, she'd distanced herself from me. Our encounters were always cordial but cold. She carried a silent grudge. And time had not erased it.

I kept my feelings about Enid to myself. What Jennifer didn't know wouldn't hurt. I responded.

"Baby, *you* don't understand. My parents are like royalty in this town. They have a social obligation to put on a show and invite every Tom, Dick, and Harry they know."

"Well, your sister didn't have a big wedding." Her tone was

confrontational.

"Marcy pissed my parents off. But she didn't care. I do. Part of my job is to make my parents look good."

Another thick wave of silence rolled over us as we neared my condo. Finally, as I pulled into the circular driveway of the majestic high-rise building, she cupped her slender fingers over my hand that was clutching the stick. I shifted into park and met her gaze. If anger had filled her eyes, it had dissipated.

"Baby, I'm sorry. I think maybe I overreacted. I've had this image in my mind of what my wedding would be like—it just wasn't a big flashy Hollywood one. But I get where you're coming from. And I don't want to let down your parents...or you."

Fuck, I loved her. And once we were upstairs in my apartment, I was going to show her just how much. The grateful kiss I smacked on her lips wasn't enough.

Chapter 5
Jennifer

After yummy morning sex with Blake, I rolled out of bed, took a shower, and got dressed. Jeans, sneakers, and my favorite USC sweatshirt. I was taking my parents to the airport.

"Jen, let me come with you. Or at least, let me get them a town car."

I gave my beautiful bedhead a peck on his forehead. "That's sweet of you, baby, but a limo is so not their style. Plus, I want to spend some time alone with them before they leave."

"Just be prepared to spend some time alone with me when you get back," Blake responded, ducking under the covers. "Quality time."

"Or do you mean quantity time?" I teased, his big dick filling my head. And in my mind's eye, my pussy too.

"Both," I heard him laugh as I waltzed out the door.

The Beverly Hills Hotel where Mom and Dad were staying was not far from Blake's condo. With no traffic on Wilshire, I got there in fifteen minutes. A feat by Los Angeles standards. I didn't even have to valet my Kia. My punctual parents were already waiting for me at the curbside when I pulled up to the entrance. Amongst the throng of trendy guests dressed in the latest designer fashions, my parents, in their simple conservative attire, stood out like a sore thumb.

"Did you guys have breakfast?" I asked as I drove down Sunset.

"No, dear," said my mother. "I thought your dad and I could catch a bite at the airport."

With light traffic and time to kill, I decided to take my parents to The Farmer's Market on Fairfax. An old tourist attraction adjacent to The Grove shopping mall, it was a hubbub for tourists from Middle America. I thought after all the Bernsteins' fancy wining and dining they would like something down to earth. Something that reminded them of home. And reminded me of home. Old-fashioned DuPar's diner fit the bill.

We settled into a booth, me facing my parents. All of us ordered good old sunny side up eggs, hash browns, and bacon. Plus OJ and coffee.

"We had such a lovely stay here, darling," said my mother over coffee.

"The Bernsteins are fine people," added my father.

"Mom, are you really okay with Helen planning the entire wedding?" The crestfallen expression on her face when she heard the news was etched in my brain.

"Yes, darling. They have so many people to invite. We could never accommodate them in our backyard. Nor could we afford the cost."

"But, Mom, Dad. You've wanted to make me a wedding your entire life."

"No, honey," said my father. "We've wanted only to make you happy our entire life. With the money we've saved for your wedding, we may do something else we've always wanted to do."

My eyes grew wide as did my mom's.

"What would that be, dear?" she asked.

"Sail to Europe on the Queen Mary."

My mother's eyes melted into my dad's. "Oh, Lordy! Could we really?"

"As soon as Jennifer and Blake tie the knot, I'm booking two first-class tickets."

Clapping her hand to her wide-open mouth, my mother let out a loud gasp.

I was brimming with happiness. My parents deserved this trip. In a way, Blake and his family were making it possible for them.

While I wanted to treat them to breakfast, my father reached for the check right away. It would be an insult to offer. My father was a *mensch* to use one of the Yiddish words I'd learned from Grandma. While waiting for the change (he had paid in cash), his eyes searched mine.

"Jennie, I want to ask you something."

"Shoot, Dad."

"Are you going to convert to Judaism?"

My mother looked at me unblinkingly; her faith and family traditions were so important to her. My stomach tightened. "I don't know. Right now, I can't fathom the idea of giving up Christmas and Easter."

My mother's expression relaxed as I continued. "Blake and I have discussed it. He's cool with that as long as we celebrate the Jewish holidays too and our kids have bar mitzvahs. I told him I want Father Murphy to officiate our wedding along with their rabbi."

My mother's eyes lit up. "That would be wonderful, darling. I think Father Murphy would really appreciate that. He's known you since you were a little girl and is such a close family friend."

My father nodded with approval. I was thrilled this decision pleased my parents so much. I made a mental note to discuss this with Enid, the wedding planner. But the discussion about Judaism wasn't over.

"Mom, Dad. I want to be honest with you. Down the line, I may decide to become Jewish. Would you be okay with that?"

My father smiled at me warmly and then clasped my hands in his. "Jennie, you must always know that both your mother and I are okay with *anything* that makes our little girl happy."

My mother grew tearful. "Honey, you're going to make a beautiful bride."

My father beamed. "And I'm going to walk my beauty down the aisle. *Zei gezunt!*"

I didn't know whether to laugh or cry. I did a little bit of both. How I loved my mom and dad! They were definitely the best parents in the world. And the most loving. Secretly, I made a wish hoping Blake and I would grow old together and have an everlasting love like theirs.

"Happy Birthday, darling," said my mother as my father placed a tip on the table.

"I'm sorry we can't spend it with you," said my father.

"Oh, Dad, it's your day too. I want Mom to film the ceremony and send it to me."

"Of course, darling," said my proud mother as she reached into the large tote bag parked between them. She handed me a package. "Your birthday present. I hope you like it."

I took the perfectly wrapped box from her and gently tore off the whimsical Happy Birthday paper. "Oh, Mom, it's beautiful! I love it!" Inside was a truly lovely ivory cashmere cardigan. I took it out of the box and brushed it against my cheek. "And it's so soft."

A radiant smile beamed on her face. "Oh, honey, I'm so happy you like it." With an equally radiant smile, I carefully folded the sweater and put it back in the box.

"And this is from me." Reaching into the tote, Dad handed me a small package. From the looks of it, it was a book. Something he always gave me on my birthday. I eagerly unwrapped it. I couldn't help but smile. It was a Jewish bible.

"Read it, Jennie. It's not that different from ours."

Tears formed in the back of my eyes. I was going to miss them terribly after I dropped them off at LAX. But hopefully, the other Jewish education lesson I'd set up would keep my mind off them.

"Bubala, they're *gawgeous!*"

Blake's grandma wasn't talking about the gorgeous diamond and tourmaline earrings he'd given me nor about the gorgeous flowers I'd brought over.

She was talking about the matzo balls I'd just made. I poked my head into the aromatic, steamy kettle of soup simmering on her old fashioned Merritt and Keefe stove, and a big smile spread across my face. My matzo balls did look perfect—big and round—just like the ones Grandma made.

But, let me tell you, I didn't get them right the first time. Something went wrong and they fell apart the minute they hit the hot chicken broth. Honestly, they looked more like vomit bits floating around in a toilet. Yes, that bad.

The second time was hit and miss. A couple worked; the rest fell apart or sunk. I was frustrated and deflated. Ready to give up.

Twice, we had to drain the broth, which earlier Grandma had shown me how to make. That part was simple. Just throw together some water, chicken parts (preferably kosher), celery, carrots, parsley, and a pinch of salt. Simmer for an hour and you couldn't go wrong. Matzo balls, however, could go wrong. Terribly wrong.

Grandma was so patient and the third time was a charm. I'd finally gotten them right. They were perfectly formed and fluffy. I'd lined up the three cherries—the right ingredients, the right consistency, the right timing.

"Trust me, Bubala, the way to a man's *shmekel* is his stomach. Blakala is going to go nuts over these."

I gave Grandma a big hug and couldn't wait to show off my new talent to my husband-to-be.

While the matzo balls cooked, Grandma and I retreated to the living room, the tantalizing aroma of the soup trailing us. After quietly asking her to show me how to make matzo balls at the end of last night's Shabbat dinner, she'd immediately invited me over to her guest quarters on the Bernsteins' property. Some guest quarters...her guesthouse was bigger than the biggest house in Boise. A mini-mansion. But unlike the Bernsteins' antique-filled palace, it was unpretentious and filled with cozy lived-in furniture and a lifetime of memorabilia. Tchotchkes and family photos were scattered everywhere. Many framed photos of a handsome man who looked a lot like Blake filled the room, including several with Blake as a toddler. And there was even an elaborately framed sepia photo of a beautiful young bride and her dashing husband on one of the walls. I studied it. It was definitely taken in the fifties. The stunning dress was Grace Kelly-like, but what most caught my eye, was the delicate lace veil that puddled all around her. It was a work of art.

"Is that you and your husband?" I asked Grandma.

Her face lit up. "Yes, that's my Leonard. The love of my life."

I didn't know much about Blake's grandma and felt a window of opportunity shining in my face.

"How long were you married?"

"Sixty-two years." Her wistful voice tugged at my heartstrings.

"How did he die?" I ventured.

"Do you really *vant* to know? Five years ago. One thrust and bada bing! I *vas* coming and he *vas* going!"

My eyes popped. Only Grandma!

She put a silencing finger to her mouth. "Don't tell *anyvon!* Our little secret. *Everyvon* thinks he died peacefully in his sleep."

Then, she clasped my hand. I promised I wouldn't say a *"vord."*

"*Oy.* Such a good man. A *mensch.* Her voice grew effusive. And oh *vhat* a *shmekel.* He *shtupped* me till the day he died." She paused and squeezed my hand. "Blakela reminds me so much of him. You've given me so much *nachas* marrying him.

Such a *bashert."*

Before I could respond, the doorbell rang. The first member of Grandma's erotica book club filed in. Fifteen minutes later, they were all here. With their canes, dentures, reading glasses, and Kindles. One hour later, after a heated discussion of one of my favorite serials, Whitney G.'s *Reasonable Doubt*, which I hoped to option, I had no doubt. The book belonged on my schedule. And I had a lot to look forward to in my old age. A lot of laughs. Good friends. And gumming my hubby.

Chapter 6

Blake

I spent Sunday afternoon at Equinox where I played a mean game of racquetball with my best bud, Jaime Zander. I kicked his ass and hence he treated us to a round of beers at the upscale sports complex bar.

"We set a date for the wedding," I told him over a frothy Guinness on tap. "Saturday, December twentieth."

"Awesome, man. Where's it being held?"

"At my parents' house." I took a swig of the golden ale. "I think Jennifer was disappointed. She was hoping it would be at her parents' house."

"She'll get over it. It's going to be the wedding of the century."

I twisted my lips. "Yeah, that's what I'm afraid of. Anything my mother plans is always over the top and you can't get in her way."

"I hope I'm invited."

I smiled at my best friend. "You're more than invited. I want you to be my best man."

"Fuck, man. Get out. I'd love to. Come on, let's toast." He lifted his mug and clinked it against mine. "To the wedding of the century."

"To making it through the wedding of the century."

We simultaneously took a slug of the beer.

Jaime set down his mug. "Let me give you a bachelor party."

"Let me think about it."

"Don't think too hard. It'll be fun. A guys' night out."

"What if you get me smashed and I go MIA?" I asked, thinking about the movie *The Hangover.* While every guy I knew found this flick hilarious, it creeped me out. I didn't want to miss my own wedding.

Jaime snorted and guzzled his beer. "Don't worry. I'll have your back. In the meantime, why don't you and Jen go out to dinner with Gloria and me tonight? Our treat. We'll celebrate."

"Thanks, but no thanks. It's been a crazy weekend. We're just going to hang out. Maybe order in and watch something on Netflix." *And fuck our brains out.*

"Sounds good, man," said Jaime, reaching for the check.

After showering, I headed home. I thought about ordering-in dinner while I was driving; I was that hungry. Maybe Thai or Chinese or something from that new Vietnamese restaurant that had opened on Westwood Boulevard. The thought of Jennifer and me feeding each other with chopsticks sent my cock into overdrive. I was hungering for her. A good game of racquetball often had that effect.

I opened the door to my condo and was greeted by a tantalizing familiar aroma. Upon hearing me enter, Jennifer came running out of the kitchen. Fuck. She looked delicious, wearing a dainty little apron over a pair of cropped leggings and barefooted.

She flung her arms around me and, on her tiptoes, gave me a kiss. "How was your game?" she breathed against my neck.

"Awesome. I creamed Jay-Z. And guess what, he's agreed to be our best man."

"That's wonderful. I'm going to ask Gloria to be one of my bridesmaids."

"Cool." With a sniff, I wrinkled my nose. "What smells so good?"

She smiled seductively. "I have a surprise for you." My eyes stayed on her as she dipped her hand into the deep pocket of the apron and pulled out a stunning jacquard tie.

"A new tie?" Jennifer loved to buy me ties.

"Mmm hmm," she purred. "I want to put it on you."

"But, baby, don't you think I should put on a dress shirt to get the full effect?"

"You don't need to right now." She stepped back up on her tiptoes, and the next thing I knew, the tie was wrapped around my eyes like a blindfold.

"Are we going to have some kinky sex?"

"Maybe. But I've got another surprise for you." She took my hand and led me in the direction of the kitchen. The delicious aroma grew stronger.

"Sit on the counter," she ordered when we got there.

I hoisted myself onto the granite countertop. My imagination was flying. Was she going to suck me off?

"Open your mouth," she breathed.

I did as she asked, and on my next breath, a spoon with hot broth filled my mouth. I swallowed.

"Jeez, Jen. This is good. It tastes just like—"

"Your grandma's matzo ball soup. She taught me how to make it today."

"You spent the day with Grandma?"

"Yes. She's amazing."

I heard a spoon clink against a bowl.

"Okay, baby, now try one of my matzo balls." I felt her warm breath against my neck as she blew on the ball. The sexy sound and sensation made my cock twitch.

"Take a bite and tell me what you think."

My lips clamped down on the fluffy ball, and I bit into it.

"Wow! It's delicious. As good as Grandma's."

Still blindfolded, I could imagine my tiger's adorable smile as I swallowed.

"She taught me the trick to the balls. You have to use club soda."

"Soda *shmoda*," I mock-mimicked Grandma. "Let me have another taste."

"My turn."

In my mind's eye, I could see her lips going down on the tender ball. Circling around it. Taking it into her mouth. My pulse sped up, and my own balls tightened as my cock strained against my jeans. What was it with matzo balls and Jen that turned me on every fucking time?

"Are there any other tricks to the balls?"

"Uh-huh. There's an art to rolling them."

Seriously? My cock was going stir crazy.

As if she read my mind, she yanked down my fly. Commando, Mr. Burns came flying out. She curled her fingers around my enormous erection, and getting down on her knees, began stroking it, hard just the way I liked it. Then, without stopping her hand action, she flicked her tongue along my smooth sack of balls, hitting a spot on the bottom that made me want to jump out of my skin. Holy shit! And if I wasn't already on my way to heaven, she wrapped her soft lips around them, rolling them around in her hot, hungry mouth, one big ball at a time. An insufferable electrical current spread from my head to my toes, the blindfold heightening every spark I was feeling. Squirming on the counter, I fisted her hair.

"Jesus, tiger," I hissed. "Is this what Grandma taught you?"

"Mmm hmm," she moaned, feverishly sucking my balls and pumping my dick. It felt fan-fucking-tastic. She was making my soup to nuts fantasy a reality. Who cared if the soup was getting cold when my balls were on fire? An orgasm of titanic proportions was not far away. That telltale tingly feeling of fullness saturated my cock, and in a harsh breath, I came all over Jen's talented hand.

Back on her feet, she undid the tie. I blinked. My river of release was seeping through her fingers. She gazed at me, her green eyes glistening with pride. "Did you like that?"

Hell, yeah. I took her into my arms. "Is this going to be one of our rituals as husband and wife?"

She smiled sheepishly. "It could be."

"What other tricks did Grandma teach you?"

"What you can do with an apron is amazing."

Leave it to my sex-crazed grandma. I glanced down at the sexy little one strewn around her waist. "I'm eager to find out."

She cocked another smile. "Come on, let's finish the soup."

I jumped off the counter. "No offense, baby. Your soup is awesome, but I'm more interested in getting a taste of your new trick and anything else you've got cooking."

Her eyes smoldering, she draped her arms around my shoulders. "Babykins, I've got a lot of things cooking."

"You're going to make one hell of a wife." I tore off her apron.

One breath later, we were fucking our brains out right on the kitchen floor. The strings of her apron bound around my wrists, I discovered what other wonders my bride-to-be had in store.

Chapter 7

Jennifer

"Happy Birthday, girlfriend!"

Libby was at the door of my office. Holding a small shopping bag, she barged in and placed the bag on my desk.

"This is for you. It's just a little something."

"Oh, Lib, you didn't have to get me anything," I protested, already dipping my hand into the bag. I broke into a smile. It was a T-shirt with "Mrs. Always Right" printed boldly on it.

"I know it's a little premature, but you need to remind 'Mr. Right' that you're the smart one."

"This is perfect. I love it." I stood up and rounded my desk to give my redheaded best friend a big hug.

"Why don't I take you out for lunch?" she asked.

"Can't," I sighed. I then explained to my future maid of honor that Blake and I had finally set a date and his mother was planning the entire wedding.

Libby knitted her brows. "Are you cool with that? What about your mom?"

"Yeah, we're both okay with it. With all the guests the Bernsteins have to invite, we don't have much of a choice." I glanced down at my watch. It was almost noon.

"Shit. I've got to go. Blake's mother set up my first meeting with the wedding planner."

I grabbed my purse and walked out of my office with Libby.

"Good luck. I want to hear everything. I can't wait to tell Chaz."

One for punctuality, I got to Enid Moore's office early. Located not far from Conquest Broadcasting's headquarters, it was housed in a lovely two-story brick townhouse right off fashionable Robertson Boulevard. Upon entering it, I was greeted by a stylishly dressed male receptionist, handsome enough to be called pretty.

"You must be Jennifer." His voice was effete yet warm.

I nodded. "Yes."

"Have a seat, sweetie. I'll let Enid know you're here. Can I get you some tea or water in the meantime?"

"I'm fine," I said, plunking down on the very formal loveseat and soaking in my surroundings.

The reception area was elegantly decorated in shades of ivory, all silk and gilt, and lit by a crystal chandelier. Antique oil paintings of aristocratic brides were artfully scattered on the walls. Soft classical music piped through hidden speakers.

The coffee table in front of me was lined with impeccably arranged bridal magazines from around the world. In the center was a thick leather-bound album labeled "Moore is More." I lifted it into my lap and began flipping through the parchment leaves. Page after page was filled with photos of events that Enid had created. My eyes widened. Each event was more extravagant than the one before—ranging from a baseball-themed bar mitzvah featuring namesake baseballs at every seat and a life-sized ice sculpture of a young boy swinging a bat—oh my God, it was thirteen-year-old Blake!—to a Cinderella-themed wedding, complete with a pumpkin-shaped horse-driven carriage carrying the bride and groom and flower-entwined cages of white mice for centerpieces. I shivered, not knowing if the mice were real or not.

The sound of an intercom buzzed in my ear. I looked up from the album.

"Enid can see you now," said the receptionist. "Her office is upstairs." With a roll of his twinkly blue eyes, he wished me good luck.

I set the album back on the coffee table and clambered up the marble stairs. As I neared the last step, a shrill voice pierced the air.

"I personally don't care if you have to rent a private plane and go to France yourself. My client wants *fresh* mussels flown in from the Côte D'Azur. Period!"

Enid was still on her cell phone when I stepped into her office. She acknowledged me by lifting a perfectly manicured bony finger that silently said, "I'll be with you in a minute." Studying her spacious office, which was even more elegant than the reception area, I took a seat on a gold-leafed velvet armchair facing her desk. I kept my purse on my lap while she finished up her call.

"I will not take no as an answer. You're fired!" With a loud, exasperated huff, she terminated the call and slammed her phone onto her pristine desk, which looked to be a museum quality antique. My eyes stayed on her as she lifted, pinky finger out, a cup of tea.

For a woman likely in her fifties, she was extremely beautiful though surely preserved with the help of some nips and tucks and the magic of Botox. Her tight-skinned face with its high cheekbones and emerald eyes was made even more regal by her tightly pulled back jet-black hair. Substantial diamonds glittered on her earlobes, and a pair of pearl encrusted reading glasses dangled from a gilt chain and rested on her ivory silk blouse. She twitched a small smile. Something told me that was as far as her mouth ever went to avoid smile lines and other wrinkles. There was seriously not a line on her face.

"Sorry about that. A ridiculously impossible vendor. Trust me, he won't be working in this town again." Her voice was now deep and breathy.

"No problem," I squeaked, admittedly intimidated by her.

"Well, let's get down to business. I'm extremely busy and am doing my dear friend Helen a big favor by squeezing you into my jam-packed schedule. Consider yourself lucky." She gave me the once-over. "I do hope you own a pair of contacts. Those hideous eyeglasses will never do on your wedding day."

"I do," I muttered, not happy with her insult. I liked my tortoiseshell glasses. They suited me.

"Good. One less thing to worry about. As you know, Helen wants her son's wedding to be the wedding of the century."

I nodded wordlessly.

She took a sip of her tea and then set the flowery bone china cup down. "I always thought my daughter would end up with Blake. Helen and I used to joke about it all the time."

A soupçon of suspicion niggled me. I wondered who her daughter was. My father's words of wisdom—curiosity killed the cat—stopped me from asking.

Enid sighed. "Bygones are bygones. Though you're not exactly in Blake's league—or my daughter's—I can't let my dear friend Helen down."

Internally, I cringed. How dare this haughty woman insult me like that? I had the burning urge to lash out at her and defend myself, but I bit down on my tongue. Starting things off badly wouldn't benefit anyone.

"Did Helen tell you anything about the way I work?"

"Not really." But I was already getting an idea.

"My motto, 'Moore is more' has made me the most sought after event planner in Los Angeles. In fact, the world. I just got back from Dubai where I created an *Arabian Nights* wedding for a young Saudi princess. At the reception, the bride and groom came flying in on a magic carpet. We're going to have to top that, aren't we?" She flashed that half-smile again.

Speechless, I nodded my head like one of those bobble head dolls. Gah! I just wanted something simple and elegant. I guess she never heard of the expression: Less is more.

"So tell me, do you have a favorite movie?"

What did that have to do with my wedding? I searched my mind. I loved animated movies and had several favorites, among them *Frozen*, *Despicable Me,* and *The Little Mermaid.* I randomly spewed the latter.

Enid's almond-shaped eyes lit up. "Fabulous. I love it. We have a theme."

"A theme?"

"Darling, all my events have themes. Yours will be an underwater fantasy. I can see it now. Guests will dance on a glass-topped aquarium filled with tropical fish of all sorts.

You'll get married under a canopy encrusted with exotic seashells. We'll do a coral and white color scheme, and at the reception, we'll have stations of seafood flown in from all over the world—from fresh sushi made by the chef I work with in Japan to a boatful of shrimp straight from the Louisiana bayou. And of course, mounds of Beluga caviar from my preferred vendor in Russia."

As I listened, unable to get a word in, her voice grew more excited, and she began gesturing dramatically with her hands. "And pearls! What fun we can have with them! Hmm. Maybe pearl encrusted invitations. Ooh! Maybe we'll place them in giant iridescent plastic clamshells. With oyster white bows! A first! And of course, edible pearls all over the ocean-inspired wedding cake. And your dress. Don't even get me started on that. I'll have to call Monique right away."

"Monique?" I peeped. Talking about clams, I was clamming up.

Enid shot me a quizzical look. "Monique Hervé. She's one of my dearest friends as well as Helen's. Anyone who's anything in this town has a gown custom-designed by Monique. I'm sure you saw the one Star Davis was wearing at her nuptials, which, by the way, I coordinated. It was on the cover of *In Style*."

No, I didn't and I didn't care. There was only one person in the world that was designing my dress. "Excuse me, Enid, but I already have a designer in mind."

She looked taken aback. Unable to lift her brows or scowl, she pursed her fire-engine red lips. "Really? And who might that be?" Her voice was frosty. She obviously didn't like being challenged.

"Chaz Clearfield."

"Who the hell is he?"

"A young, up-and-coming designer. He's very talented and happens to be one of my best friends."

Enid's eyes bugged out. Suddenly, she reminded me of Cruella de Vil, and in fact, they could have been separated at birth.

"I. Don't. Think. So." Each word was a sharp staccato.

"What do you mean?"

"Monique is already committed. And the publicity this wedding will get will assure her hundreds of thousands of dollars in business. You should know she is a very big supporter of Helen's charities."

"But—"

Enid rudely cut me off. Her eyes flared. "Let's get something straight, Jennifer. I'm in charge here. Helen has put her trust in me to create a spectacular wedding. There are no buts. Are we clear on this?"

Shriveling in my chair, I nodded.

"Good. With the ridiculously tight time frame, there's absolutely no room for second guessing."

I twitched a nervous smile, acknowledging her. In the near distance, I heard footsteps—the clickety-clack of high heels on the hardwood floor in the hallway.

"My assistant should be here any second. With my hectic schedule, she will be your point person." She directed her gaze at the doorway. "And here she is."

I swiveled my head and my jaw crashed to the floor.

Enid's voice drifted into my ears. "This is my daughter, Katrina, who will be working with you."

Shooting eye daggers my way, Enid's daughter faced me.

Blake's ex hook-up.

Kitty Kat.

Chapter 8

Jennifer

I couldn't get my mouth to close. I was in a state of semi-shock. I just couldn't believe who was standing at the entrance to Enid's office. Kitty Kat. The catty bitch who had butted heads with me the night of Jaime Zander's art gallery gala and then kissed Blake at some black tie affair while we were broken up. The photo of her all over Blake had appeared in numerous magazines, including *The Hollywood Reporter*. If it hadn't been for Chaz, who'd been at the event and witnessed her aggressiveness, Blake and I might have never gotten back together.

Dressed to the nines in a body-hugging black mini-dress and six-inch stilettos, she was as stunning as ever. A tall, blond, D-cupped goddess who could have easily been a supermodel. The epitome of every woman Blake fucked until he met me. Her cat-green eyes, identical to her mother's, continued to clash with mine.

Enid's face lit up at the sight of her daughter. "Darling, don't just stand there. Do come in."

My gaze stayed glued on her as she slinked into her mother's office. Her lustrous, shoulder-length tresses bounced like the hair you saw in one of those shampoo commercials. And her bountiful boobs bounced along in perfect rhythm. She held up her head proudly. Everything about her oozed confidence and sex. *And* trouble. My stomach twisted into a painful knot.

"Why, hello, Jennifer," she huffed, as she lowered herself into the armchair next to mine. Her cloying floral scent, the same as her mother's, assaulted me.

"Oh, I didn't know you two knew each other," chimed in Enid.

"Yes, Mommy. We met on one occasion."

One time too many, I thought to myself.

Enid continued while my blood curdled. Her words about a potential marriage between Blake and Katrina whirled around in my head. Did Blake have some kind of history with her?

Enid cut my disturbing thoughts short. "Since you'll be working so closely together, I thought it best you get to know each other. I've arranged a lunch for the two of you at The Ivy."

"And when would that be?" I asked, hoping the answer would be never.

"Why today, of course. With the wedding so close, we can't waste any time."

"But—" I had a boatload of work with deadlines.

Enid's eyes narrowed. "Jennifer, I thought we agreed. The word 'but' is no longer in your vocabulary. We must work on a very strict schedule."

"Right."

I didn't know whom I despised more. And even worse, feared. Enid or her daughter.

The Ivy, the original outpost of the popular Santa Monica restaurant Blake and I frequented, was located on Robertson Boulevard, walking distance from Enid's office. Except I needed to drive. Not thinking our initial meeting would last long, I'd parked my car in a metered space with a thirty-minute time limit. There was an underground parking structure located just down the street and that's where I went. As I exited my car, a sharp pain stabbed at my gut. I winced. Just nerves, I told myself. The thought of having lunch with Kitty Kat was stressing me out.

I arrived at The Ivy before Kat and was shown to the umbrella-shaded patio table that had been reserved for us. As the waiter handed me a menu, I took in my surroundings. The place was bustling. Filled with slick Hollywood mover and shaker types, supermodels, and those philanthropic, fashionable ladies who lunched like Helen. I even spotted a couple of celebrities. I could handle coming to one of these Hollywood hot spots with Blake or Chaz, but by myself, I felt uncomfortable. Out of my league to use Enid's phrase.

My eyes darted to the street, and I saw Kitty Kat pulling up to the valet in her black Mercedes convertible. An attendant ran to open her car door and she gracefully stepped out of it. She kissed and made small talk with a couple of stylish women, who were waiting for their cars, and then loped up to the equally attractive hostess. They hugged. Obviously, she was a regular here. She spotted me and strode over to our table. All eyes turned to look at the long-legged beauty.

Taking a seat across from me, she set her monstrous designer bag on the brick patio floor and began, "I hope you know what you want because I don't have a lot of time. I have a mani-pedi I can't be late for."

The less time I spent with her the better. I immediately opened my menu and made a selection. A young waiter came by.

"Well, hello, Ms. Moore. Will you be having your regular?"

"Yes. A small plate of asparagus and a glass of champagne. The Perignon, please."

The waiter turned to me. "And you, madame?"

"I'll have the crab cakes and a passion fruit iced tea." Truthfully, I craved a glass of champagne to calm my nerves and numb my mind, but I didn't want to drink at lunch. I had a lot of scripts to get through today and needed to be clearheaded.

The waiter came back quickly with our drinks. Without any kind of toast, Kitty Kat raised her flute to her full glossy lips and took a sip. I latched on to my iced tea and curled my lips around the straw, taking sip after long sip so I didn't have to make any small talk with my companion.

Kitty Kat set down her champagne. "So, Jennifer, has Blake fucked you every which way?"

I gulped. The tea went down the wrong pipe, and I began to choke, spraying the amber liquid all over my silk blouse and the vintage floral tablecloth.

"Has he fucked your tits? He loves doing that."

I was coughing too hard to respond.

Her venomous eyes glared at my tea-stained chest. "I bet he hasn't. You're way too flat-chested."

My blood was bubbling with rage. I finally caught my breath. "Can we please talk about the wedding?"

It was as if she had deaf ears. Her eyes bore into me. "Did Blakey tell you we were an item?"

What?

"We both went to Buckley. He was crazy about me. Head over heels."

Wait! Blake didn't do love until he met me! "I don't believe you!" I snapped.

Kitty Kat smirked. "Oh, he never showed you any of our love letters?"

My heart skipped a beat and my chest tightened. I parted my lips, but words failed me.

"I'll take that as a no. So, I brought one along to show you." She lifted her purse onto the table and slipped a hand into it. A few rapid heartbeats later, she was holding a white manila envelope. My stomach churned as she pulled out the contents. A single piece of notebook paper.

"Take a look-see," she purred as she handed it to me. I instantly recognized the handwriting. The almost illegible scribble. Unmistakably Blake's. My heart clenched. And as I read the words of a poem, my hands trembled.

A million stars light up the sky;
One shines brighter I can't deny.
A love so special, a love so true;
A love that comes for very few.

At the bottom, it was signed in large block print letters: ITALY~BB

The letter slipped out of my shaking hands onto the table. I was having difficulty breathing. Finally, I managed a few words. My voice quivered. "It doesn't say anywhere that he loves you."

A poisonous smile slithered across Kitty Kat's face. "ITA-LY."

"That's a country," I countered defensively.

"Ooh. You're a smart one." Her voice was dripping with sarcasm. "And FYI, that's where we fucked for the first time when our families were vacationing together in Capri. We signed all our love letters that way. It's an acronym that stands for *I Totally Always Love You.*"

Tears were forming in my eyes, but I fought them back. *Don't let her get to you, McCoy.*

"Blake only loves me." My voice was desperate and watery when it should have been convincing and strong. I anxiously fiddled with my engagement ring.

A throwaway "ha" spilled from her lips. "He still loves me and I'm going to prove it to you. Besides, you're all wrong for him; he needs Hollywood royalty not some Middle America farm girl." She snorted like a pig. "He's just blindsided. You'll see."

Rage whipped through my veins like a rollercoaster. Impulsively, I grabbed my glass of iced tea, ready to toss it at her. However, my hand was shaking so vehemently the glass tumbled onto the table. The tea spilled everywhere, soaking Blake's poem. The words dissolved into an unreadable inky blur.

Kat's eyes flickered with fury. She screwed up her face, her lips snarling. "Look what you've done!"

"I-I'm sorry," I stuttered, springing to my feet. "I have to go."

Leaving Kat fuming, I skirted past the waiter, who was bringing what we'd ordered to our table, and sprinted down Robertson to my car. Tears were falling.

I desperately needed to talk to Blake.

Chapter 9
Jennifer

B lake was at his desk, his eyes glued to his computer, when I stormed into his office. His face looked intense.

"Blake!"

Upon hearing my voice, he looked up at me, startled as if I'd taken him out of deep thought.

"What's up?" He was being terse with me, something I'd never experienced.

"We need to talk," I replied, marching up to his desk.

"I can't right now. I'm in the middle of getting last minute P&L numbers together for my father's board meeting. He needs them by three o'clock to review. The meeting's at four."

"But it's important."

"This is more important. I can't be distracted. It's going to have to wait till later."

"When's later?" The testiness in my voice was thick.

"I don't know. The meeting could go late." He paused. "Come over here. Let me give you a birthday kiss."

"I can't right now," I snipped, mimicking the tone of his earlier words.

"Fine." He stabbed the word at me and immediately returned his eyes to his computer screen.

Through pent-up tears, I stormed out of his office as fast as I had stormed in. So, work came first.

I spent the rest of the afternoon in my office, my door locked and my office phone set to "do not disturb." I pored over several scripts, in various stages of development, for the erotic romance block I'd developed for MY SIN-TV. I had a hard time concentrating. And I think I was being overly critical because I was in a bad mood. I'd desperately wanted to talk to Blake about Kat, but he was too busy. Okay. I got that, but it was the way he handled it.

After giving script notes, I watched a rough cut of an episode of *Shades of Pearl* based on Arianne Richmonde's popular trilogy. It was the sixth installment. Pearl (Cameron Diaz) was slow dancing with her now husband Alexandre (Gaspard Ulliel) in their suite at the Hotel George V. Goose bumps spread across my skin, and I was verging on tears. My viewers were going to love it. It was so sensual and romantic! I could feel what Pearl was feeling. The lust. The love. I'd gone to France last Spring to supervise the shoot. My first time in Paris. On my last day there, Blake had flown in and surprised me. And just like Alexandre, he'd taken me into his arms to dance and shown me that Paris was the City of Love. Our mind-blowing Bateau Mouche ride was just the beginning. Over the weekend, he'd fucked me senseless, sending me into outer space. There were not enough Michelin stars in the world to rate the delicious orgasms he'd given me. He knew every romantic hot spot in the city—from the most intimate restaurants to the expressive Wall of Love. A shudder ran through me. I now wondered—had he made love there with well-traveled Kat? I couldn't get her out of my mind.

Blake didn't bother to call or text me the rest of the afternoon. I guess he was still in the "very important" board meeting with his father. I glanced at my watch. It was after six. I decided to give his secretary, Mrs. Cho, a call to find out if she knew when the meeting would end.

"Me have no clue. Meeting go for very long time," she said in her charming Korean accent. "You want I tell Mr. Blake you call?"

"Don't bother," I told her. "I'll be heading out soon." We exchanged good-nights, and I hung up the phone.

My blood pressure was rising like bread in an oven. I needed to talk to someone. Unload. Impulsively, I dialed Libby's extension. I inwardly sighed with relief when she picked up on the first ring.

"Jen. What's up? I'm about to leave."

"Do you have dinner plans?"

"I'm meeting Chaz for sushi at Roku. Isn't Blake taking you out for your birthday?"

"Can't. He's got a board meeting."

"That sucks. You can't be alone on your birthday. Have dinner with us."

Just the words I wanted to hear. And seeing Chaz would certainly cheer me up and set me straight with his brutally honest advice. "Really?" I responded.

Libby laughed. "Get over yourself."

I laughed back. The first time all day. I so loved Libby.

Roku was a popular Japanese restaurant located near the Beverly Center, not far from the house I used to share with Libby. Despite Don Springer's vicious sexual assault that almost cost me my life, Libby had chosen to stay when I moved out and moved in with Blake. She'd made the owner put metal grilles on the windows and added an alarm system for protection. She felt safe there and had turned my bedroom into an office.

Chaz ordered for all of us. Three large sakes and an assortment of delectable sushi, served in an extravagant bamboo boat. Libby and Chaz dug in right away with their chopsticks, consuming piece after piece of the artfully arranged rolls of raw fish. I picked at a California roll.

"You better have some more, Jen, before Chaz and I eat it all."

I took a sip of my hot sake. "I'm not that hungry."

"What's wrong, Jenny-Poo?" asked Chaz.

Guzzling the rest of my sake, I told Libby and Chaz about my meeting with Enid. And then about my lunch with Kat.

"She's just trying to intimidate you," said my analytical friend Libby.

"I'd like to slap the bitch," chimed in Chaz, who despised Enid's daughter.

"Why didn't Blake tell me about her?"

"You need to talk to him," quipped Libby, the researcher. "Find out what really went down between them."

"I tried to talk to him this afternoon, but he was too busy with last minute stuff for some board meeting. He practically ignored me."

"You can't blame him. The Conquest Broadcasting board meeting is super important."

Always rationale, Libby had a point. Maybe I overreacted. Yes, love was putting the needs of someone else before your own, but maybe that wasn't always possible.

I sighed and helped myself to more sushi. The hot sake was taking its effect, relaxing me a little. "How am I going to work with Kat?"

"You're not," chirped Libby.

"Easier said than done," I replied glumly. "It's not like I can tell her mother that. And I'm not comfortable getting Blake's mother involved. She and Enid are best friends. Enid handles all her events."

Chaz reached for another piece of sushi. "Wait till she sees you in the wedding gown I'm designing for you. It's going to be so faboo. The bitch will positively die over it."

My heart stuttered. I chewed down on my lip and swallowed hard. "Chaz, I've got some bad news." I paused, struggling to tell him the inevitable. "I won't be wearing your dress."

Libby's twin brother shot me a puzzled look. "What are you talking about?"

I felt tears clustering behind my eyes. "Enid has already commissioned some other designer. Monique Hervé." I didn't tell him how she'd dismissively blown him off.

"But, I've already started it. It's going to be everything you and I talked about and so much more."

Libby's eyes narrowed with rage. "Fire the bitch."

"I can't. Remember, I didn't hire her. Blake's mother did.

And to make matters more complicated, Monique is a big supporter of Helen's charities."

Libby folded her arms across her full-sized chest. "That sucks. But there's no fucking way I'm wearing anything else but one of Chaz's dresses. I'm not taking any orders from the Beverly Hills mafia."

Maybe Libby could be a rebel, but I couldn't. I met Chaz's chocolate gaze. "I'm so sorry, Chaz."

"Don't be, Jenny-Poo." His boyishly handsome face softened. "I'm going to make sure you get your dream dress regardless of whoever designs it. I'm going to be there every step of the way even if I have to smack one of those bitches till they get it right."

Libby slapped one chopstick against the other. "Smack the shit out of them, bro."

Oh, Chaz! Always there for me. Giggling, I felt so blessed to have him and Libby, my two best friends in the world, in my life.

We polished off the sushi (befitting given the theme of my wedding), and to my surprise, a small piece of complimentary birthday cake arrived at the table. After my two friends sang "Happy Birthday" at the top of their lungs and totally off key, I blew out the sparkling single candle and made a wish—I hoped my wedding would be perfect. And my dress too. Over the third large sake, we joked about the underwater theme of my wedding. Leave it to Chaz to make me laugh. We were pretty smashed and singing our version of "A Sailor Went to Sea, Sea, Sea"

"And all that he could see, see, see, was the bottom of Enid's ass, ass, ass!"

Chapter 10

Blake

The board meeting was long and tried my patience. While my father, as always shined, I was distracted. I felt bad. I'd been short with Jennifer—on her birthday of all days. Maybe later, I could make it up to her. Lately, the pressures of work had interfered with our social life. My father was under a lot of pressure to live up to Wall Street's expectations for our fourth quarter earnings. The new Fall season had started out a little rough, but fortunately, Jennifer's block of programming was going through the roof. Daytime ratings for MY SIN-TV were the highest among all broadcasters, network and cable alike. The advertising dollars were pouring in, and we were seeing revenue from the joint online venture with Gloria's Secret. There was considerable talk in the meeting about spinning MY SIN-TV into its own 24/7 cable channel. I couldn't wait to share this news with Jennifer.

When the meeting finally broke at seven p.m., I immediately called Jennifer. No answer. Maybe she didn't have her cell phone with her or maybe she just wasn't answering. She was probably pissed at me. I was eager to get home, but my father insisted I join him and the board members for dinner at Maestro's, an expensive steak joint in Beverly Hills. He was the boss. I had no choice.

It was after ten o'clock when the dinner ended. I cruised down Wilshire Boulevard in my Porsche, the convertible down, keeping my eye out for a flower shop where I could stop and pick up a dozen fragrant pussy pink roses—Jen's favorite—along with a "Happy Birthday" SpongeBob balloon. Unfortunately, while I passed a few, not one was open.

When I got home, Jen was curled up on the couch, already in her SpongeBob PJs, reading a script. "How was the board meeting?" she asked without looking up at me or prefacing her question with a simple, endearing "hi."

"Long," I told her, trying not to react to the coldness in her voice. "I tried calling you, but you didn't pick up."

"I was in a noisy restaurant and had my phone on silent," she replied, her head still buried in her script though I didn't think she was actually reading it.

"I want to share some exciting news with you, but first I owe you an apology."

For the first time, she looked up at me. Her green eyes searched mine.

"I'm sorry I was so short with you this afternoon. I was under a lot of pressure."

"Well, it seems like you can always find the time to fuck me over your desk, but when I have something important I need to share with you, you're always too busy."

Lately this was true. Work always seemed to come first.

I sat down next to her, my body brushing against hers. I nuzzled her neck. Instead of enjoying my company, she flung her script on the couch and jumped up.

"I'm going to sleep."

I leapt up from the couch and trailed her. "No, you're not. Not until we talk."

"Leave me alone, Blake. I'm tired."

Fuck. I wasn't going to leave her alone. Catching up to her, I flipped her around and walked her backward until she was flat against the hallway wall. I held her pinned against it by her shoulders. The cherry vanilla scent of her freshly washed hair drifted up my nose. Almost a head shorter than me in her fuzzy slippers, she gazed up at me and shot lasers out of her eyes.

"Blake, why didn't you tell me?"

"Tell you what?"

"That you and Katrina Moore were a couple in high school."

"That's so fucking untrue. And what makes you say that?"

"She told me over lunch."

"Lunch?"

"Just for your information, she's going to be working with her mother planning our wedding."

"Shit." I let go of Jen's shoulders, but she didn't budge.

"She told me how she lost her virginity with you in Capri and how you wrote her love letters."

"What?"

"She even showed me one. It was a poem. I recognized your handwriting. I didn't know you wrote poetry."

My poetry skills were limited to dumb-ass limericks. I searched my memory.

"Jen, it was a twelfth grade homework assignment. We had to write a poem and then the teacher made us do an exchange. I got stuck with Kat. And I didn't write that poem. I copied a fucking Hallmark card. And FYI, I got a 'D.'"

My answer didn't seem to satisfy her. Distrust was written all over her pretty face.

"And what about Italy?"

"I was thinking maybe we'd honeymoon there," I said, glad she'd changed the subject.

Jen scowled. "I-T-A-L-Y as in *I* *T*otally *A*lways *L*ove *Y*ou."

"Tiger, I have no idea what you're talking about. I've never written that in my entire life. She must have imitated my handwriting and made that up. I swear I'm telling you the truth. That girl is delusional. Yes, I did fuck her in Italy. It was a summer fling. And yes, I did screw around with her a little in high school."

I paused, the next words, ready to explode like a Molotov cocktail on my lips. I bit back my tongue.

"But nothing more. She's not even one of my hook-ups."

"Right." She stabbed the word at me. "You want me to believe that after I saw you together at Jaime's art gallery opening?"

"Jen, I was there alone. She happened to be there. She's a fucking stalker. She even followed me home that night. I swear I almost had to call the police."

Jen's eyes stayed steady on my face as she digested my words. It was hard to read what was going through her head. I couldn't blame her for distrusting me with my checkered past. Her silence was killing me.

Finally, she parted her lips. "Why didn't you tell me about her?"

The softness in her voice and yearning in her eyes pro-voked me to run my hand along her jaw line. She didn't flinch. I looked deep into her soulful green orbs. "Because she means nothing to me, tiger. She's ancient history. I didn't want to upset you." *And I didn't want to go there.*

She fluttered her long-lashed eyelids. My cock tensed. I had to claim her. Let her know she was mine.

"There's only you, baby. I totally always love you. Only you. Every waking minute of the day. You do things to me no other woman ever has." I put her hand to my cock. It was as hard as rock. And then I put her other hand to my heart. "My heart only beats for you. You own it. No girl has ever owned my heart except you. I want you to believe me."

"I do." Her voice was a whisper.

The sweet innocence of her voice aroused me. I pushed my hips against her, pressing my erection firmly against her center.

"You're the only one I want to fill. I want to fill your mouth. Fill your pussy. And fill your heart." Impulsively, I crushed my mouth against hers and gave her a fierce, passionate kiss as my hands slid down her pajama bottoms. I fiddled with my pants button and fly, and out sprang my cock ever so ready for her. With the help of my hand, I shoved it inside her, surprised she was so hot and wet. Placing my palms against the wall for support, I began thrusting into her forcefully, filling her to the hilt, while I tongue fucked her mouth and groped her tits. Groans escaped her throat and her breathing grew ragged. I picked up my pace, making my thrusts harder and faster. Her breaths came in pants and her groans became whimpers. She pressed hard against my shoulders, pushing me away and forcing me to free her mouth. Her face looked heated and impassioned. So fucking beautiful.

"Blake," she panted out. "Is this makeup sex?"

"If. You. Think. We. Had. A. fight," I grunted back with

each successive, hard, long stroke.

"I'm not sure."

"Just shut up and let me fuck you." God. No one felt as good as my tiger.

"Okay," she groaned, letting me reclaim her mouth.

Without losing contact, I lifted her up against the wall. Wrapping her legs around me like a warm pretzel, she splayed her hands on my ass, and rocked her hips forward to meet my thrusts. Her whimpers morphed into shrieks, and I knew she was close to coming. Hard. I wanted to hear my tiger roar my name. So, I released her mouth again, not caring if she woke up the neighbors.

"Come for me, tiger," I urged, banging her into submission.

"Blake!" she cried out as she let go, her body shuddering inside and out with spasms of ecstasy. She clung to me as my own epic climax took hold of me, my load bathing her with sweet bliss.

Catching her breath, she rasped, "We should fight more often."

I smoothed her damp hair while she held on to me. "Nah, baby. We should just talk more often." And then I smacked my lips against hers so she couldn't say another word.

We fucked our brains out again and talked some more in my— I mean, *our* bedroom. Pillow talk was something new for me. Before Jen, I'd never spent the night with a woman. I had a rule. My hook-ups were plain and simple not allowed to share my bed.

The room was pitch black except for a sliver of moonlight that peeked between the curtains. We were spent and naked; while Jennifer was totally adorable in her SpongeBob pajamas or in a pair of my boxers, I'd take her in the buff any day of the week. She rested her head on my chest, my arm wrapping around her warm body. My fluffy duvet covered us midway.

She told me more about her meeting with Enid. Fortunately, Kat didn't come up again. The thought of her made me sick. She was trouble with a capital T, and I wasn't sure how far she'd go with Jen. I was going to have to deal with her and the past, but I wasn't sure how and when. Hopefully, she'd keep her fucking mouth shut. I forced myself to focus on what Jen was telling me.

"Are you shitting me? An underwater adventure?" Jokingly, I told her we could put SpongeBob blow-up dolls as centerpieces on all the tables.

She laughed. "I don't think so. Disney Ariel dolls are more like it. And she'll probably coordinate some kind of synchronized swimming production in your pool."

"Why didn't you tell her your favorite movie was *Jungle Book*, tiger? We could have had a zoo in our backyard, and you could have had Katy Perry show up and sing 'Roar' Or you could have sung it to me."

She playfully punched my chest. "Very funny."

I stroked her hair and got serious "Jen, you shouldn't have to be dealing with this bullshit." *And especially Kat.* "This wedding is stressful enough as it is."

She sighed. "I don't think I have a choice."

"I'm going to talk to my mother. It's your day. You should have the wedding you want."

While it was dark, I could feel Jen's eyes on me. "Blake, it's not my day. It's *our* day. We're in this together. I want to come with you to talk to your mother."

"Are you sure?"

"Yes, I'm sure."

"Okay, I'll try to set up something for tomorrow." Maybe the power of two would work. My mother was a force to be reckoned with, and Jen had only gotten a little taste.

I kissed my bride-to-be good-night and wished her a very happy birthday.

Chapter 11
Jennifer

B lake managed to set up a meeting with his mother on Monday at lunchtime. We left together from work and drove to Hillcrest, the exclusive country club the Bernstein family belonged to. Not far from Conquest Broadcasting, we drove into the gated property down a long tree-lined road to the entrance where a valet took Blake's Porsche.

Although the Bernsteins had a tennis court on their property, Helen preferred to play tennis at the club where she socialized with her society friends. She had agreed to squeeze us in after her game. I'd learned from Blake that his mother had a very full life—every minute of the day was scheduled from the time she woke up to the time she put her sleeping mask back on. In addition to playing tennis and bridge, she chaired and sat on numerous cultural and philanthropic boards. The galas she organized were the talk of the town and raised hundreds of thousands of dollars for the charities they supported. Her other standing appointments included weekly visits to her hair stylist/colorist, manicurist, and facialist. She was so busy, Blake joked, that his father had to schedule sex with her. I believed him.

Helen was already seated at a linen-covered table when

Blake and I, hand in hand, breezed into the club's busy, posh restaurant. Straight off the court, she was still in her tennis whites and wearing a visor. Her face brightened when she glimpsed us coming her way.

"Hi, Mom," said Blake, embracing her.

"Hello, darling. And hello, Jennifer," she added while Blake pulled out a chair for me. He then sat down next to me. A waiter came by with menus and told us about the specials. The poached salmon sounded good.

"I had a wonderful match with Lenore Waxman. I won both sets. Six-three."

"That's great, Mom," Blake said, studying the menu.

"She's so excited about the wedding. She even postponed her trip around the world to attend it."

Not wasting a second, Blake closed the menu. "Mom, Jen and I are having some issues with the wedding."

Helen's eyes grew wide. Like Enid, she couldn't lift or knit her eyebrows together. They probably went to the same skin doctor for Botox.

"I'm surprised to hear that. I just spoke to Enid who told me things are going swimmingly. No pun intended. The underwater theme is divine."

I built up the courage to open my mouth. "I mean, it's very creative and everything, but I'd like something simpler and more understated."

Helen fluttered her eyelids as if she'd just heard her best friend had died.

Blake came to my rescue. "Mom, this is Jen's special day. She should have the wedding she wants."

"Blake, darling, it's a little too late. Jennifer should have spoken up."

Yeah, right. Dragon lady would have fried my ass.

Helen continued. "With the wedding less than two months away, Enid is moving at a very rapid pace. She's already started to design the invitations—the idea of encrusting them with pearls and delivering them in simulated seashells is positively divine—and she's ordered bolts of coral Thai silk for the tablecloths and tent draping from her vendor in Bangkok. And what do you think of this? She's lined up the U.S. Olympic Synchronized Swim Team to perform in our pool while our guests enjoy pre-wedding hors d'oeuvres and oyster shooters."

Blake and I shot each other an oh-my-God look. I was only kidding when I mentioned that possibility. A sinking feeling settled in. I was swimming up a stream without a paddle. No laughs. No pun intended.

Blake tried to reason with her again. "But Mom—"

I cut him off. It just wasn't worth it to create friction with his mother. I got it. Helen's way. Or no way. Things could get ugly quickly.

"Blake, we'll work with the theme. The wedding will be wonderful."

Helen flashed a smile. "Dear, it's going to be the wedding of the century. Generations will talk about it in years to come. I've lived for this day. My little boy's wedding."

Blake flushed while I forced a smile back at her. There was still one other big issue.

Blake read my mind. "We have one other issue."

"And that might be…?"

"Kat." Just the mention of her name on his lips made my

blood boil.

"What about her?"

"She's assisting her mother with the wedding plans. She's Jen's point person."

"Excellent. Enid could use some help. She's juggling so many events at once, including two I'm co-chairing in January."

Blake held his ground without getting into explicit details. "She's making Jennifer very uncomfortable. You know we have a history."

Helen flinched and then dismissively waved her bony, perfectly manicured hand. "Darling, let's not go there. That was ages ago. High school. I think it's wonderful she's following in her mother's footsteps. God knows, this town will need another Enid once she retires."

Our waiter returned to our table with a bucket of champagne. He set down three fluted glasses and then poured some into each.

"Children, let's end this discussion and toast." She lifted her champagne glass. "To the wedding of the century."

Reluctantly, Blake and I raised our flutes and clinked them against hers.

Blake's mother had defeated us in our verbal tennis match.

"Well, that didn't go well," I said as Blake drove out of the club.

"It went well for my mother," he replied.

"Is she always like that?"

"Yes. Welcome to my world."

I'd spent some time with Blake's mother over the last few months at Shabbat dinners and a few events, but I actually hadn't gotten to know her.

"She's very set in her ways," Blake added.

"And your father puts up with her?"

"He more than puts up with her. He worships her. She's like a piece of jewelry. They have the perfect marriage."

"Elaborate," I said as we zipped down La Cienega. I wanted to know what he meant by the "perfect marriage."

"It's simple. Their roles are clearly designated. He's the king and the provider. She's the queen who makes him dazzle."

I deconstructed his words. What he said was true. I'd been to their home countless times and to several of Helen's events. She made everything beautiful. Including her husband. A shudder of self-doubt ran through me.

"Blake, I can't be that to you. I don't know how. Plus, I have a career I'm not giving up."

As we cruised down the busy thoroughfare, Blake was pensive. Finally, he responded. "Tiger, you're more to me than a piece of jewelry. *You're* my shining star."

I looked his way. Our eyes met briefly and then his returned to the road.

The words of his "poem" vaguely whirled around my head. "What do you mean?"

"You light up my life."

"I do?"

"Totally. You give me direction when I'm lost. You set me straight when I stray. And you take me places no one else can."

Tiger, tiger, burning bright. Oh, Blake!" His heartfelt

words tugged at my heartstrings and sent a stream of tingles through me from my head to my toes. I had the burning urge to ask him to pull over and fuck him right in his car when I realized we had turned onto the 10 Freeway heading east.

"Blake, what's going on? Where are we going?"

"Vegas. My grandma was right. Let's elope."

Shock bolted through me like lightning. "Blake, that's crazy!"

"Jen, all I want is to marry you and for you to be happy. I don't need my mother's over-the-top wedding. I just need you."

My emotions swirling, I digested his words as he continued.

"We can get married at the Hard Rock. That place has meaning."

Indeed it did. It's where I totally fell in love with Blake Burns after a weekend of working, gambling, and dancing in his arms to Roberta Flack's "The First Time Ever I Saw Your Face." Every moment of that unforgettable weekend danced in my head.

"We'll get one of those Elvis impersonators to officiate," he said, cutting into my delicious memories and bringing me back to the moment. Reality set in.

"Blake, we can't do that. It would upset your mother and break my mother's heart as well as my dad's. My parents have lived to see me get married. And it would break *my* heart if they weren't at our wedding."

It was Blake's turn to think about my words. "I guess you're right," he mumbled, preparing to turn off the next exit.

As much as I loved him for caring so much about my happiness, I was glad he hadn't lost his mind and pursued the Vegas idea. Eager to get back to the office, I got another surprise when he made an unexpected screeching turn into the parking lot of one of those roadside motels. The turn was so sharp my head swung out the window.

"Sheesh, Blake. You practically gave me whiplash."

"Sorry, baby. Between work and this wedding, I'm just really stressed out." He pulled the car into an available parking spot.

"Why are we stopping here?"

"Because there's a vacancy. And I need to de-stress and fuck your brains out. And fuck myself senseless."

Oh.

Chapter 12

Blake

Ten minutes later Jen and I were checked into Room 202. Trust me, with its cheap brown wood furniture, dingy floral bedspread and curtains, and worn out pea-green carpet, it was no suite at The Beverly Hills Hotel. But something about it made me fucking horny as hell.

I plopped down on the edge of the rickety wood-frame bed while wide-eyed Jen explored her surroundings. God, she was adorable.

"Blake, they have free SIN-TV here," she pointed out.

I wasn't going to need any porn. Just my tiger. "Baby, I want you to strip for me. Like a strip teaser."

Jen raised her brows and then quirked a sexy little smile. "Really? Are you going to compensate me?"

"Oh yeah, I'm going to compensate you big time."

"Some music would be good," she replied with a wink.

To get her in to the mood, I pulled out my phone and searched my iTunes app. "Bang Bang" fit the bill. My tiger loved this song.

Strutting around the bed, she began to undress. My eyes stayed riveted on her slender figure as she slowly and sensuously unbuttoned her silk blouse, taunting and teasing me. The

temperature in the room was rising by the minute. Hot damn. I
loosened my tie and opened up my shirt. I was unwinding, but
my dick was winding up. Way up.

"Bang, bang," Jen mouthed, her voice all breathy, as she
sensuously slipped the blouse off her shoulders, whirled it
around above her head, and tossed it to me. It was an easy
catch. I kept it in my lap as I watched her massage her lace-
encased pert breasts; her full lips parted in a sexy pout. God,
she was good, totally getting into it. I knew from the day she
stepped into my office and pretended to have a major orgasm
there was more to this sweet little Boise girl than met the eyes.
Yeah, I needed a good girl to blow my mind.

Thinking her bra would go next, she surprised me by taking
off her pencil skirt, slipping it seductively down her hips. She
gracefully stepped out if and stood before me in just her lace
bra and panties and her heels. She splayed her fingers on her
hips and gyrated. Bang, bang went my heart. Bang, bang went
my cock. Mr. Burns was totally enjoying the show. Then she
did something that totally drove my cock crazy. She pulled the
elastic out of her hair and her perennial ponytail fell loose, her
soft dark waves cascading over her shoulder like a sexy cape.
She flung her head forward, her locks falling over her tits, and
then flung it back, raking her fingers through her mane while
she licked her upper lip with her talented tongue. Man, this
show kept getting better and better. My cock was raging.

"Do you like what you've seen so far, Mr. Burns?" she
purred.

"Come here, tiger," I growled, crooking my index finger.
She sashayed up to me until she was standing between my
spread legs. I dipped my hand into my pocket and pulled out a

crisp one hundred dollar bill. I slipped the bill into her soaked panties, brushing my fingertips along her hot wet folds.

She shot me a satisfied, seductive smile and proceeded to expertly unhook her lacy bra. It slithered down her arms and, in the blink of an eye, it was sitting in my lap.

I studied her. Oh, my sexy tiger—clad only in her scrap of lace panties and her heels. I inhaled. Mmmm. She already smelled of sex. So fucking intoxicating. On my next heated breath, I shoved her bikinis down and buried my face in her pussy.

I couldn't get enough of her. I licked, sucked, flicked, and circled. She tasted as good as she smelled. So sweet. So fucking sweet.

I planted my hands on her hips, and she gripped my shoulders as she let out moans. Rocking into me, she was enjoying every minute of this game as much as I was.

"Oh, Blake," she panted out. "You're going to make me come."

Not the time to stop my ministrations. That was the point. I wanted to give my tiger a mind-boggling orgasm and feel her pussy throb all around my tongue. I darted my tongue into her pussy while my right hand moved to her clit and took over.

"Oh God, Blake!" she shrieked.

Just hearing her say my name sent me orbiting. How the words of only one woman could send me flying into outer space. With a pinch of her clit, I sent her over the moon. As she came, she roared my name, and I looked up just in time to see the rapture on her face. Man, what a fucking beautiful sight!

Now it was my turn. Though she had barely recovered from her mega-orgasm, I flung her onto the bed. She was so spent she didn't resist. I frantically pulled down my pants and briefs and then mounted her. The bed made a strange creak.

Spreading her beneath me, I tore off her panties and plunged my hungry cock deep inside her entrance. Dripping wet, she didn't even yelp. I began to pound her. I mean *really* pound her.

Having one of those expensive memory foam mattresses at home, I wasn't prepared for this thrill ride. Man. Sex on this decrepit spring mattress was fucking unbelievable. The bounce was practically sending me flying, and I didn't have to work hard at pumping away. I don't know what was louder—the sound of our harsh pants, the rattling of the swaying bed, or the creaks of the ratty mattress. And I seriously wasn't sure which would last longer—the mattress or me.

Jen was thinking the same thing. Between pants of ecstasy, she breathed out, "Blake, I think we're going to break the bed."

Bang, bang. I didn't give a flying fuck. If the damn bed went down, we were going down with it. I picked up my pace, ramming ruthlessly into her at full throttle. What a cacophony of sounds—my body slamming against hers, our harsh breaths mingling with grunts and groans, and that damn boing-boing of the cheapo mattress springs.

And then one sound overtook them all. That of my tiger screaming to come. I moved my fingers to her clit, working it vigorously in circles the way she adored, and in a few breaths, she came with a roar. Craving my own release, I gave her one more forceful thrust, and as I exploded, the mattress crashed to the floor. Bang bang. Boing boing.

"Oh my God, Blake!" shouted stunned Jen as we went down.

"Fucking shit!" I growled, my cock still inside her.

Then we both burst out in hysterical laughter. I was laughing so hard it hurt, and Jen was practically in tears. After the stress of the last few days, laughing our asses off felt so fucking good. Still roaring with laughter, I cradled her head in my hands.

"Baby, we're going mattress shopping right after this."

"To replace this one?"

"No, baby, to buy us one just like it."

Chapter 13

Jennifer

O ver the next few weeks, I learned that planning a wedding was a lot like producing a movie. It was a huge ordeal with much to commission, coordinate, and approve. Except unlike the erotic romance telenovelas I was overseeing, I was not the executive in charge of production. I would sum up the credits as follows:

Slate: Jen's Wannabe Wedding

Executive In Charge of Production: Enid Moore

Co-Producer: Helen Bernstein

Associate Producer: Katrina Moore

Gopher: Yours Truly

I was the bride. I was supposed to be the star *and* executive producer. The one in charge. Making the decisions. Selecting and approving invitations, flower arrangements, the menu, and lots more. Even being catered to. But this was hardly the case. I was more like a dispensable extra from Central Casting.

Because of the tight time frame, much of our correspondence and decision-making was done online. And it wasn't like I had a say. Whenever I got an e-mail from Enid regarding the wedding, it started off with two words "We have" As in…

We have created a Pinterest board to keep you abreast of our creative decisions. Please check it regularly. Today, I posted the most positively divine floral arrangement for the tables. A seascape of exotic flowers and seashells. Don't you just love the coral pedestal?

I must say, however, she worked at breakneck speed and was super organized. She'd created a To Do List and a timeline. Within one week, the following had been accomplished:

* A Save the Date had been sent to all twelve hundred potential guests via a Paperless Post custom design. Rather than a virtual envelope, a virtual scallop shell opened when you clicked on "You're Invited."

* A caterer was in place. Claim to fame: the coveted *Vanity Fair* Oscar party.

* A florist had been selected: "The Florist to the Stars."

* Extras had been hired to be part of my bridesmaid troupe. Per Enid, having only three—Blake's sister Marcy, Vera Nichols, and Gloria Zander—would look "positively pathetic" in publicity photos. I only hoped none of Blake's blond bimbos were among them.

* Photographers were in place. A dozen of them. Many would be shooting photos for various magazines, including *In Style.*

* A videographer was in place. Actually, it was the production team from one of Conquest Broadcasting's reality series.

*   A twenty-piece band had been hired. But Enid was still hoping the Disney orchestra would come perform.

*   Security was in place. There couldn't be enough. Paparazzi and wedding crashers were likely to abound at the Hollywood wedding of the century.

And that was just a partial listing. There was so much more to do—or should I say sign off on—including the final wedding invitation (to Enid's chagrin, the "right" pearls from her "preferred" supplier hadn't yet arrived), setting up a wedding registry, locking the menu, and putting together a play list. I wouldn't be surprised if Enid picked out all the gift items and decided what songs I should dance to with Blake and my father.

Last but not least, there was still the issue of my wedding dress. My dream dress. Or so I hoped it would be. Monique was out of town. I should have been thrilled at the prospect of meeting with her, but instead, the more time that passed by, the more I dreaded it.

My mom called me every day to find out how things were going. So much of me wanted to unload on her. I missed her so much. I so wish she lived close by and could be here for me. I'm sure, if I asked, the Bernsteins with their billions would put her up (and my dad too) in a nano second, but that was so not my humble parents' style. Nor mine. Moreover, Enid, the shark, would likely eat my poor mother alive. I assured her everything was going well. The truth: I felt overwhelmed and disconnected from my own wedding. The most important day of my life. To make matters worse, Blake had to embark on his yearly round of meetings with SIN-TV affiliates, which meant he was going to be out of town, traveling across the country for two weeks.

"Tiger, I'm going to miss you," he said on the morning of his whirlwind trip. Earlier, we'd fucked our brains out as if there were no tomorrow. "Are you going to be okay?"

I nodded. "The telenovelas are moving along great."

Standing at the doorway, his roll-away bag by his feet, he tilted up my chin with a thumb. "I mean about the wedding and everything."

I met his gaze. "Yes, baby, I'll be fine, but I'm going to miss you terribly."

"Same. I'll text you whenever I can and let's try to Skype every day. And you let me know if Enid or Kat cause you any problems."

The thought of "sexting" him every day and Skyping him—and having virtual sex—cheered me up a little, but I knew the brunt of Enid and Kat was mine alone to bear while he was gone. Thank goodness, I hadn't had to deal with Kat since that horrific lunch, but who knew how long that would last. Standing on my tippy-toes, I kissed Blake for a long time, not wanting to let go of his kissable lips, and not wanting to say good-bye.

That morning I got into my office, feeling overwhelmed and downtrodden. I already missed Blake. I booted up my computer. My inbox was besieged with a barrage of e-mails from Enid, all *Subject: Wedding Detail*. One, in particular, marked URGENT, captured my attention and I opened it immediately. It was straight and to the point.

We have our first dress fitting today. Details below. It's imperative you be there. Be sure to bring a nude strapless bra and heels.

Where: L'Atelier de Monique Hervé

Address: 8420 Melrose Place, 2nd floor

Time: Noon

My stomach bunched up. With nerves, not excitement. What was wrong with me? I should have been excited about picking out my dream gown but strangely wasn't looking forward to it. Not one bit. And didn't Enid have any idea I had a high-powered job? She just assumed I could drop everything I was doing and race to meet her. Two words resounded in my head. *No buts.* I checked my Outlook Calendar, and luckily, my schedule was open at lunchtime, though I had no time to fetch the heels and bra. I immediately speed-dialed an important number. I wasn't going there alone.

I arrived at Monique's atelier early. Having boned up on my French in preparation for the *Pearl* telenovela, I know that atelier meant studio. It was located just above her eponymous boutique on chic Melrose Place—a short drive from Enid's office.

My eyes took in my surroundings. I felt like I was in some kind of fairy tale. Everything was white, gilt, and velvet with accents of girly hot pink. A regal crystal chandelier bathed everything in a warm glow, including breathtaking arrangements of fragrant white flowers on scattered pedestals. Above a glass console sat a huge, almost ceiling-high gold-leaf mirror, and in the corner, there was another massive tri-fold mirror. Bolts of tulle, lace, silk, and other fine fabrics were stored on built-in glass shelves, and elegant mannequins were clad in the most extravagant bridal dresses ever. There were also several racks of gowns gracing the marble floor.

A familiar breathy voice caught my attention. "Hello, dear." Theatrically stepping out from a pair of pink velvet curtains was Helen, wearing a stunning one-shoulder coral gown and flanked by Enid and Kat, dressed almost identically in designer black V-necked body-hugging silk dresses. My jaw dropped.

"Oh, Helen," I gushed with sincerity. "You look beautiful." She truly did, the magnificent silk-satin gown accentuating her svelte figure and the color complementing her platinum hair, cerulean blue eyes, and alabaster skin.

"Thank you, my dear," she beamed. "Monique is absolutely brilliant. She came up with the idea of the scalloped edges—so in tune with the theme of your wedding. By the way, Monique needs your mother's measurements. She has an equally wonderful idea for an oyster-white suit for the mother of the bride."

"Sure," I murmured, wondering how my mother would take this and wanting her to look as fabulous as Helen. I suddenly missed her. Terribly. Wishing she was here with me on the day of my first fitting.

An attractive petite brunette woman emerged from a back room. She was clad in a stunning chartreuse sleeveless sheath with matching heels. A tape measure was draped around her neck.

"Helen, darling, you must take a look-see in the mirror." I assumed she was Monique Hervé. I expected her to have some kind of foreign accent, but she didn't. She instead sounded very Valley.

Helen slinked over to the three-way mirror to admire herself. "Oh, Monique! It's positively divine."

Enid echoed the sentiment while Kat's poisonous eyes stayed focused on me. Monique turned her gaze to me and gave me the once-over. "So you must be the bride-to-be."

"Yes, I'm Jennifer."

She plastered a big fake smile on her face. "Wonderful. I have another very important client coming in shortly so let's get started."

"If you don't mind, I'm waiting for someone." *Where was he?*

Enid sneered at me. "Dear, we can't be wasting Monique's precious time. She squeezed you in today as a favor to me."

"Well, I guess I can start looking through the dresses on the racks." Having perused bridal magazines, I had in mind what I wanted—something with a vintage feel, either flapper-like from the twenties or Grace Kelly-like from the fifties.

Monique rolled her eyes. "Please, darling, there's no need. Enid and I have already chosen your dress."

I felt my blood bubbling. Didn't I—hello, the bride!—get a say?

My stormy eyes stayed fixed on Monique as she waltzed over to one of the racks and pulled out a gown. Folding it over her arm and not giving me the slightest chance to view it, she headed back my way and ushered me into the fitting room.

Fifteen minutes later, I shuffled out of the fitting room wearing "my" wedding dress and a pair of heels that were three sizes too big for me. Monique trailed behind me. Kat shot me a smirk.

"Take a look-see," trilled Monique.

I wobbled over to the tri-fold mirror. I glimpsed all three angles of my bridal self and not one put a smile on my face. My heart sunk.

"It's *magnifique!*" I heard Monique say.

Yes*, maybe* the dress was magnificent, but it was just not right for me. It was an extravagant shimmering white satin sheath that flared out in a cascade of ruffles below the knee. A mermaid-style dress, apropos to the wedding's under-the-sea theme. I could barely fill out the strapless top, which was encrusted with crystal starfish, and what was supposed to be a body-hugging column hung loosely on my petite, boyishly narrow body. It was so baggy you couldn't even see my panty lines. The dress was definitely made for someone much taller and curvaceous. Someone like—

"Katrina, what do you think?" asked Enid, cutting my thoughts short.

She smirked again and snickered. "Personally, Mommy, I think it would look much better on me."

Her words stung me like a stingray but ran true. That's who this dress was made for. Blake's wannabe bride.

Enid absorbed her daughter's words and then turned to Monique. "Monique, darling, it *is* a little big."

A little big? I was swimming in it. No pun intended.

Grabbing a heart-shaped pincushion from a nearby table, Monique asked me to step up onto a pedestal and began sizing the dress. "Don't move," she murmured, pinning the edges. My eyes stayed on my reflection in the three-way mirror. Even with all the nips and tucks (there were almost as many pins as there were crystals), the dress did nothing for me.

Monique admired her handiwork. "Much better. And we'll pad the top, maybe add a couple of spaghetti straps to hold it up, and sew in a butt pad to give you some curves."

"A butt pad?"

"Of course, darling. Everyone's wearing them ever since Pippa wore one to the royal wedding."

So I was going to be sitting on some kind of whoopee cushion at my wedding. My heart sank deeper as if an anchor was pulling it down. This was supposed to be one of the best days of my life, but it was so far from it. I felt like the Titanic.

Blake's mother glanced down at her gold and diamond beveled-faced watch. "Oh, dear, I'm going to have to say ta-ta. I have a board meeting downtown for the Philharmonic at one thirty." She scurried back into the dressing room and five minutes later, reappeared in her gazillion dollar designer pink silk suit.

She kissed me good-bye. "Darling, it's going to be perfection. Sorry to have to go, but I'm leaving you in good hands." Hugging Enid and then Monique effusively, she asked them to send her a photo when all was said and done. In a breath, she was gone. I was shocked she wasn't staying for the entire fitting and more than ever wanted my mom to be here. Along with the other person I'd invited. Coming from downtown, maybe he was stuck in traffic. *Hurry!*

Monique made a few final nips and tucks. "You know, Jennifer, given how close your wedding is, you are *so* lucky this dress was available. I custom-designed it for a very famous rock star—whose name I can't divulge—but TMZ caught her equally famous fiancé in bed with an even more famous supermodel so she called the wedding off."

Great. So, I was going to be wearing someone's doomed hand-me-down.

"It would have taken months for the silk fabric to get here from Italy and forget about the genuine Swarovski crystals."

I gazed down at the glittery crystal starfish cupping my tits and hugging my hips, thanks to the pin-job. They did little to cheer me up. A welcomed familiar voice, however, did.

"Oh my frickin' God! That is so wrong!"

Chaz! Finally! Tearing my eyes away from the sad image in the mirror, I watched him storm into the atelier. His eyes clashed with Kat's. Poison daggers were going back and forth. Kat's lips snarled.

"What the hell is he doing here?" she snapped at me.

"I invited him. I wanted him here to give his opinion."

Chaz jumped back in. "Jenny-Poo, you look like Bridezilla! Take that hideous thing off immediately."

Monique's face darkened. "Excuse me? Did you just insult my one hundred thousand dollar creation?"

Gah! One hundred thousand dollars? Maybe some of the crystals were real diamonds.

Chaz held his own. "I don't care if it cost one dollar. A Las Vegas showgirl wouldn't be caught dead in that rag!"

God, I loved Chaz. He just told it like it is. He was so brutally...no, beautifully honest. He was right. Who was I kidding? The dress was *vomiticious.*

Flustered and obviously having a hot flash, Enid began to

fan herself. "Jennifer, who is this intruder?" she panted.

Kat retorted before I could say a word. Her scrunched up expression was one of pure disgust. "Mommy, he's that man I told you about who called me rude at that Beverly Hills Hotel event back in January. The one Blake was at."

"Shut up, bitch!" Chaz barked. "Or I'm going to have to slap you."

All at once, Kat, Enid, and Monique gasped. I stifled a laugh.

Monique was the first to respond. "Whoever you are, I'd like you to please leave."

"My name is Chaz Clearfield, and I happen to be LA's hottest new designer and one of Jennifer's best friends. And she's going to wear *my* dress."

"Excuse me?" breathed Enid.

Kat turned to her mother. "Mommy, do you want me to call 911?"

My heart was in a flurry and my stomach twisted. A sharp pain stabbed me in the gut. Clutching my belly, I winced.

Chaz's eyes grew wide with alarm. "Are you okay, Jenny-Poo?"

I nodded, still in pain; I was sure, just stress. "Chaz, why don't I meet you at El Coyote. I'll be done here soon."

"Sure, honey." After a bear hug, he proudly sashayed out of the atelier, leaving me alone with the three barracudas.

Fifteen minutes later, the fitting was done and I was back in my work clothes. I grabbed my bag and headed to the stairs.

"Don't forget, Jennifer. Geary's at three o'clock sharp," Enid called out.

I stopped dead in my tracks and flipped around. "What do

you mean?"

Enid scowled, making the tiniest crease in her Botoxed forehead, while Kat smirked. "Darling, don't tell me you've forgotten."

"I don't know what you're talking about."

"Didn't you read Katrina's e-mail? I've set up an appointment at Geary's to create your bridal registry."

"I never got it."

"Well, I sent it," snapped Kat in a snide singsong voice. "Maybe you need a new pair of eyeglasses."

Inside, I was fuming. She was lying. She *never* sent it. And probably deliberately.

"Where's it located?" I asked, trying hard to mask my anger.

Enid rolled her eyes in disgust. "Seriously, darling? It's on Rodeo Drive. I'm sure you'll find it. Helen is meeting us there, so please don't be late."

My eyes clashed with Kat's before I powered out the door.

"Oh God, Chaz. You're so lucky you missed the headpiece. It's some super-weird sequin headband concoction with this ugly rhinestone starfish that sits in the middle of my forehead." Another leftover from the rock star, who was obviously in love with being a star.

Seated in a booth at the popular Mexican restaurant El Coyote, I was on my second margarita and my thoughts were flowing freely. I dug into my tostada.

"Thank you, honey, for sparing me," replied Chaz, helping

himself to another shot from the pitcher we'd ordered. He took a long sip and set his margarita glass on the table.

"Jenny-Poo. Listen to me. Go along with those bitches. I've moved forward on your dream dress and I'm not stopping."

My heart fluttered with happiness. "Oh, Chaz! Really?"

"Trust me, they're not going to stop you from wearing it on the day of your wedding."

Where there's a will, there's a way. Blake had ingrained these words in me. Chaz and I would make things work. Somehow. Someway.

A delicious lightness swept over me. I was going to be a beautiful bride after all. Wearing my dream dress. I couldn't wait to marry my Blake.

"When can I see it?"

"In a few weeks." As Chaz reached for the check, he looked at me sheepishly. "I have a big favor to ask."

"Anything."

"Would you find out if Jeffrey, Monique's receptionist, is single? He's so cute."

"Sure." A big smile lit my face while Chaz blushed. My father always said something good always comes out of the bad.

Geary's in Beverly Hills was a glittering spectacle of china, crystal, and silver. It smelled of money. I was sent to the second floor where Enid, Katrina, and Helen were already gathered with a spindly silver-haired sales woman, who was holding an iPad. I recognized her. She was the woman who'd helped me at Bloomie's earlier in the year with picking out a gift for Gloria. And the woman who'd assisted my ex, Bradley, and his new fiancée, Candace, with their registry. She must have switched jobs.

"You're late," snapped Enid.

I glanced down at my watch. It was 3:05.

"We don't have all day so let's get started." She introduced me to the woman who would be working with us. Her name was Bea.

"Lovely to see you again," she said in her husky smoker's voice.

Enid looked puzzled. "Do you two know each other?"

"Yes, we met last year when I was still at Bloomingdale's"

"Such a despicable store," huffed Enid.

"Can I offer you ladies some champagne?" asked Bea, ignoring the putdown.

Everyone except me agreed to a glass. I still had a buzz from the margaritas. Bea sauntered off, telling us to start earmarking items while she got the champagne.

"Shouldn't we wait to do this until Blake gets back in town?" I thought engaged couples were supposed to pick out their registry together.

Helen laughed lightly. "Puh-lease, darling. Men have no clue whatsoever when it comes to these kinds of things. You're so much better off he isn't here."

"And Blake obviously doesn't have a handle on the finer things in life," added Kat with a smirk. It was clearly an insult directed at me. It took all my effort to let it go.

"Jennifer, chop chop. Stop wasting precious time and get moving," urged Enid with a clap-clap of her bony hands. "I'm going to use the restroom and then I'll be right back." Helen and Kat joined her.

Truthfully, I didn't know where to begin. All around me were hundreds of dazzling china patterns, crystal glasses, and silver settings. Fit for royalty. Truthfully, I didn't want or need any of this stuff. Blake and I needed basics. Things like everyday china, dishwasher-safe silverware, pots and pans, and the like. Being a player and dining out most of his adult life, Blake had very few of these things, and we'd purchased just a few essentials when I'd moved in with him. I should be at Crate & Barrel. Not here.

I forced myself to meander through the store. My eyes bugged out. Everything was so super expensive. Can you imagine—three hundred dollars for a teeny weenie eggcup? I mean, who in their right mind would gift such a thing? None of my friends or my parents' could afford even one. If they asked what to get us, I was just going to tell them whatever. Or to make a small donation to a charity in our names.

Examining a silver-rimmed dinner plate that at least re-minded me of my mother's lovely Lenox china, I was distracted by a familiar voice.

"I should be registering, not you."

I spun around. Kat with a flute of champagne in her hand.

"What are you talking about?" My tone was sharp.

"Blake should be marrying me. I'm the one he really loves. You whored your way into his heart."

At her untrue words, a deluge of anger swept through me. "You're delusional. Blake even told me himself."

She narrowed her eyes at me. "Oh, and did he tell you about—"

"Darling." Kat's mother cut her off. "That's wonderful you're working with Jennifer. She can learn a lot from you."

She smirked again. "Yes, Mommy, she *can.*"

Enid sauntered off to join Helen and Bea.

Kat glowered at me. "Good luck, delusional one."

To my utter shock, she flung her glass of champagne at me and strutted off. My mouth hung open.

One soaked hour later, Blake and I had a registry that came close to $500,000. It included three sets of hand painted Limoges china (breakfast, lunch, and dinner), the finest Christophe cutlery, matching Baccarat wine and water goblets plus a set of flutes, a dozen Buccelati silver picture frames along with a complete tea service, and twenty-four of those little egg cups. Guilt rippled through me. Maybe after we were married, Blake and I could return all this shit. A half a million dollars would feed a lot of hungry children. And they sure didn't need eggs in eggcups.

Chapter 14

Blake

B y the time I checked into my hotel, The Walden, where I always stayed in New York, it was going on eight o'clock. The rush hour traffic on the expressway from Kennedy into Manhattan had been nightmare. And made worse by some badass accident that every Tom, Dick, and Harry stopped to gawk at.

I plopped down on the king-sized bed, and propping myself against a mountain of fluffy pillows, I speed-dialed the top number on my contact list. That of my tiger. I hadn't even been away from her for twenty-four hours and I fucking missed her. She picked up on the first ring.

"Hi, baby. You landed okay?" She sounded tired.

"Yeah. I'm here. Are you okay?"

She launched into her afternoon. Shit. Fucking Kat was antagonizing her again. Every muscle in my body tensed. Sooner or later, the psycho bitch was going to let the cat out of the bag. While Jen went on about her disastrous dress fitting and the ridiculous wedding registry, I half-listened, debating whether I should tell her what had happened. Nah. It had to be done face to face, plus, I didn't want to ruin my little surprise. My cock jumped at the thought.

"Baby, I need you to do me a favor. Go to my office. And when you get there, lock the door."

A minute later, she was just where I wanted her. "Blake, what's this all about?"

"Open my top desk drawer. Inside you'll find a DVD. Insert it into my computer and watch it."

"Hold on." I heard the beginnings of a familiar theme song. I knew she was watching the DVD—various sexy poses of yours truly (including some photos from my modeling days) that I'd strung together with my own narration. Damn, I was good. Tom Cruise would be fooled.

"Good evening, Ms. McCoy. *That* man you're looking at is Blake Burns, one of this country's most dangerous sex addicts. Your mission, Jen, should you chose to accept it, is to capture Mr. Burns and make him come in his pants. As always, should you be caught in the act, my secretary will disavow any knowledge of your actions. This tape will self-destruct in five seconds. Good luck, Jen."

Jen's laughter mixed with the sound of a loud explosion. The DVD had faded to black, but Jen was still laughing.

"Are you kidding me, Blake?" she managed.

"Mission accepted?" I asked matter-of-factly.

"Accepted." Her voice was an octave lower and as sexy as sin.

"Excellent, Agent McCoy. You will need a special weapon to take him down." *After getting him up.* "Open the bottom drawer."

My cock already flexing, I waited impatiently as she did as I asked.

"Blake, a dildo?"

It was the biggest one I could find in the Gloria's Secret catalogue and even had one of those rabbit attachments.

"Suck on it."

Silence.

My cock rose another few inches. It was almost at full mast and as hard as a rock.

"Lick it all over. Make it really wet. And don't forget to kiss those cute little bunny ears. For. Me."

While the line stayed quiet, I wished I'd Skyped with her. But as my father said, some things were best left to the imagination. Let me tell you, my mind's eye was getting a workout. A wild one.

"Now what, Blake?" Her voice was breathy.

With my boner straining against my fly, I shifted a little on the bed. "I want you to pull up that pretty little skirt of yours and bend over my desk. Click on your weapon and aim for your clit. Keep the phone on speaker nearby. I want to hear you loud and clear."

The buzz of the dildo sounded in my ear, but it was soon washed out by her loud whimpers. I'd preset the vibration mode to extreme pulsation.

"Good job, baby. Now for phase two of your mission. Stick your weapon up your pussy."

"Okay," she breathed. I could hear her panting and imagine the glorious sheen on her face as well as her adorable ass up in the air.

"Oh my God" were the next words I heard. I could no longer keep my throbbing cock in my pants. With a hiss, I zipped down my fly and out popped my whopper. Holding the phone to my ear, I began to stroke it with my free hand to the beat of her desperate whimpers. I squeezed my eyes shut as my balls tightened, and the madness between my thighs intensified with each long, hard stroke. Close to the edge, I picked up my pace, stroking fast and furiously. My breathing grew ragged.

"Blake, I can't take this anymore," she moaned into the phone.

"Stay with me, baby. You're almost there." My hand galloped along my massive shaft as I imagined her soaked, throbbing pussy. My head lolled back as my pulsing cock raced to climax. Oh, sweet Jesus. Filling and swelling. On the next harsh breath, I exploded with an epic release that could make the Guinness Book of Records.

"Fuck," I muttered under my breath as a sweet cry of ecstasy sounded on the other end. I slowly peeled open my eyes and caught my breath.

"Tiger, are you there?"

Silence. Shit. Maybe she'd passed out. I imagined her collapsed over my desk.

"Tiger?"

"Blake." Her voice was just a tiny whisper. "That was amazing."

"Yeah, fucking amazing. You okay?"

"Yes. How did I do?"

"Baby, you can be on my team any day." I glanced down at my glistening semi-erection. *Mission accomplished.*

"I miss you, baby."

"The same." I crawled out of the bed, leaving my khakis behind though taking my phone with me. "I've got to wash up (oh boy, did I) and go out for dinner with my New York manager. I'll call you later. Where are you going to be?"

"I have my rape support group after work."

"Be careful. You know I don't like that neighborhood at night." I'd become as protective of her as I was possessive.

"Don't worry. I'll be fine. And then I'll be home dealing with wedding stuff."

At the word wedding, a chill skittered down my spine.

"Baby, if Kat harasses you, let me know. And don't believe a word she says. There's only you. Only you."

Chapter 15

Jennifer

I missed Blake terribly. He'd been away for over a week. Yes, he "sexted" and Skyped me, and we'd even had outrageous phone sex, but this didn't make up for not having him around. I missed falling asleep in his arms and waking up on his chest, his heartbeat singing in my ears. And I missed seeing him at the office, sneaking kisses whenever we could. The touch and taste of his lips. Those kissable lips that had kissed me everywhere.

I was lonely. And a little on edge. Having Blake around made me feel safe and protected. The Springer incident had messed with my head. While we lived in a secure doorman building, an unexpected sound outside our apartment caused my heartbeat to accelerate, thinking someone might be trying to break in. And sometimes, I thought I was being followed, though when I glanced over my shoulder, no one was ever there. Other girls in my rape support group shared these insecurities. Dr. Williams, our group leader who had been a rape victim herself, said they were common.

Both Libby and Chaz were on the road—Chaz for trunk shows in major cities across the country and Libby for focus groups. Libby's findings along with ratings and quantitative survey research would determine which Conquest Broadcasting shows of the new Fall season would stay on the schedule and which would be canceled. I was thrilled my innovative block of women's erotic romance programming—MY SIN-TV—had tested through the roof. To my utter delight, Blake had told me there was talk of expanding the block and even creating a spin-off 24/7 women's erotica channel.

The only good thing about having Blake away was that I could focus on the wedding, especially at night. Every day after work, I came home to a boatload of gifts—so many that one of the building attendants had to pile them up on a dolly and cart them up to our apartment. Thank goodness, Blake had a spare bedroom. There was no place else to store all the boxes. It was almost filled to the hilt. The gifts came from all over the world, including a complete set of the eggcups from a Duchess in England who unfortunately couldn't attend the wedding. I'd become a master of writing thank you notes to people I didn't know.

E-mails from Enid besieged my inbox, and quite truthfully, I didn't have the time to open and respond to all of them during my busy work day. Every day, she updated me on the RSVP list. The pearl encrusted invitations had finally gone out—yes, packed inside giant iridescent seashells, twelve hundred in all. The betrothal of Blake Adam Burns to Jennifer Leigh McCoy was now official.

We were already at six hundred twenty guests. The list was growing exponentially and that meant yet more gifts. More thank you notes. I seriously couldn't believe how many people the Bernsteins knew. Well-known television producers, directors, and stars were coming to the black tie affair from all over the world. And many politicians too. I perused the latest list. Oh my God. Even George Clooney and his new wife were coming. And so were Brangelina and the Clintons. I only hoped my mother could take a photo with Hilary.

Surveying the "C's" on the latest RSVP list, I spotted Libby Clearfield's name and wrinkled my brows. I'd invited both her and a guest—her longtime boyfriend Everett—but the response was not for "plus-one." Libby, my maid of honor, was intending to attend my wedding solo. I immediately speed-dialed her cell phone, having no idea where or what time zone she was in. She picked up on the second ring.

"Hi, Jen. I just got home. A quick break until I do my Midwest groups. What's up?" Her voice, so unlike her, sounded weary.

I got straight to the point. "Why aren't you coming to my wedding with Everett?"

Silence. A long, tense silence. Finally, my bestie broke it. Her voice was small and shaky.

"Jen, I think I need to break up with him."

I reflected on her word choice...*need.*

"What do you mean?" Libby and Ev had been together forever, and despite the more than five thousand miles that separated them—she in LA and he in London on a Fulbright—neither had strayed from the other to the best of my knowledge. A moment of doubt hit me like a lightning bolt.

"Oh my God. Did Everett cheat on you?"

"Hardly," she said, her voice now tearful. In a heartbeat, she began to cry, sobs beating into my ear. Something so, so out of character for my sassy best friend. My heart was splintering.

"Lib, do you want to come over and talk?"

"I don't want to intrude on you and Blake." As close as we were, she was uncomfortable spending time in our condo. And because of the Springer shit that'd happened back in our little rented cottage, I was unable to go back there. Too many bad memories that ended in nightmares.

"Listen, Lib. Blake is out of town. Get your red curls over here, NOW."

She was on her way.

Libby looked tired. Her eyes were bloodshot—either from crying or the lack of sleep or both. The glut of focus groups, incessant travel, and whatever she was going through emotionally had taken a toll on her. Dressed casually in jeans and a USC sweatshirt, my curvy full-figured friend plopped down on one of Blake's oversized Italian leather armchairs while I went to the kitchen to fetch a bottle of white wine and a pair of goblets.

I curled up on the matching leather couch catty-corner to her and filled the glasses.

She took a couple of slugs and her freckled face brightened. "Wow, this is good stuff."

"Blake belongs to a wine club." I took a sip. "But to be honest, I kind of miss our Two Buck Chuck."

Libby smiled. "I'm still drinking it, but it's not the same without you."

I smiled back and then turned serious, ready for some answers. "Lib, what's going on with you and Everett? Why isn't he coming to the wedding?"

She exhaled. "It's complicated. I still love him, but it's not going to work out."

I knitted my brows. "What do you mean?"

"He wants to stay in Europe. He's been offered some associate professor position at a university in France. He's been pressuring me to quit my job and join him." She paused and took another sip of the wine. "Jen, I can't. My life is here."

"How long has this been going on?"

She ran her free hand through her flaming red mane. "A while."

"Why didn't you tell me?"

"With all that's going on with your job and the wedding, I just didn't want to bog you down with my mess of a life. We've been fighting a lot. In fact, we just had one tonight."

That explained the tears. Suddenly, I felt bad. Libby had always been there for me, but somehow I hadn't reciprocated. At least, recently. I mentally kicked myself.

"You should have told me. But I'm glad you're telling me now."

Setting her depleted glass on the coffee table, she reached for the bottle and took a chug straight from it. So Libby. So us. I grabbed the bottle from her and did the same.

"Maybe it would be good if Everett came to the wedding and you could talk things through." Poor Libby hadn't seen him for almost a year. Her joke that her vagina was going to shrivel if she didn't get laid was no joking matter.

Snatching the bottle from me, she shook her head. "I don't think so. The wedding will give him the wrong idea. And it would be very hard on me. I'm going to break up with him. I just don't know when, where, or how. I need to do it face to face. I owe him that."

Her hazel eyes grew watery. An unsettling thought entered my mind. "Lib, are you okay with me getting married?" I wondered if maybe she was jealous or threatened. Or just plain sad.

She set the bottle down. "Oh, Jen, of course, I am. I'm so thrilled for you and Blake."

A bright smile lit my face. Despite initially not caring for my fiancé boss because she thought he was an arrogant, self-centered, egotistical jerk, which he sometimes still could be, my best friend had warmed up to him. Especially after he'd saved me from the monstrous Don Springer. A man who would slay for his woman scored big points in Libby's book.

"I'm so happy you're going to be my maid of honor," I said, the warmth of her words spreading through me.

Libby's lips flexed with a genuine smile. "Me too. I just wish I could be there for you more. This time of year is so busy for me. The focus groups won't let up until right before your wedding." She twirled a long, springy curl. "How's it going with Enid and the bitch?"

I caught her up on the dress situation and the latest developments. Her freckles practically jumped off her face.

"Oh my God! It sounds hideous. There's no way I'm letting her turn me into some sleazy sea siren. Chaz is going to design my dress too."

"With your red hair, you'd make the perfect Ariel."

"No fucking way." She playfully threw a pillow at me.

"And listen to this, at each place setting, there's going to be a snow globe with a live tropical fish inside. The take-home party favor."

Libby made fish lips and held up the bottle. "To my best friend's wedding!"

It was time to uncork another.

Maybe Enid could dictate almost everything about my wedding from the invitations to the décor. But there were two things she wasn't going to have any control over: the dress I was going to wear and the person I was tossing my bouquet to.

In my heart, I wanted Libby to have her happily ever after just like me.

The next evening when I came home from work, I received the first wedding gift I wanted to keep. A splendid silver-plated, engraved wine cooler from Crate & Barrel and two cases of Two-Buck Chuck from Trader Joe's. A big smile warmed my lips as I read the enclosed note.

To My Bestest Friend in the World~

I can't wait to stand with you.
Cry with you.
Laugh with you.
And hold up Chaz's dress while you pee.

I love you so much~ xo Libby

Chapter 16

Blake

I used to love these two weeks of visiting affiliates. It was a glorified road trip—I flew first class, stayed in five-star hotels, and ate in the finest restaurants. I visited my stations, wined and dined my managers, and usually found some babe to fuck and forget. Just last year at this time, I was having the time of my life.

But all that was before Jen. I couldn't wait for this trip to be over. I got in and out of every city as fast as I could. Acting like an old fart. I visited each station, went out to dinner with the general manager, and then feigned fatigue so I could go back to my hotel room and catch up with my tiger. We "sexted" and Skyped, but nothing compared to having her in the flesh in my bed. Wanking off wasn't cutting it.

After a quick visit with my Sacramento affiliate, I'd flown to the East Coast and then worked my way back to LA. My last stop was Las Vegas. I was actually looking forward to being there. Not only because I was one stop away from seeing my tiger, but because I also got to spend time with my favorite affiliate manager, Vera Nichols.

Vegas was our top market, thanks to Vera. She ran her station with both an iron fist and a big heart. Her staff adored and revered her. And rightfully so. Her inspirational style of management was one for the books.

"You should have had Jennifer fly in," she told me over lunch at an Italian restaurant close to the station. "And by the way, Blake, her erotic romance block is killing it here. So many viewers have told us they want more."

I grinned. My tiger was brilliant. A star. And not just in bed. All across the country, I'd gotten the same reaction. A 24/7 erotica channel targeted at women was inevitable.

"I wish she could have, but she's so tied up with production. She's trying to get everything wrapped before our wedding."

"How's the wedding shaping up?"

I told her how my mother's event planner was putting it together at lightning speed and that it was going to be very over the top. I also told her about Kat's involvement.

"Geez, Blake. That must be awful for Jennifer to have to deal with her."

"It sucks for both of us." I wanted to tell Vera more. I knew I could trust her with my heart, but my father's words of wisdom resounded in my ears: "When in doubt, leave it out." I should have heeded them in the first place when it came to Kat.

Vera took a last sip of coffee. "I'm so honored Jennifer chose me to be one of her bridesmaids. I just need to figure out when I can fly into LA to be fitted for my dress."

"She's so honored you accepted. She thinks the world of you, Vera. Like I do." Vera was like a sister to me. And even more so than the one I actually had. I fought the urge to confide in her.

"Steve wants to take you out for drinks tonight," she said as

I took care of the check. "He's going to call you later."

"Awesome." I looked forward to spending my final night in Vegas with Vera's husband. Tomorrow, I would be back in my office. First thing, I was going to have a closed door meeting with my Director of MY SIN-TV. I was going to fuck her over my desk.

I was staying at the Bellagio, one of the swankiest hotels in Vegas. While the Hard Rock was Conquest Broadcasting's preferred hotel, I made a point of not staying there because of the special memories it held for me. One day, Jen and I would go back there and fuck our brains out.

At nine p.m., Steve called me to let me know he was here. When I got downstairs to the sprawling casino, not only was Steve waiting for me. Surprise. So was Jaime Zander. And an even bigger surprise—so was Jake, my roommate from college. The one who'd made me enter that crazy America's top model contest. Now that he was living in Silicon Valley, I hadn't seen him for over a year. He'd been through some bad shit but came out smelling like a rose. Something good had come out of the bad. Success agreed with him.

"You look fucking good, man," I said, giving him a man-hug. Along with Steve and some guys from the office, he was going to be one of my groomsmen.

"Where are we going?" I asked as the three of us, all casually dressed in jeans, headed toward the entrance to the bustling hotel.

I quickly learned we were going to have a guys' night

out—a bachelor party so to speak.

"C'mon, man," said Steve as we filed into the Lip Service limo, courtesy of Jake, so we didn't have to think about drinking and driving. "You're going to sow your wild oats tonight."

"Don't lose me, dudes." Scenes from *The Hangover* flashed into my head. "I don't want to be hanging with any tigers." (Well, except the adorable one I was craving back home.)

The strip joint the guys took me to was off the beaten track. Despite being high-end, it was in a word—raunchy. All dark and smoky. Jaime had gotten us a reservation in the upstairs VIP room. The two of us nestled on the gaudy red velvet U-shaped couch while Steve and Jake plunked down on over-stuffed club chairs. We shared two cylinder-shaped tables. A big tit cocktail waitress in a skimpy leather mini dress that barely covered her ass brought us a thousand dollar bottle of Cognac to go with our Cubans and filled our crystal snifters.

"To *that* man!" Jaime toasted, aiming his balloon glass at me. We clinked and chugged the shots.

As the velvety orange liquid warmed my blood, swirls of colorful disco lights bathed the scarlet walls and music piped through the speakers. Wouldn't you know it? "Bang Bang"— the very song Jen had stripped to a few weeks ago.

"Here comes your girl," sang Steve, refilling our glasses.

"Whoof!" mumbled Jake, blowing a ring of smoke.

Strutting my way was five feet ten inches of pure plastic. Bikini clad, tatted, and wearing tacky as shit platforms. I gulped my drink. Fuck. I recognized her. She was one of the blond bimbos who'd assaulted me at the Hard Rock pool and put a rift of misunderstanding between Jennifer and me.

Jennifer's stinging words whirled around in my head. "No girl means anything to you." What a difference a year could make. And what a difference one special girl could make.

"Hiya, handsome," she cooed, hurling me into the moment with a seductive come-on. "Nice seeing you again."

"You know each other?" laughed Jaime, sucking on his cigar.

"Oh yeah," said Kelly or Keely or whatever the fuck her name was. "But now we're going to get to know each other better."

Downing their cognacs, the boys roared as she straddled her long legs over my lap. She was in my face. Her musky scent nauseated me. She smelled nothing of cherries and vanilla.

She began to do her thing. Pouting. Licking her lips. Gyrating her hips. Grinding my thighs. Swinging her melon-sized tits. Brushing them against me. Flinging her brassy mane. Touching herself all over. Smashed, my buddies were getting off on her, howling, "Whoo hoo! Fuck! Go, baby!" If only Gloria and Vera could see them.

You'd think my cock would be in overdrive. Bang bang. Don't let my genitals fool you. Forget it. Not even a testicular tingle. Not one urge to get my dick wet. Not wanting to be a killjoy, I plastered a fake smile on my face. I fucking wasn't into it. In fact, I felt sick and wished I could take her by the haunches and shove her aside. Even pass her over to one of my stag mates. Out of the corner of my eye, I saw cameras on either side of the room. Damn. She could touch, but I couldn't. Physical contact wasn't allowed. I put my clammy palms under my ass so I wouldn't be tempted.

Seamlessly, a new song started up. Enrique Inglesias's "Bailando."

"I wanna be *contigo,*" purred my private dancer, in her cheap, nasal voice. To my utter horror, while she circled her soaked center around my cock, her Miley Cyrus length tongue trailed up my neck to my lips. While my pals howled like animals, I squirmed, forcing myself not to turn my head to avoid looking like a pussy. She might want to be with me, but I didn't want to be with her. Not one repulsive bit.

And then, I heard the hiss of a zipper. The sound of metal scraping against my dick. Shit. She was pulling down my fly. That did it. With a powerful thrust of my knees, and without touching her, I bounced her off my lap. Stunned, she fell onto one of the cylinder tables.

"What the fuck?" she hissed, collecting herself.

Not aware of what was really going on, shit-faced Jaime, Steve, and Jake applauded and blew wolf whistles.

"Give our boy a table dance," shouted Jaime, tucking a hundred dollar bill into her skimpy wet bottoms. He must have blown several thousand dollars at this pop stand.

I bolted to my feet.

"Where you going, dude?" asked Steve. "Need to wank off in the little boys' room?"

I tried to keep my cool but was sweating like a pig. I felt dirty and claustrophobic. Feigning fatigue once again and citing an early morning flight (which was, at least, true), I thanked my buds for my stag night.

"She's all yours, dudes." I didn't want to come across as a jackass.

"Man," said Jaime, his voice hoarse. "Are you wussing out

on us?"

I missed my tiger. It was as simple as that.

I got back to the Bellagio at midnight. While I couldn't get the Presidential Suite reserved for high rollers, I had an almost as luxurious penthouse unit on the same floor. Wearily, I inserted my key card into the door, debating whether to call my tiger after taking a quick shower to rid myself of the stench of stale booze, smoke, and bad pussy. At this late hour, she could be sound asleep.

Except for the dazzling Vegas skyline shining through the floor to ceiling windows, the suite was pitch-black. I swear I'd left the lights on. Maybe the turndown service maid had turned them off. Whatever. I headed straight to my bedroom, ready to collapse into bed.

As I stepped into the dark room, a familiar voice sounded in my ears.

"Hi, Blake. Did you have fun?"

My nerves shorted out. I flipped on the light. "What the hell are you doing here?"

It was fucking Kat. Wearing nothing but a black lace push up bra and matching thong along with black patent stilettos. Perched on my bed with her knees bent and endless legs spread. She licked her lips.

"You could be a little happier to see me and say hello." She slid a hand beneath the lace bottoms.

My blood was sizzling. "How did you know I was here?"

"From your friend Jaime Zander. When I called him to

discuss a bachelor party, he told me all about the one he had planned for you tonight."

"How did you get his number?" My voice was rising with anger.

She smiled smugly. "Daddy. Jaime handles all his advertising."

Mooreland Realty was one of the biggest realtors in the country. I had no idea Clayton Moore was one of Jaime's clients. That explained why Kat was at his art gallery opening last December.

"How did you get into my room?"

She batted her eyes. "It's amazing what a hundred dollar bill given to the right person can get you."

I'd give as many hundreds at it took to get her out of my room. And out of my life for good. It was time to cut to the chase.

"Kat, what the fuck do you want?"

"I want what we once had." She was fingering herself.

"We had nothing."

"We had Capri."

"It was just a summer fling. I ended it, but you have some kind of weird-ass obsession with me. You should be in therapy."

She let out a mocking laugh. "I've been in therapy my whole life. It's a joke."

Obviously, it was. She was still one sick chick.

She narrowed her eyes at me "You ruined it for me with all other men. No one fucks the way you do."

"I'm sure you can find someone," I said, wondering why the hell I was even having this conversation with her.

"We could have had it all, Blake. But you fucked it up."

"You fucked yourself." I spat out the words.

Anger washed over her face. Her eyes flared with fury. I was beginning to think she was bi-polar. I'd had enough.

"Please get the fuck out of here before I call security." I had to control myself from physically throwing her out the door.

Slowly and wordlessly, she made her way out of my bed. My eyes stayed fixed on her as she donned her pencil skirt and tight V-neck sweater. She grabbed her monstrous purse and marched to the door to my suite. At the doorway, she turned and glared at me. A sinister smile curled on her lips.

"I'm going to prove how much *I* love you, Blake. I'm going to let *you* tell that classless, mousy fiancée of yours *all* about us."

I clenched my jaw and my fists. I'd never been this close to punching a woman. My blood pressure soaring, I held my breath and then let it go through my nose.

"Get the hell out of here, Kat. NOW!"

"Bye, Blakey," she retorted, her voice saccharine sweet. She turned on her heel and disappeared.

I sunk down on the couch and rubbed my temples. Tomorrow, when I got back to LA, I was going to have a heart-to-heart talk with my tiger. It was time she knew.

Chapter 17

Jennifer

Thank God, Blake was coming back tomorrow morning. The two weeks he'd been away felt like an eternity. And this last week had been pure misery.

I was bloated. Achy. Irritable. And tired. A total emotional wreck.

I cried at the littlest things. For no reason.

I yelled at sweet Mrs. Cho when she couldn't reach Blake.

I scribbled red-ink notes all over one of the scripts I was reading and couldn't focus on another.

I broke down and bawled in my support group when a new member shared her horrific story of being beaten and raped.

The pressures of work and the wedding were getting to me. And so was something else. I was over a week late for my period. *Stress?* Tossing the script I was reviewing, I googled my symptoms.

Oh shit!

If things couldn't get more complicated, an unexpected e-mail popped up in my inbox. The hair on the back of my neck bristled. It was from my ex-fiancé, Bradley Wick. I hadn't seen or heard from him since the time I ran into him and his fiancée Candace, registering at Bloomingdale's, and that was almost a year ago. I stared at my computer screen, my fingertips lightly drumming the keyboard. The only thing keeping me from deleting it was the subject line said URGENT in big shouty caps. With reservation, I opened it. The long and short of it— Bradley wanted to see me. He had something important he wanted to share. Despite my angst-out state, I agreed to meet him at lunch—at a nearby vegan restaurant. Some things never changed.

Mr. Punctuality was already seated at a table in the small, uncrowded restaurant. He'd already ordered one of those green soymilk concoctions he favored. Taking a seat across from him (yes, still the same ungentlemanly Bradley), I rested one hand on the table and the other, with Blake's ring, on my lap. I studied his face as he flashed that big toothy smile. The smile hadn't changed but his face had—he looked like he'd put on a fair amount of weight. He'd gotten jowly, and his receding hairline had receded further.

"Hi, Jennifer," he said, handing me a menu. "Thanks for coming."

"Sure, Bradley. No problem." Interestingly, I no longer felt anything toward him—neither rage nor contempt for having cheated on me with his hygienist. "You said it was urgent. Is something the matter?"

"I made a mistake."

I cocked my head. "What do you mean?"

"I should have married *you.*"

"Bradley, what are you talking about?"

"It didn't work out with Candace. She was a money grubbing wench. We just finalized our divorce. The bitch got the condo."

"I'm sorry to hear that." Okay. I had to admit it. My heart was doing a little jig. He'd gotten his comeuppance.

"I want us to get back together. Give it another chance." To my shock, he reached across the table and palmed my hand. I yanked it away.

"Bradley, I'm afraid that's not possible." My other hand flew up from under the table. I held it up, the glimmering snowflake diamond facing him. "I'm engaged."

Bradley's beady eyes darkened. "To who?"

"To my boss. Blake Burns."

Bradley's lips snarled. "To that fucking psychopath who practically bit off my fingers?"

I nodded. Bradley's face reddened with rage. He slammed his juice on the table.

"You're making the biggest mistake of your life."

"No, Bradley, the biggest mistake of my life would have been marrying you. Thank goodness, Blake sent me that video of you and Candace all over each other."

Bradley's eye grew wide with shock. "What! That bastard shot that footage?"

Enough of this lunch; it was beginning to nauseate me. "Excuse me, Bradley. I'm going to use the restroom, and then I'm splitting."

Grabbing my shoulder bag, I stood up and then hurried to the restroom located in the back of the restaurant. Frequent urination. Another symptom. Fortunately, the small one-person unisex bathroom was vacant. I emptied my bladder, washed my hands, and unlocked the door. As I opened it, Bradley came charging in and pushed me backward until I was pinned against the wall. His newly flaccid body pressed against me and his small hands fondled my swollen breasts.

"Bradley, please let me go," I pleaded, trying to stay calm.

Madness flickered in his eyes. "No, not until you get another taste of me." He leaned into me with his mouth parted. His antiseptic breath skimmed my cheeks. To my horror, his repulsive lips were about to touch down on mine. *No fucking way.* Without over thinking, my knee came up and jabbed his groin. I heard him groan. *Bingo!* I'd gotten him right where I wanted. Right in the balls! The self-defense class Blake had made me take had paid off.

"Fuck!" he roared as he crumpled to the tiled floor. Clutching his crotch, he writhed in pain.

A victorious smile shimmered on my face, and then it fell off like a scab, giving way to cold fury. "Don't you ever contact me again, Dickwick. I'm so done with you."

He glared at me. "You're going to pay for this, Jennifer Fucking McCoy."

Without another word, I scurried out of the restroom, my stomach cramping.

On the way back to the office, I made a stop. At a CVS drugstore. There was something I needed to buy. There was something I needed to know.

And soon enough I did.

Chapter 18

Blake

I got on an early morning flight and was back in LA by seven a.m. I had my driver take me straight to my apartment. I couldn't wait to see my tiger. I was going to fuck her senseless, and then I was going to tell her. The sour taste of Kat was still in my mouth. I had to cleanse myself of her. I'd buried the truth six feet under, but now I had to expose it before it blew up in my face. My stomach knotted as I inserted the key into the door lock. A cocktail of guilt and anxiety coursed through my blood. I hadn't rehearsed any kind of confession, nor did I have any idea how she would react to what I was about to tell her. I'd made a stupid, stupid mistake.

Expecting to see my early riser in the kitchen making coffee, I was surprised when she wasn't there. Dropping my bag, I padded to our bedroom. With the blackout curtains drawn, the room was dark. I could hear her soft breaths. Quietly, I traipsed over to the bed. She was still sound asleep, a script by her side. She looked so beautiful and peaceful. Despite my physical and emotional needs, I couldn't wake her. I headed to the bathroom to wash up and then I shed my clothes and crawled bone naked into the bed. Before I could get under the covers, she stirred.

"Blake?" she said sleepily. Her eyes fluttered open and she

twitched a small smile.

"Baby, what are you still doing in bed? I thought you'd be getting ready for work."

She groaned. I smoothed her hair. "Are you okay?

"I got my period. It's super heavy and I have really bad cramps." She grimaced. "I'm almost two weeks late."

My stomach twisted. While she was still on the pill, I hadn't used a condom in almost a year. The chances were slim but still possible.

"Do you think you had a miscarriage?" Saying that last word pained me.

She shook her head. "No. I took a pregnancy test yesterday. It was negative."

I felt partly relieved, but worry still gnawed at me.

She sat up slowly. The pinched expression on her face told me she was in pain. She held a hand to her belly.

"I'm going to head into the office a little later if that's okay with you."

"No, it's not okay. I want you to stay home and rest."

"But Blake, I've got so much to do. And with the wedding and everything—"

"Fuck it. It'll all get done. And I want you to see my sister. She's the best gynecologist in town."

I held her in my arms. "I've missed you, baby."

"The same," she said softly as I planted a kiss on her scalp.

Fucking my tiger wasn't happening. And the dreaded conversation I wanted to have with her would have to wait.

Chapter 19
Jennifer

"Hi, Marcy. Thanks for seeing me on such short notice." I'd actually had to wait almost two weeks for my lunchtime appointment—until my much longer than usual period subsided. I'd been so looking forward to accompanying Blake at lunch to pick out a new tux for the wedding, but he was insistent on me seeing his sister at the very first opportunity. Health came first.

"Not a problem, Jennifer. Fortunately, I had a cancellation." Her voice was professional but warm. Clad in a stylish slacks outfit under her lab coat, she looked a little trimmer since I'd last seen her, and she was wearing more makeup. She actually looked very pretty.

She continued. "What brings you here?"

Sitting with one leg folded over the other on an examining room table, I told her that I hadn't been to a gynecologist since grad school, and that I was experiencing some cramping and heavy bleeding with my period. It had lasted ten days.

"Are you on the pill?" she asked.

"Yes." I nodded.

"Okay, what I'd like you to do is to undress and put on the robe, leaving it open in the front. I'll be right back." She ambled out of the small room, closing the door behind her.

I eyed the blue paper robe sitting next to me on the table. In no time, I was undressed and wearing the flimsy contraption. Still seated on the table, I surveyed my surroundings. Unlike the campus doctor's examination room, it was full of personality. Marcy's numerous degrees and awards took up space on the walls along with many charming framed pieces of artwork done by her children. One, a painting of SpongeBob, brightened my spirits.

Blake's sister returned in no time. She shot me a small smile. I think this was a first.

"Jennifer, I'd like you to lie down."

Doing as she asked with my knees steepled, I watched as she slid out two metal stirrups from the examining table.

"Now slide your rear down to the edge and put your feet in these."

Familiar with this routine, I did as she asked. The jolt of cold metal against the heels of my bare feet sent a shiver up my spine.

"Perfect." Facing me, she inserted a gloved hand into my center, gently pressing and moving around it. She closed her eyes while doing the pelvic exam.

"You're very tiny," she commented.

"Yeah, I know," I replied, hoping she wasn't going to say something like: "How does my brother get his huge cock inside you?" Or: "Does it hurt when he fucks you?" The truth: Blake fit inside me beautifully, and it felt fucking great.

As Marcy probed with her gloved fingers, I suddenly imagined Blake here doing the same. Feeling me up and then fucking me wildly with my feet anchored in these stirrups.

He'd once told me he'd done that to a high school teacher and had gotten caught by his sister. Such a bad boy. A sudden distraught thought made me shudder: Had he ever done that to Kat?

"Are you okay?" asked Marcy, obviously feeling me squirm.

"Yes, everything's good." I forced Kat to the back of my head. Whatever she had with Blake was ancient history. I shouldn't care. Yet, I did.

Marcy continued to probe.

"Did you find anything?" My voice was peppered with concern. She seemed to be spending an unusually long time exploring my privates.

She opened her eyes and removed her hand. "So far, everything seems normal."

Relieved, I kept my eyes on her as she reached for the speculum on the mobile tray table beside her. I hated this part of the exam.

"Now, I'm going to insert this into your vagina and then do a pap smear. Let me know if it hurts," she said as she adjusted the metal clamp between my legs.

While it was definitely uncomfortable, it didn't hurt. Marcy had a very gentle touch. My eyes stayed on her as she swabbed me twice, once with a small spatula and then again with a small bristle brush. She dipped each into separate vials that were filled with liquid and labeled with my name.

"Are we done?" I asked, eager to leave.

"I'd like to do one more thing. An ultrasound just to do a double check."

I'd never had one before. "Isn't that what they do for pregnant women?" I shivered. Maybe I was pregnant and that stupid store-bought test was wrong.

"Yes," she said, first pressing down on my abdomen. "Does this hurt?"

I had to be honest. "Just a little."

Her lips pinched, she pressed down harder. I gave a little yelp. A frisson of fear rippled through me. "Is that normal?"

"Yes. Some women are just very sensitive. If you really had a lot of pain, you would have jumped off the table."

Inwardly, I sighed with relief as Marcy wheeled the ultrasound machine closer to me. It consisted of a monitor and some kind of computer with lots of buttons and attachments. She then lifted up my paper gown and rubbed some gel on my tummy. The surprising warmth of it contrasted sharply with the chill of the air conditioning.

"Is this going to hurt?" I asked, fear creeping into my voice.

"Not at all." She smiled again. "It may even tickle."

I watched as she glided the head of a shaver-shaped probe around my belly while her other hand fiddled with the buttons and keys on the computer. She was right. It did tickle.

Her intense blue eyes alternated between my abdomen and the screen as did mine. I was intrigued by the volcano-like image on the screen, but had no clue what it was.

"Hmm," she murmured, her eyes on the monitor.

My muscles tensed. "Is something wrong with me?"

"You have a number of fibroid tumors on your uterus." She pointed them out to me on the monitor. They looked like shadowy dark spots. There were five in total.

"Oh my God. Are they dangerous?" Panic shot through me.

Tumors? The C-word was on the tip of my tongue.

"Actually, they're very common and benign. Many women have them although they're a little unusual for someone as young as you. They explain your heavy, irregular period and the cramping."

"What should I do?" I asked anxiously as she cleaned off my shiny tummy with one of those moist wipes.

"Really nothing. We'll just have to monitor them to watch how fast they grow and see if they affect your ability to get pregnant."

My panic button sounded. I was such an alarmist. "Does that mean I won't be able to have a baby?"

"Not at all. Most of the time, they're harmless and very slow growing. If they do interfere with your ability to conceive, they can be laparoscopically removed."

"Laparoscopically?" I could barely pronounce the scary-sounding word.

"It's a noninvasive surgical procedure. It's rather painless and can be done as an out-patient." She set the probe down on the ultrasound stand while I lay there motionless. Worry was etched on my face.

"Jennifer, honestly, there's no need to worry at this point," Marcy said with a comforting smile. "I want you to stay on the pill and eat foods rich with iron so you don't get anemic. Just let me know if you experience any unusual discomfort." She took off her latex gloves and washed her hands as I collected myself.

"Would you like to have lunch?" she asked. "I close the office and take an hour break every day. There's a great little coffee shop downstairs."

I was pleasantly surprised by her offer. I'd never spent a lot of time with Blake's sister. And Blake rarely socialized with her. Maybe this would be a good opportunity to get to know her and learn more about their brother-sister relationship. And she was, after all, going to be one of my bridesmaids.

The coffee shop Marcy took me to was right next door to her office. It was small and totally unpretentious and kind of reminded me of the old fashioned coffee shops in Boise. We both ordered iron-rich medium rare burgers and kale salads, along with Cokes—she, a diet one, and I, a cherry one.

I anxiously bit into my delicious burger, not quite knowing what to say to her. Marcy, on the other hand, wasted no time starting a conversation.

"I thought we should get to know each other since we're going to be sisters-in-law."

Swallowing, I agreed. "Thanks for inviting for me for lunch."

"My pleasure." She took a sip of her soda through her straw. "You're probably wondering why Blake and I don't get along that well."

Ten years younger than Marcy, he had mentioned once that the two of them fought all the time as children. "He doesn't really talk about it much," I replied. "Mostly, he refers to you as being the best gynecologist in all of LA." *The truth.*

Marcy's eyes widened with surprise. "He said something nice about me?"

"Yes. He's very proud of you."

With that, Marcy began to tell me what it was like growing up with Blake. She had enjoyed being an only child, and though never the beauty her mother was, her parents lavished her with attention. She was quite the bookworm and pleaser, always studying and scoring high grades. She sounded a lot like me.

When Blake came along, everything changed. The beautiful blue-eyed baby was the apple of everyone's eyes. The center of attention. No matter how mischievous he was, he got away with everything. Marcy grew jealous of Blake, who knew how to wrap both his father and mother around his little finger. And his grandma too. While sixteen-year-old Marcy was going through an awkward stage with raging hormones and pimples, six-year-old Blake was getting more adorable each day.

"I felt threatened by him," Marcy sighed. "I was the smart one, but I really wanted to be the beautiful one." She paused to sip her Coke. "Thank goodness, I have identical twins. And even if they weren't, I'd never pit one against the other that way. Or lavish more attention on one over the other."

I processed what she'd said. Being an only child, I had no clue about sibling rivalry. I stored her information in my mind for the future.

"How are Jonathan and Jackson doing?" I interjected.

"Thanks for asking. They're actually doing surprisingly well. In fact, better now that Matt and I are separated. I think all our fighting really affected them. Kids model themselves after their parents' behaviors."

More words of wisdom. And so true. I was so much like my pleasing mother, so non-confrontational. And I dissected things like my father. I told Marcy I was sorry about her marriage.

"Don't be. We weren't good for each other. It was a marriage of rebellion and convenience—he was a good-looking poor guy and I came from a lot of money. But we didn't make the other half better."

I thought hard about what Marcy had just said. Blake was still cocky, stuck-up, and arrogant. Maybe we weren't meant...

Before I could finish my thought, Marcy jumped in. "Jennifer, I just want to tell you that you are so good for Blake. You make him better. I see the way he acts around you. He's sweet, considerate, and loving. He's more patient and so much less into himself."

"But he's still so cocky and self-assured."

Marcy rolled her eyes. "You have no idea. And those bimbos he used to hang with..."

"Do you know Kat Moore?" The question slipped out of my mouth.

Marcy's blue eyes darkened. "That girl is pure trouble. Stay away from her."

"She's helping plan our wedding."

"Be careful. Don't let her manipulate you." She pressed her lips thin as if she wanted to tell me more and was holding back words. Before I could ask her what she meant, she changed the subject.

"The boys are so excited about being the ring bearers. But they've been fighting over who's carrying which ring."

Still mulling her previous words, I feigned a chuckle. The check came and Marcy reached for it. Her treat. She smiled warmly at me and then did something unexpected—she affectionately clasped my hands in hers.

"Jennifer, I'm so glad you're marrying Blake. You're the best thing that's ever happened to him. I'm thrilled you're going to be my sister-in-law."

We ended lunch with a hug. A new mission impossible awaited me. I was determined to get Blake to like his sister as much as I did.

Chapter 20

Blake

I owned half a dozen tuxes, but Jennifer was insistent I get a brand new one for our wedding. One that had never been photographed at the many galas I'd attended or touched by one of my former hook-ups.

Driving my Porsche with the top down, I headed to Beverly Hills where I was going to meet with my personal shopper, Daniel, at the Saks Fifth Avenue Men's Store. I was actually looking forward to it. Unlike a lot of men who hated shopping for clothes, I actually loved it. And I especially loved buying beautiful Italian designer suits. I must have owned over two hundred of them. Jennifer's analytical friend Libby called me a metrosexual, and one night when we went out for dinner, she made me take a *Cosmopolitan* magazine quiz.

1. You just can't walk past a beauty supply store without making a purchase. *True.*
2. You own fifty pairs of shoes, a dozen pairs of sunglasses, just as many watches and you only wear Calvin Klein briefs. *True.*
3. Mani-pedi is part of your vocabulary. *True.*

4. You shave more than just your face. You also exfoliate and moisturize. *True.*

5. You can't imagine a day without hair styling products. *True.*

6. You spend more time in the bathroom showering and grooming than your girlfriend. *True.*

7. You carry a man bag. *False.*

Okay, so, I blew one question (guess which one), but I was a high maintenance kind of guy. Trust me, any rich, good-looking guy who tells you he isn't is full of shit. Jennifer couldn't believe I had to annex my closet to make extra room for all my suits—and all my grooming products. She'd threatened to buy me a man bag for Christmas. But that's where I drew the line. No fucking way. Our silly squabble flashed into my mind as I valeted my car at the back entrance of the venerable department store. As competent as I was when it came to suiting myself up, I wished she were here with me. But I didn't want her to miss her hard-to-get appointment with my sister, and she didn't want me to postpone the fitting with the wedding so close. It was less than a month away.

The valet attendant welcomed me warmly as I stepped out of the car. I was a familiar face. While a lot of guys I knew, including Jaime Zander, preferred to shop at hip Barney's down the street, I liked Saks. Because all three floors of the store catered only to men, it was kind of a refuge. The last place I'd get assaulted by a blond bimbo. Besides, this is where my father shopped and his father before him. Legacy.

Upon entering the store, I headed to the elevator and took it straight to the third floor. Daniel met me quickly. To my astonishment, I was the sole customer. Well, at least I'd get done quickly. In fact, I knew what tux I liked already—it was draped on a mannequin. Simple. Elegant. A one-buttoned tapered jacket and a thin satin stripe along the pants leg. The kind Brad Pitt might wear.

"An excellent choice," commented the perfectly groomed, androgynous Daniel. "An Armani. It just came in. I'll retrieve one in your size and send Luigi to the dressing room to tailor it."

Five minutes later, I was looking, if I had to say so myself, damn good in my new tux, complete with a slick new tux shirt and bow tie as well as a snappy pocket square in my signature blue. The spacious dressing room was the size of a guest room, done up in soothing shades of gray. Standing before the tri-fold mirror, I watched as Luigi, my tailor, expertly made some alterations. A stocky Italian craftsman in his late seventies with a shock of never-graying jet black hair, he'd been with the store forever and had tailored both my father's and grandfather's suits. He was practically family.

"*Howsa* your grandma?" he asked in his still thick Italian accent as he squatted down and let out the hem of the pants to accommodate my long legs.

"She's great." I'd long suspected that Luigi had a crush on Grandma.

"You tell her Luigi said to give her his love." I made a mental note: Invite Luigi to the wedding. Grandma needed a date. *And* sex.

Luigi stuck a few pins along the legs of the pants, taking them in. I always took one size bigger because I needed the extra crotch room. While the crotch could be let out, having pins anywhere near my dick gave me testicular tingles—not the good kind.

"So *who'sa* the lucky girl?"

"Her name is Jennifer. You'll meet her, Luigi, at the next fitting."

"Luigi cannot wait." He finished up. "*All-a* done." The jovial Italian reassembled his tailoring kit. He carefully helped me off with the jacket and then left me alone in the dressing room, closing the door behind him.

About to unbutton the pinned-up trousers, I heard a knock on the door. I recognized the voice. Daniel.

"Mr. Burns, your fiancée is here. May I send her back?"

"Of course." That was just like my tiger to surprise me. A rush of tingles spread from my head to my toes. The thought of having a little quicky with her right here in this dressing room sent my dick into a dither. I could feel it rise and harden against the fine wool fabric of my trousers. Maybe I'd wall-bang her or fuck her over the velvet bench or have a roll on the carpet. We could even watch ourselves come in the tri-fold mirror. My pulse quickened as the unlocked door swung open.

"Hi, Blake."

My jaw dropped to the floor and so did my cock.

I watched in the mirror as one of her long, toned bare arms wrapped around my shoulder while the other one grabbed my crotch. Hot kisses singed the back of my neck. Every muscle in my body clenched.

"Kat, what the fuck are you doing here?" Rage fueled every word, but I didn't move, afraid her claws would dig into my balls.

"You know you want me." Smirking, she squeezed my

equipment harder. I yelped. And then, in one swift move, she unbuttoned the tuxedo pants and unzipped the fly. The pants slid down to my feet. She worked her hand under my briefs.

"Fucking let go of me." Impulsively, I jerked myself free, almost smashing into the mirror.

I turned to face her. "Get the hell out of here."

Her fierce green eyes pierced me like poisonous darts. "You should be marrying me, Blake, not that pathetic excuse for a woman. You need a Rolls Royce, not a pickup truck."

"Don't you ever fucking talk about my future wife like that." Seething mad, I clutched the tails of my tux shirt so I wouldn't raise a hand and slap the shit out of her.

Another smirk flashed on her face and then she huffed. "Are you threatening me, Blake?"

I didn't respond. "Just. Go."

"Does Jennifer know yet what *really* happened?"

My blood curdled. I still hadn't told her. I sucked in a gulp of the thickening air. "We don't sit around talking about you. We're too busy fucking like bunnies."

"Ha! Aren't you the funny one? Well, you're fucking with the wrong person."

Her double entendre wasn't lost on me. "You mind your own damn business, Kat, and keep your fucking mouth shut. And if you come near me one more time, I'm going to get a restraining order."

Collecting herself, she smirked yet again. "Oh, is that another threat? Don't worry, Blake."

With a fling of her mane of hair, she slithered out the door.

Chapter 21

Jennifer

I wove down trafficky Santa Monica Boulevard en-route to my office. Adele's "Rumor Has It" was playing on the radio.

My mind occupied, I forced myself to pay attention to the congested road. The findings of Marcy's examination were unsettling. While she seemed nonplussed, I was concerned. A new F-bomb. Fibroids. As I sat at what felt like forever at a red light, I debated whether or not I should tell Blake about them. With the wedding getting closer, we just didn't need more stress.

And while our lunch had drawn us closer, one of his sister's remarks had made my blood bubble. Yes, it didn't take a rocket scientist to figure out Kat was trouble...but what did she mean about not letting her manipulate me? The way she immediately switched the subject made me think there was something more. Something she wasn't telling me.

My mind drifted to Blake, and I glanced at my dashboard clock. It was almost one thirty. I wondered—was he still at his tux fitting? Maybe there was still time to show up and surprise him. Saks was only one turn away. Using my Bluetooth, I speed-dialed him. It went straight to his answering machine. I bypassed leaving a message. When the light turned green, I decided to take a chance. I made a sharp right onto Beverly Drive and headed south toward Wilshire.

My cell phone rang. A familiar number. I hit answer. My heart leapt into my throat.

Horns blared at me as I ran a red light.

Oh. My. God. *No!*

THAT
MAN
5

NELLE L'AMOUR

PRAISE FOR THAT MAN 5

"With *THAT MAN 5*, Nelle L'Amour proves she's the Queen of Sexy Romantic Comedy. Blake Burns will once again make you laugh, cry, and swoon."

—*Arianne Richmonde, USA Bestselling Author of The Star Trilogy*

"Holy mother of a finale! *THAT MAN 5* just filled my heart with pure joy and happiness. And the writing, the one-liners, the hot crazy sex...I cannot even begin to articulate what an amazing storyteller Nelle is, and I'm in awe of her ability to have made this series get better and better, hotter and hotter with each book."

—*A is for Alpha, B is for Books Blog*

"Way worth more than 5-stars. A MUST READ!!! So right up there with the *Stark* series and the *Beautiful Bastard* series."

—*Johnnie-Marie Howard, Reviewer*

"Author Nelle L'Amour is on top of her game. Right up there with Emma Chase and Christina Lauren. There's no funnier, sexier, or more original book boyfriend than Blake Burns."

—*Adriane Leigh, USA Today Bestselling Author of Beautiful Burn*

"*THAT MAN* has it all—love, drama, mystery, craziness, heartbreak, sweetness and lots and lots of scorching sex scenes that made me a hot me a hot mess. Bravo, Ms. L'Amour, for such an amazing, beautiful love story!"

—*Give Me Books*

"WOW! Let me tell you you're in for a thrill ride. This series is in my Top 5. You won't be able to get enough of Blake and his tiger!"

—*Summer's Book Blog*

"A perfect way to end the series. Be prepared to cry, throw things and swoon over Blake once again."

—*Book Avenue Reviews*

"An emotional rollercoaster. A kickbutt hero. It's been an absolutely amazing journey witnessing Blake and Jen's love flourish."

—*Fairest of All Reviews*

"A sweet, crazy, and dynamic love story. One I soon won't forget."

—*Love Betweeen the Sheets*

"An awesome end to a fantabulous series. This is one series that will definitely stay in my hoard of books."

—*My Book Filled Life*

"Flove this series! Nelle warned us to 'Be prepared to laugh, cry, and swoon.' Boy did I!!!"

—*Chasing Orion's Rouge Odyssey*

"I experienced every emotion possible reading this last installment. Jennifer and Blake's passion and energy make for unforgettable scenes. As Blake's Grandma always says: *Zei gezunt.* Enjoy!"

—*As You Like It Reviews*

**To join my mailing list for new releases, sales, and giveaways, please
sign up here:**
NEWSLETTER: nellelamour.com/newsletter

NICHOLS CANYON PRESS
Los Angeles, CA USA

THAT MAN 5

Cover by Arijana Karčic, Cover It! Designs
Proofreading by Karen Lawson and Gloria Herrera
Formatting by BB eBooks

To THAT MAN...Blake Burns

I will miss you.

And to all of you who fell in love with him.

Chapter 1

Blake

S peeding back to my office, my pulse was in overdrive. My unexpected encounter with Kat at Saks had unhinged me. The fucking bitch!

My nerves were buzzing. I couldn't trust her. Not one bit. I hadn't yet told Jennifer a thing. The timing sucked. Fatigued and frazzled by her heavy period, the pressures of work, and all the wedding craziness, she just didn't need to hear something that might send her over the edge. In retrospect, I should have told her a long time ago. What had happened wasn't really my fault, but it was something I wasn't proud of. I wanted to forget. Keep the memory buried.

Should I tell her now? Fuck. I had to. Before she heard it from that sick bitch, who I knew would twist the story and make me look like a total shit.

At the first red light on Wilshire Boulevard, I reached into my pants pocket for my cell phone. Balls. It wasn't there. It must have fallen out in the dressing room at Saks. I made a sharp U-turn and headed straight back to the store. My heart was racing. I'd given Kat plenty of lead time.

Foregoing the slow elevator, I bounded up the emergency stairs to the third floor, taking two steps at a time. Working out weekly at the steep Santa Monica Stairs had its benefits.

"Looking for this?" my personal dresser Daniel asked as I exited the stairwell. My phone was in his hand.

I was breathing hard, not because I was winded, but because I was stressing.

I huffed a loud breath of relief as he handed me the phone. "Thanks, man," I said and then hurried to the elevator. Before I could speed-dial Jen's number, the phone rang. I glanced down at the caller ID screen and hit answer. It was Mrs. Cho.

"Mr. Burns, Jennifer call me. She say to tell you she going home."

"What do you mean?" My heart was hammering.

"She cry on phone. She say something bad happen."

God damn it. I was too late. Kat had gotten to her.

I repeatedly pounded the down button but with no results. Fucking worthless piece of shit. Impatient, I flew back down the emergency stairs.

Fifteen minutes later, I pulled up to my condo building, relieved I hadn't gotten a speeding ticket. Leaving my car with the valet, I raced up to my apartment.

Silence.

"Jen! Jen? Are you here?" Frantically, I dashed from room to room, calling out her name. Fuck. Where was she?

I phoned her again. Her cell went straight to voicemail. I left her an urgent message, telling her to call me back right away. A chill skittered down my spine. Maybe, she'd never want to talk to or see me again. Once again, I'd deceived her.

Impulsively, I called my sister at her office. Perhaps, she knew something.

"Hi, Blake. What's up?" Her voice sounded unusually

warm and friendly.

"Marcy, while she was there, did Jennifer get a call or text that upset her?"

"No. We had a lovely lunch, and then I believe she was heading back to her office. What's going on?"

Rushing my words, I told her what I believed had happened. My sister was one of the few people who knew what had gone down between Kat and me. Kat's file was sealed in her office.

"Jeez, Blake. Why didn't you tell Jen?"

"I don't know. I should have. But I didn't." *Stupid me.*

"Blake, it wasn't all your fault." Marcy's voice was softer and compassionate.

"I know. But I'm sure crazy Kat twisted things. With all her trust issues, Jen probably believed her. She didn't go back to the office."

"Shit. Blake, you've got to find her and explain what happened before everything blows up again."

Pacing my bedroom, I blew out a heavy breath of air. "My secretary said she was going home, but she's not here." My heart beat into a frenzy. Maybe the news had upset her so much she got into a car accident. She was, after all, Calamity Jen. But then I calmed down. For sure, I'd know that by now. "Marcy, what should I do?"

"Try calling her again, and then try one of her friends. Maybe they know something."

Marcy was always the smart one. Made sense. After trying Jen one more time, I'd try Libby.

I thanked my sister and told her not to say anything to our parents…at least not yet.

She assured me she wouldn't. "Good luck, Blake. And call me the minute you hear from her." She paused. "Love you, lil' bro."

Her unexpected affectionate words touched me, and I thanked her again. I quickly ended the call and speed-dialed Jen one more time. Shit. Nada. Wasting no time, I scrolled through my contacts and hit Libby's name. Fortunately, Jennifer had given me her number in case of an emergency. This was an emergency. Jen was leaving me.

Libby's phone, like Jen's, went straight to voicemail. Damn it. She was probably in a focus group or traveling. In a state of panic, I redialed Mrs. Cho. Perhaps she knew more. And had heard from Jen.

"Mrs. Cho, you said Jennifer went home, but she's not at my condo."

"No, no, Mr. Burns. She go home to her mother. She say big emergency."

Jesus. It was worse than I thought. Yup. A big emergency. I'd broken her heart.

"Cancel all my meetings and get Travel to book me on the next available flight to Boise."

Quickly, I changed from my suit into a pair of jeans, a T-shirt, and my leather bomber jacket. I retrieved my overnight bag from my closet and hastily threw in a hodgepodge of cool-weather clothes and bare necessities.

One hour later, I was on Delta Flight 4820, heading non-stop to Boise. I was comfortably seated in first class. But my heart was painfully seated in my throat.

Chapter 2

Jennifer

I immediately spotted my mother sitting in the waiting room of St. Luke's and sprinted up to her. The minute I'd heard the news, I'd headed straight to LAX, running a red light and narrowly missing a head-on collision. I didn't even go home to pack a bag. I needed to get to Boise as fast as possible and could always borrow some of my mom's clothes. My heart hadn't stopped galloping.

"Mom!"

My mother sprung from her chair at the sound of my voice. Her eyes were swollen red, and tears were swimming down her face. We exchanged a hug.

"Oh, honey, I'm so glad you're here," she sniffed.

"How's Dad?"

She dabbed at her tears with the dainty lace-trimmed hankie she was holding. Her lips quivered. "I don't know yet. He's still in surgery."

A horrific, freak thing had happened. While he was taking an afternoon stroll through our neighborhood, a car had hit him. The driver's brakes had given out, and he'd lost control. The car had swerved off the road, pinning my father against a telephone pole.

"The driver feels so bad. He wanted to stay until Dad got out of surgery, but I told him to go home to his family."

I squeezed my mom's free hand. That was so like her. To be forgiving, no matter what the circumstances. Deep inside, I hoped this virtue had been passed on to me. I encouraged her to sit down and took the vacant seat next to hers.

"Honey, does Blake know what's going on?"

"I tried to call him, but haven't been able to reach him." As much as he depended on it, Blake was forever forgetting, misplacing, or losing his cell phone. Retrieving my phone from my shoulder bag, I tried him one more time. No answer. Straight to voicemail. Instead of leaving a message, I hung up and texted him.

In Boise. Desperately need to talk to u.

In my anxious state, I inadvertently hit send before adding my customary "*xo.*" And then my cell phone died. Without my charger, I now wouldn't know if he received my text or was trying to reach me.

I held my mom's hand as we waited patiently for news. My stomach was in knots. The minutes crawled by like hours, and from time to time, I could hear her soft sobs.

"Oh, honey, I'm so scared. What if—"

I cut her off. "Mom, he's going to be okay. I know it." I squeezed her icy hand, trying hard to believe my own words.

At close to six, a doctor met us in the waiting room. He introduced himself—Dr. Kumar. His accented voice was soft and melodic and suggested he was likely from India. He was wearing scrubs and a surgical mask atop his head. With his boyish good looks, the handsome physician looked too young to be an accomplished surgeon, but I reminded myself that St. Luke's was the best hospital in Boise and was, in fact, one of the top surgical hospitals in the country. I'd been here once when I'd gotten my tonsils out as a child.

My mom jumped to her feet and met his gaze. "Is my husband all right?" Her voice was small and shaky, and her eyes were still watering.

The brown-skinned doctor pressed his lips thin and swiped sweat off his forehead. "He's in critical condition."

"What does that mean, doctor?" I asked before my trembling mother could say a word.

"He sustained a head injury. We did an MRI and there's brain swelling. We won't know until tomorrow if he has sustained permanent damage."

His words were like a knife to my heart. The thought of my dad the professor not having his faculties was unbearable. Like my mother, I was an alarmist, but I had to be brave for her.

"Oh dear Lord," she muttered. Her hand flew to her mouth, and a new torrent of tears poured down her cheeks. All air left my lungs as tears rushed to my eyes too. Afraid my mother might faint, I wrapped my arm around her frail shoulders as the doctor continued.

"He also sustained multiple fractures to his right leg. We did a bone graft and set it with pins."

Words were trapped in my weeping mom's throat. Holding it together as I best as I could, I asked the doctor if we could see him. The only good news, if you could call it that, was we could.

They had transported my dad from recovery to a small room in the intensive care unit. Still unconscious, he was hooked up to a myriad of bleeping monitors and IV bags, and an oxygen mask covered his face. His breathing was labored. A wide bandage swathed his head, and beneath the fabric of his blanket, I could see the outline of a thick toe-to-thigh cast.

"Oh, Daddy!" I cried silently. Tears stung the back of my eyes, and a painful lump filled my throat. I wasn't prepared for seeing him like this. So lifeless and vulnerable. All my life, my handsome, brilliant dad had always been strong and there for me. He almost never got sick. And now this. There were no Scrabble words in the world to describe the tangle of emotions that ate away at my heart. Sobs clogged my throat, but I held them back to be a pillar of strength for my mom.

"Oh, Harold, darling," she choked, gently running her fingertips along his slack jaw. "Can you hear me? I love you so much. So very much."

My father stirred just a bit as if he'd heard her. At that moment, I was overwhelmed by the love my parents shared. A love so pure, so deep, so everlasting. A love for richer and poorer. In sickness and in health. I thought about Blake. And wondered—would this be us?

A sweet voice intercepted my thoughts. A nurse. She told us visiting hours were over.

My mother dabbed her tears with her soaked hanky and searched the nurse's kind, dark eyes. "Please, can I stay? I want to be here for him when he wakes up."

If he wakes up.

A warm smile flickered on the nurse's face. "I don't see why not. I'll order a cot."

"Mom, I want to stay too."

The nurse responded. "I'm afraid, dear, we can allow only one person to stay in the room. Hospital regulations."

Disappointed, I cupped my mother's shoulders. "Are you going to be okay, Mom?"

She nodded. "I'll call you, honey, if there's any change."

For the better, I prayed silently. I hugged her good night. Then, lightly, I kissed my father on his cheek.

"I love you, Dad." My voice was a soft whisper, but I knew he heard me.

Chapter 3

Blake

Where the fuck was she? I'd landed in Boise over two hours ago and taken a cab straight to Jen's house. The lights were on, but the house was vacant.

Sitting on the front step next to a large carved pumpkin leftover from Halloween, I tried her cell for the umpteenth time. No answer. And then I texted. Again no response. It was going on eight o'clock. The temperature had dropped significantly, and the damp autumn air sent a chill to my bones. My stomach rumbled with hunger as I hugged myself to keep warm.

Finally, a car pulled into the driveway. The headlights glared in my eyes; it was for sure Jen's dad's station wagon. Squinting, I jumped up as a familiar slim figure slid out of the driver's side door.

"Jen!" I sprinted up to her.

"Blake! Oh my God. What are you doing here?"

I searched her face. I could tell she'd been crying. Her green eyes were glazed and her thick layers of lashes were soaked. I took her in my arms and drew her close.

"I'm so, so sorry." Stroking her hair, I could only imagine what garbage Kat had told her.

Shivering, she leaned into me, resting her head against my leather jacket, her arms wrapped around me. "Oh, my love. Thank you for being here. It means so much to me." She began to sob softly.

I fluttered my eyes in confusion as I held and caressed her. "Tiger, why are you crying?"

"My Dad. He was hit by a car."

Holy. Fuck. Shit. I mentally hit the reset button. I had it all wrong. This was no time for me to tell her about Kat. And I wasn't even sure if Kat had contacted her.

"Jeez, Jen. I didn't know. Why didn't you call me or respond to my texts?"

"My cell phone died. And I don't have my charger. I'm sorry, baby."

Her snivels were gutting me. "No apologies necessary. How's your father?"

"Oh, Blake. It's not good. He may have sustained brain damage, and his leg is in bad shape. My mom's spending the night at the hospital."

"Fuck," I mumbled, bowing my head until my lips skimmed her scalp. Mr. McCoy had championed me when I was courting Jen, and I plain and simple adored him like a second father. I held her tighter.

A clap of thunder sounded. And a sudden downpour fell upon us. The pitter of the heavy rain striking my leather jacket reverberated in my ears. I lifted up Jen's chin with my thumb. And crushed my lips against hers. Her hot tears mixed with the cold raindrops. Another burst of thunder exploded while my heart thundered too.

Believe it or not, I'd never kissed a girl in the rain before.

Yet another first with my tiger. As the angry sky showered us with nature's tears, our lips melded together, our tongues entwined in a slow, sad dance.

Chapter 4

Jennifer

B lake filled me in on how he'd found out from Mrs. Cho that I'd flown to Boise. He'd been waiting for me on the front steps for more than two hours. After a long passionate kiss, I unlocked the front door and headed to the kitchen to whip up a quick dinner. We both hadn't eaten for hours and were famished. A beef casserole was in the refrigerator— probably the dinner my mother had prepared for my father. *His last supper?* While Blake washed up and changed into some dry clothes, I heated up the dish in the oven and choked back tears.

Blake met me in the dining room. "What's all this?" he asked as I padded in with some plates and silverware.

I eyed the dining room table where Blake and I had shared our first memorable Christmas Eve dinner almost a year ago. That magical snowy night he'd shown up at my doorstep to tell me he loved me. My heart was bursting with emotion. Lined up on the polished tabletop were hundreds of three inch square hand-painted frames encrusted with seashells and dusted with glitter. I set the china and silver on the credenza and made my way to the table. I picked up one of the charming frames. Inside it was an ivory place card with *Ms. Libby Clearfield*'s name elegantly scrolled in gold ink and printed below it: *Table 1.*

The rush of emotion surged through me. My creative mother, the ultimate DIY'er, had secretly taken it upon herself to make keepsake place card holders for all our wedding guests. *Oh, Mom!* My heart pitter-pattered, but then my moment of joy succumbed to an unbearable sadness. The dam holding back my tears broke loose, and I began to sob uncontrollably.

"They're place card holders my mom made for our wedding," I spluttered, my heart in my stomach. Now, everything was so up in the air.

Blake immediately took me in his arms and let me heave tears.

"Oh, Blake, I can't go through with this wedding if my dad's not there."

"Baby, we'll call it off. My mother will get over it. I'll do whatever you want to do. We're going to get through this together."

He tenderly kissed the top of my head, leaving his warm lips there as I continued to weep against his soft T-shirt. His muscled arms held me tight. It felt so good to be blanketed in his warmth. His manliness. And his love.

After dinner, which we ate in the kitchen, we unwound in the living room. The beautiful plaid cashmere blanket Blake had given my father last Christmas was draped over Dad's favorite reading chair. The sight of it sent another ripple of sadness through me. In my mind's eye, I could see Dad reclining there with his reading glasses parked on his nose and a book in his hand. I had to blink my eyes several times to banish the illusion. And to blink back more tears.

While Blake plopped down on the comfy floral couch with his laptop to catch up on work-related e-mails, I meandered over to the easy chair. A thick, leather-bound volume of Shakespeare's sonnets was sitting on the cushion. The edges were frayed, indicating to me it had been read many times. Lifting it into my hand, I curled into the chair and wrapped myself in Blake's buttery blanket. There was something so comforting about being shrouded in this luxurious fringed cover, imbued with his love and my father's familiar pipe-smoker scent. I opened the book; it was a gift from my mother. The inscription was dated: *November 16, 1974.* My lips transitioned into a melancholic smile. The day my parents got married. Their fortieth anniversary was coming up soon. My eyes traveled down the page, and I drank in the words she'd written by hand:

To My Darling Husband~
My bounty is as boundless as the sea,
My love as deep; the more I give to thee,
The more I have, for both are infinite.
With eternal love~Meg

My eyes watered. I recognized the passage. It was from *Romeo and Juliet.* My dad, the English professor, and I shared a passion for Shakespeare, and I knew many of his brilliant lines by heart. These, in particular, resonated with me. I'd been struggling with writing an original marriage vow...and now I'd found it. The mention of the sea fit in well with the underwater theme of my wedding and the fact that my mom had shared these beautiful words with my dad on their wedding day made them even more special. I began to leaf through the delicate yellowed pages of the book. As I read one exquisite sonnet after another, the words of another English poet whirled in my head. Chaucer.

If love is not, Oh God, what feel I so?
And if love is, what thing is it?

Shakespeare, however, did know what love is. My mother's chosen words softly formed on my lips.

Blake looked up from his computer. "Jen, are you okay?"

"Yes, baby." God, how I loved him. *Hear my soul speak. The very instant that I saw you did my heart fly to your service.* That first kiss. The first time ever I saw his face.

My eyes grew heavy. The next thing I knew I was in Blake's strong arms. He was carrying me upstairs. I must have dozed off. My sleepy gaze met his. Neither of us said a word.

Sometimes, words unspoken are the loudest. I knew Blake could intuit everything my weary mind was thinking. My love. My fear. My grief. He intermittently kissed my hair as we wound up the stairs.

When we crossed into my small bedroom, he set me down on my bed and tenderly undressed me, holding me in his gaze while he did. Our eyes never lost contact as he slid off my garments until I was fully unclothed. I sat motionless as Blake reverently cupped my breasts in his palms. And then he peeled off his clothes.

The first and last time Blake slept in my twin-sized bed, barely big enough for someone as petite as me, he'd fucked my brains out. Tonight was different. Bared to each other, he cocooned me in his arms, spooning me next to him. The warmth of his body blanketed my cold numbness.

On my side, I pressed my hands together. Closing my eyes, I silently prayed. *Oh, please God, make my dad okay. Please! For my mom. For me. For us.*

"Be brave, my tiger. It's going to be okay," Blake whispered in my ear, holding me tight. His big warm hands folded over mine. A final round of tears made their way down my cheeks. Oh, Daddy! Oh, Mom! Oh, Blake!

The music of Blake's heartbeat and soft breaths lulled me to much needed sleep.

When Blake and I arrived at my dad's hospital room at seven the next morning, my mother was still sound asleep in an armchair, a small Bible folded over her lap. But Dad's hospital bed was gone. I gasped and clung to Blake, my worst fear rolling through me like a tidal wave. I began to breathe heavily and was close to hyperventilating.

In a state of panic, I woke my mom up, gently shaking her. "Mom, where's Dad?"

Startled, her eyes fluttered open. "Oh, Honey. Blake?"

Blake bent over and hugged my mom. "I'm so sorry to hear about your husband."

My heart was in my throat. "Mom, is he okay?"

"They took him for another MRI."

Relieved, my breathing calmed down. Blake and I took a seat on the cot that had been brought to the room. It looked as if my mother hadn't slept in it at all.

Blake drew me close to him and wrapped his arm around my shoulders. I was wearing one of his heavy cashmere sweaters over the skirt I'd worn yesterday.

"Has there been any change in his condition?" I asked my mom as my husband-to-be soothingly brushed his long fingers along my upper arm.

She shook her head. Her usually wide blue-gray eyes were bloodshot slivers and her pale cheeks hollow. Purple shadows lined her lower lids. She looked like she'd gotten very little sleep. On a deep breath, she added, "But the good news is his vitals are stable."

I sighed another shaky breath of relief, but the worst wasn't over. We spent the next fifteen minutes making small talk to pass the time. After Blake told my mom how he'd found out I was in Boise, he offered to go to the cafeteria and bring back some coffee. Exhausted and drained, we were grateful.

"Mom, Blake called his sister last night, and she did some research. According to her colleagues at Cedars, Dr. Kumar is top notch. Dad's in good hands."

"I'm so glad to hear that. Blake is such a good man," my mother murmured. "And he adores you, my sweet girl."

A small smile flickered on my lips. "Yeah, Mom. I'm so lucky to have him. In many ways, he reminds me of Dad."

She smiled back. It was the first time I'd seen her smile since the accident.

Blake returned shortly with the coffee. Not the best I'd ever had, but the strong bitterish brew instantly seeped into my veins and revitalized me. After a few sips, a clamor outside the room caught my attention. My eyes flew to the door. It was my father. Still hooked up to a portable IV unit, he was being wheeled back in. Holding a clipboard, the young doctor, who I'd met last night, accompanied the attendants and a nurse. With butterflies in my stomach, I watched as they reattached him to all the beeping machines.

I stood up and treaded to his bedside. Though the oxygen mask was off and he seemed to be breathing evenly on his own, his eyes were still shut. A light layer of graying stubble lined his peaceful face. My mother joined me. Her lips quivered as the nurse hooked him up to the last of the monitors. I squeezed her hand as Blake hovered behind me.

"Mrs. McCoy," began the doctor.

"Yes?" responded my mother, her voice trembling.

"I have good news for you and your daughter."

My rapidly beating heart was already dancing.

"The MRI shows the swelling in his brain has gone down. There's no permanent damage."

"Oh, dear Lord. Thank you!" Bursting into tears, my mother hugged the doctor. Whatever prayers she said must have worked. Tears of relief flooded my eyes too. Wrapping his arms around me from behind, Blake kissed the top of my head.

"When will he wake up?" I asked the doctor, leaning into Blake's hard body.

"It could be in a few minutes. Or in a few hours. Whenever he does, be sure to give him a little water." From the corner of my eye, I saw the nurse refill his plastic water cup on the nightstand next to his bed.

The doctor and his team excused themselves after telling us

they'd be back later to check up on my dad. We returned to our seating positions, all keeping a vigilant watch on him. I gripped Blake's hand.

"Mom, I need to tell you something."

Her gaze shifted to me. A small smile played on her face, and serenity now filled her tired eyes. "What, honey?"

"On our way here, Blake and I had a discussion. We've decided to call off the wedding."

"Over my dead body, young lady."

The voice was a hoarse whisper but unmistakable. Dad!

He was awake and talking!

"Oh, Dad!" I ran over to his bed and kissed him, gushing with happiness.

My speechless, teary-eyed mother leapt up from her chair and caressed his face. "Oh, darling!" With the push of a button, she raised the bed just a smidgeon and lovingly held the cup of water to his lips.

"But Dad," I contested as he took a small sip through the straw. "You may not be well enough in time for the wedding."

"My Jennie, I have every intention of walking you down the aisle." He turned his bandaged head toward Blake. "And you, son, better be sure she's there."

"Yes, sir." They exchanged a conspiratorial wink.

My heart swelled with love for the two men I loved most in my life.

My beloved dad. And my soon-to-be husband.

Chapter 5

Blake

Knowing Jen's dad was going to be okay, I flew back to LA the next day. I had too much shit to take care of at work. Heading up a porn network came with its share of hard-ons and hardships. Jen, however, decided to remain in Boise until her father was released from the hospital later in the week. He was going home but would need a lot of physical therapy—especially since he was so intent on walking Jen down the aisle. I fucking loved this man.

I missed my tiger and was distracted. A weight hung over my head like a ticking time bomb. I still hadn't told Jen the truth about what had happened between Kat and me at the end of high school. I just couldn't break the news to her in Boise with what had happened to her father. I was certain it would make her an emotional wreck and dredge up all her trust issues. And knowing how Jen often overreacted, she might even call off the wedding—and break her father's heart and her mother's. And, last but not least, mine.

Every ring of my phone, ping in my mailbox, or ding of a text made my nerves zing with anxiety and apprehension. At any time, I was expecting to hear from a hysterical Jen. That Kat had gotten to her. That she knew. But each time we spoke or texted, which was often, not one mention of Kat. I took one day at a time. Maybe, Kat hadn't been lying that afternoon at Saks and had no intention of sharing our past any further with Jen. I just couldn't be sure—she was a psycho bitch—and there was nothing I could do to stop her.

On Thursday, I had my weekly evening chat with my dad. True to fashion, we sat outside on my terrace and caught up over fine cigars and brandy. Unlike chilly Boise, the early November Los Angeles air was still balmy. Darkness, however, was descending.

"How's Jennifer's father doing?" asked my old man, after pouring the brandies.

I'd told my parents what had happened. Both were genuinely heartbroken and had not only called Mrs. McCoy but had also sent an array of exotic get-well flowers to his room that must have cost a small fortune. I filled my father in on the latest—that Harold had been released from the hospital and was determined to walk his little girl down the aisle.

My father chuckled and took another puff of his Cuban cigar. He blew out a curl of smoke. It faded into the night air. "I'm glad to hear that. If there's anything your mother and I can do to help, just let us know."

"Thanks, Dad." I smiled. My billionaire parents were generous to a fault.

We imbibed our brandies in unison. My dad set his tumbler down on the round table between us. "So, how's the wedding shaping up?"

My father hadn't been involved. It was my mother's thing and he gave her total control. Not wanting to create any kind of friction between my parents, I hadn't told him about the issues we had with Enid and Katrina. Fucking Kat. The velvety brandy seeped through my veins and warmed me. It had been a stressful week, but now I was loosened up. The urge to tell my dad about Kat's antics burnt my tongue and the words tumbled out. My father listened intently, his lips pressed into a thin grim line. He plunked his tumbler down on the table again—this time with a loud, angry bang.

"You should have had security arrest her," he grumbled when I finished relaying the Saks incident. "She's pure trouble, that girl." Dad had never liked or trusted Kat despite the friendship between her mother and mine.

"Yeah, I should have." I took another sip of my brandy. "Dad, could you talk to Mom and try to get Kat out of our lives?"

My father flicked a thick layer of ashes into the Baccarat ashtray on the table. "Son, I don't think that's a good idea. It'll blow up in our faces. That crazy girl might go to the tabloids, and that's the last thing we all need."

My wise old man hated negative publicity. It wasn't good for our family or the company. Fortunately, the incident was handled in a way that had kept it out of the press all these years. I sucked in a deep breath. There was more than just negative publicity at stake.

"Dad, what if she tells Jennifer?"

My father's steel-gray eyes narrowed as he furrowed his bushy brows. "She doesn't know?"

I told him how I'd flown to Boise to tell her, but with Jen's dad's accident, it just wasn't the right time. And though Harold was now on the way to recovery, I didn't want to shake things up by phone or e-mail.

My understanding father nodded his head of silver hair. "When is she coming back?"

"Tomorrow." *Friday.*

"Skip Shabbat and take her out for a nice dinner. She's got to hear it from you. Don't waste any time."

My stomach twisted. Just as fast as my tiger had walked into my heart, just as fast she could walk out. "What if she—"

My father cut me short. "Blake, no amount of guilt can solve the past, and no amount of anxiety can change the future."

My old man's words of wisdom. I hoped he was right.

Friday couldn't get here soon enough or late enough. As much I coveted Jen in my arms—and in my bed—my stomach was in knots. Tonight, I was going to tell her the truth about my past with Kat. I wasn't sure how she was going to take it. Yes, the past was the past, and with Jen, I'd turned over a new leaf, but I'd kept it from her. My father had once said, there are two different types of sins: sins of commission and sins of omission. I'd committed both.

We touched base in the morning before she left for the airport. Upon landing, she was going straight to the set of *Bound to You*, the latest erotic romance we were shooting. She'd managed to score Jessica Chastain and Alexander Skarsgård to play the lead roles. I told her I wanted to meet her for dinner and picked a small romantic French restaurant not far from the set. I couldn't wait to hold her in my arms and fuck her brains out, but I had to get the truth out first. I owed it to her; she had to hear it from me. It was fucking killing me.

Shortly after I made an eight o'clock restaurant reservation, an unexpected e-mail showed up in my inbox. My chest tightened. Balls. It was from Kat and marked URGENT in shouty caps in the subject line. Fuck. Had she contacted Jen and told her the story? With apprehension, I opened it.

Dear Blake~

I'm really, really sorry about what happened at Saks last week as well as in Vegas. My behavior was totally out of line, and I would like to make it up to you. I hope you'll agree to meet me for a quick drink so I can apologize in person. There are also some important wedding details I'd like to share with you. I'm planning a big surprise for Jennifer and I'd like to get your input. Please don't let me down. I hope you don't mind meeting at Greystone at 6:00 p.m. as I have dinner plans there immediately following with another client.

Yours~ Kat

My fingers drummed the keyboard while I stared at the e-mail. Should I agree to see her? Hear her out? Had *she* finally turned over a new leaf? Or was this just another ruse? Torn, I finally hit reply, driven by my curiosity to find out what surprise she had in mind for Jennifer. I typed three words: *See you there.* I could spend an hour or so with her and have time enough to meet Jen for dinner. While the bistro I'd chosen was not far from Greystone, traffic in LA on a Friday night was usually brutal, and I didn't want to be late. In the blink of an eye, Kat replied with a smiley face emoticon.

"Good to see you, Mr. Burns," said the flirty mini-skirted blond hostess, who stood by the entrance to Greystone Manor. "I haven't seen you for a while."

The truth, though I still had a membership, I hadn't been back to the trendy club since the Conquest Broadcasting Christmas Ball last December. That night I'd fucked my tiger for the first time. Following that unforgettable night, I had no need for my fuck pad. I made a mental note to give it up permanently.

I told the attractive hostess I was here to meet Kat Moore. Smiling, she told me she was already here and led me through the uncrowded club (which wouldn't start filling up until much later). She deliberately swayed her hips. While her sexy walk got my attention, it didn't turn me on. I might still be a looker, but only one woman aroused me.

A big toothy smile flashed on Kat's face when she caught sight of me. She was seated at my regular table in the corner. There were plenty of empty tables in the vast club at this hour, but she'd chosen this one. An uneasy feeling settled in me. I was having second thoughts. Maybe agreeing to meet her here was a bad idea.

My skin prickling, I sat down facing her and crossed my legs under the table. Call it cock protection. My eyes took her in. Dressed in a strapless black dress, she looked, as usual, like a sophisticated goddess. Her wavy blond hair fanned over her broad shoulders, and she was perfectly made up. A bottle of champagne was anchored in an ice bucket beside the table. Kat was already sipping a fluteful of bubbly and had poured one for me.

"Blake, thank you for meeting me here on such short notice. I hope you don't mind I ordered a bottle of champagne."

She took a small sip. "Your favorite. Cristal."

"Actually, I appreciate it. I don't have much time. I've got to be somewhere at eight." I raised my crystal flute to my lips.

"Wait, Blake. Don't drink it until we toast to your wedding."

Hesitantly, I clinked my glass against hers, and as the crystal tinged, another smile slithered across her face. I guzzled my champagne as if it were soda water while she took another dainty sip. She then set her glass down and licked her upper lip.

"So what are you planning for Jennifer?" I asked, wanting to get straight to business. Her body language was unnerving.

She ran a hand through her thick mane of golden hair. "Oh, Blake. First things first. I'm terribly sorry for what happened in Vegas and at Saks. I spoke to my shrink about the incidents, and he insisted I apologize face to face. I hope you can forgive me."

"Apology accepted. Now, what do you have in mind?" My words were rushed. Despite what sounded like sincerity, I wanted to get out of here as fast as I could.

Smiling, she circled the rim of her champagne flute with her long manicured finger. "Well, this is what I was thinking. Why don't we put together a video montage of you growing up to show at the wedding? I bet Jennifer would get a kick out of that."

I thought about the idea. Not a good one. I was sure even if I scrutinized it, Kat would find a way to slip in footage of the two of us. Especially Capri. I still didn't trust her one fucking bit.

"I don't think so. I'd prefer if you did one starring her."

"Blake, a wonderful idea." Still smiling, she paused. "And Blake—"

"Yes?"

"You have my word I won't ever tell Jennifer about our little secret. My lips are sealed." She slid her finger across her glossed lips.

I twitched a small grateful smile. "I really appreciate that, Kat."

Relieved, I reached into the ice bucket to refill my champagne glass. I fucking loved Cristal. A few more sips and I was out of here. Was I still going to tell Jen about the past? My thinking had grown cloudy.

As I poured the champagne into my flute, my hand shook. A sudden rush of nausea like I'd never known rose to my chest. The room began to spin. The bottle slipped out of my hand. I heard it shatter, and then everything faded to black.

Chapter 6
Jennifer

I got to Le Petit Café, the small intimate French restaurant where Blake had made a reservation, just a little before eight. I was the first to arrive, and the hostess showed me to our corner table. Blake knew how much I loved this restaurant with its candlelit, red-checkered-clothed tables and bistro menu; it reminded me so much of Paris where we'd filmed part of *Shades of Pearl*. Though we'd spoken and Skyped several times a day while I was in Boise, I was so eager to see Blake. I missed him terribly. My blood was streaming through me like champagne—happy little bubbles zapping me with giddiness.

Over a glass of Bordeaux, I perused the menu and thought about my day. It felt good to get back to work and be on a set. The filming of the first episode of the delightful Vanessa Booke's *Bound to You* had gone off without a hitch. I was so excited about this telenovela which we would be airing in the Fall. Today we had filmed the opening scenes that took place in Los Angeles. Rebecca, the spunky curvy heroine played by redhead Jessica Chastain, had said good-bye to her actor boyfriend Miles, played by Matt Bomer, after discovering he was cheating on her with his sexy co-star Scarlett—supermodel Kate Upton. The way Jessica had powerfully delivered the closing line—"I gave you everything, Miles, but you ripped it away. You chose her instead of me."—had me close to tears. My viewers were going to swoon over this adaptation of this popular erotic romance. Next week, pre-production started up in New York City where the rest of the filming would take place after the holidays. *After I got back from my honeymoon.*

The handsome, sandy-haired waiter, who looked to be an aspiring actor, came by and asked if I wanted an appetizer. Though ravenous, I passed and told him I was waiting for someone. I glanced down at my cell phone. It was 8:15. Blake should be here soon. He must be tied up in Friday night traffic. I called him. No answer.

Taking a small sip of the velvety red wine, I decided to catch up on e-mails. Intermittently, I called and texted Blake. Still no answer. I was growing edgy, and the wine did little to take the edge away. My eyes kept darting to the front of the restaurant, with the hope of seeing Blake fly in.

It was now going on nine p.m. I was worried. Worried sick. Where was Blake? I called his cell phone every five minutes, but each time it went to his voicemail. I texted him. No response. I called his office and our home phone. No answer. I called Mrs. Cho and then his best friend Jaime, but they hadn't heard from him either and had no clue where he was. Mrs. Cho, however, did mention he'd left the office early for a meeting. *What meeting?* He hadn't mentioned one to me, and unfortunately, Mrs. Cho didn't know the details. *Strange.*

The server came by again to take my order. "I'm still waiting for someone," I told him glumly. With an irritated shrug, he marched off, leaving me alone. I tried all of Blake's numbers one more time, but still no Blake. A sudden chill ran through me. My heart hammered. Maybe something had happened to him. Like he'd gotten into a bad car accident. Or mugged. Maybe, I should call the police and all the local hospitals. Oh, God, please, please, please no! And then another equally horrible thought hit me with the force of an avalanche. His secret meeting. Blake always kept Mrs. Cho abreast of his whereabouts. My blood ran cold. Was he seeing someone else? Someone new he met while I was in Boise? All my insecurities and trust issues flooded my brain, and nausea rushed to my chest.

My cell phone pinged. An e-mail. From Blake? I glanced down at the screen. It was from the last person I wanted to hear from. Kat. She was probably just e-mailing me to confirm my fitting appointment tomorrow. With reluctance, I opened it. The body of the message was all of two words: *Please review.*

There were several attachments. All jpegs. Bridesmaid dresses? Seating arrangements? The latest tropical fish that would be swimming in the Bernsteins' salt-water pool?

While I was in no mood for wedding detail, I opened the attachments, one at a time. My heart fell to my stomach. And all air left my lungs. The phone shook in my trembling hands.

"Oh my God," I heard myself say as I viewed one photo after another of Blake and Kat bared to each other and entwined in a familiar bed. The satin-sheeted one in his fuck pad at Greystone Manor—where he'd fucked me for the first time the night of the Conquest Broadcasting Christmas party. The photos ranged from heated embraces to Kat sucking his cock. And so much more. By the fifth photo, I'd had enough. Scorching tears poured down my face. Oh my God. How could I be so blind? In so much denial? Reality hit me like a crashing meteor. Blake was still into her.

The server came by again. "Have you decided what you want to order? The kitchen will be closing down soon."

I looked up at him with my tear-flooded eyes. "I-I'm sorry. I won't be staying for dinner." My voice was a mere rasp. Barely a whisper.

The server regarded me with compassion. I guess he'd seen a lot of girls stood up in his time. But none as crestfallen as me.

"No problem, madame."

Madame. The French word for "Mrs." Mrs. Blake Burns was not in my stars.

"Thank you for understanding." I dug through my bag and found my wallet. I pulled out a hundred-dollar bill. The hundred-dollar bill Blake had given me when I'd stripped for him in that seedy motel; I'd kept it as emergency money. This was an emergency of the worst kind. I plunked it down on the table.

"I'll be right back with your change," the sweet waiter said.

"No need," I stammered. While my glass of wine came to only twelve dollars, the hardworking server deserved the money for his time, patience, and compassion.

"Are you sure?" His eyes lit up with surprise.

"Yes, please." I rose from my seat, my knees so weak I thought I'd fall down. The kindly waiter pulled out my chair and helped me up.

"Merci, madame. I hope you have a lovely evening."

That wasn't happening.

❧

I don't know how I made it back to Blake's condo. Tears blurred my vision, and twice I almost got into a major auto accident. The ache in my heart was so great I thought I might have a coronary. First, Bradley. Now, Blake. But the pain this time was exponentially worse. Unbearable. I needed windshield wipers to wipe my tears away.

Fortunately, Blake's condo was not far from the restaurant, and traffic along Wilshire Boulevard was light. I got there in no time. I valeted my car, skirted past the doorman, and hurried upstairs. I made a couple of calls and then collapsed onto the couch. I could no longer share Blake's bed. It was already ancient history. Tomorrow, I would be gone.

You chose her instead of me.

Chapter 7

Blake

"Fuck," I heard myself murmur. *Fuck, fuck, fuck.*
My head was spinning; my mouth felt like the Mohave Desert, and nausea consumed me. Slowly, I peeled my eyes open—well to be honest, only one. It took me several long, nauseating moments to realize where I was. I was in my Greystone fuck pad, sprawled naked on my bed. I had no fucking idea how I'd gotten here, and the shitfaced way I felt didn't make remembering any easier. I glanced at my watch. Squinting with the one eye open, I made out the time. It was six o'clock. Except in my windowless suite, I had no idea if it was six in the morning or the evening.

The bed was a rumpled mess with the covers half off, and I noticed my clothes were strewn on the floor. How did they get there? How did I get here? I hadn't been back to my fuck pad since the time I'd fucked Jennifer at the office Christmas party. And that was almost a year ago.

I crawled out of bed. In my sorry state, I could barely stand up. My legs felt like Jell-O and another tidal wave of nausea descended on me. Close to passing out, I collapsed onto the floor and crawled on my hands and knees to the adjacent bathroom. Frankly, I wasn't sure I'd make it to the toilet in time, but thank fucking God I did. Perched on my knees, I puked my guts out until my throat burned and my insides were torn. Believe it or not, I actually felt a little better. And despite my headache the size of Texas, a little more clear-headed. But I still couldn't piece together how I'd gotten here or what had happened in the last twenty-four hours.

I managed to get to my feet and noticed my cock was flaccid. I'd never woken up without a big boner. Poor Mr. Burns was as wasted and confused as I was. This was bad. Really bad. I quickly brushed my teeth and then staggered out of the bathroom after passing on a hot shower. I didn't think I was steady enough. One glance in the bathroom mirror confirmed that. I looked like death warmed over. Like someone had painted me with chalk and left me in Death Valley to die. Roadkill.

Back in my fuck pad, I gathered up my suit in slo-mo. I slipped on my dress shirt first, unable to button it with my shaky hands. Then the slacks and jacket. At last minute, I threw my tie around my neck. In a moment of panic, I slipped my hand into my slacks pocket where I kept my wallet and cell phone. To my relief, both were there. I pulled out my cell phone, and immediately checked my texts, e-mails, and phone messages. There were dozens. All from one person. My Jen— wondering where I was and asking me to call her. I immediately speed-dialed her number, but there was no response. I texted her and e-mailed her. Zilch again. Maybe it was six o'clock in the morning and she was still sleeping. And then an unnerving thought punched me in the gut—I hadn't gone home to her. What could she be thinking?

Without warning, my cell phone died on me. I stared at it blankly. What did it matter?

I didn't have an explanation.

Chapter 8
Jennifer

My sleep was tearful and restless. I don't know why I bothered. I fumbled for my cell phone, which was tucked under my pillow, and glanced at the screen. It was going on five a.m. If it weren't such an ungodly hour, I would have called Libby or Chaz or even my parents. I had the burning urge to talk to someone. Anyone. Blake had never called or texted me. Shutting my eyes, I tried to fall back to sleep on the couch, but it was futile. My throat was raw from crying, and the ache in my heart was palpable.

Light shortly filtered through the floor-to-ceiling windows. My burning eyes took in the dawn of another day in LA. Beautiful as usual, but not beautiful for me. In a few hours, I would be on a plane. Away from LA and the man I thought I loved with my body and soul. Except he'd betrayed me. I pulled the blanket over my head, and then forcing myself off the couch, I stumbled to the bedroom Blake and I shared. Or should I say once shared. My eyes stinging, I gazed at the king-sized bed where we had made beautiful, endless love countless times. There was no more "we." Painfully, I retrieved a small suitcase from the walk-in closet and tossed it onto the duvet. I needed to pack. I was going back home. To be with my parents who needed me—but only a fraction of how much I needed them.

Halfway done packing, I heard the door to the apartment unlock. And then I heard it slam shut. A shiver skittered though me. Blake! I continued tossing a week's worth of clothing into my suitcase. While I hadn't informed HR of my sudden leave of absence, I was positive I could convince them I could work from Boise, given my stellar job performance. MY SIN-TV ratings were though the roof. And right now, most of our telenovelas were in post-production, not im-mediately demanding my attention. I just wasn't going to tell them that most of my time would be spent looking for a new job.

I heard a shuffle of heavy footsteps approach. I ignored them. I was almost packed. And then he called out to me.

"Jen." His voice sounded worn and hoarse.

I refused to acknowledge him and continued with my packing. Every muscle clenched. The pain was so great. Treacherous tears cascaded down my face.

"Jen," he murmured again, this time, his voice a desperate croak.

I couldn't help but face him as he staggered my way. I soaked him in with my watering eyes. He looked awful. His hair was a wild mess, and his complexion had a ghoulish green cast. His suit was wrinkled, his creased shirt opened, and his tie hung loosely and unevenly around his neck.

"Where are you going?" he rasped, eyeing my suitcase.

"Home." I stabbed the word at him and impulsively tugged at my engagement ring. With my finger swollen, the damn thing wouldn't budge. I was going to have to mail it to him.

He gazed at me imploringly, his bloodshot eyes blinking

for an explanation.

"I'm moving out, Blake."

"Why, tiger? Why?"

I answered his question with another a question. A Jewish thing to do, so I'd learned. "Where were you last night?"

He shook his head. "I don't fucking know."

Bullshit. I tossed my cell phone at him. He caught it…barely. His reflexes were not what they normally were. Of course. Kat had fucked his brains out.

"Just click the first e-mail. And then any attachment. I'm sure they'll trigger your memory."

My eyes stayed fixed on him as he did as asked. His glazed eyes grew round.

Raking his hand though his disheveled hair, he groaned, "What the fuck?"

"What do you mean?"

"What I mean is I have no recollection of being with the bitch."

The angry way he said "bitch" struck a deep chord. His gaze met mine. I swiped at my tears.

"Honestly, tiger, I have no memory of the last twenty-four hours. Everything's a blank."

His sunken eyes bore into me like a puppy looking for love. I searched them, seeking the truth.

"I swear to God, Jen. You have to believe me."

My inner conscience went into war-mode. There was the me who distrusted and the me who wanted to believe. My mind was a battlefield. But, one by one, the soldiers of distrust were being knocked down by the true believers. A mental massacre led by my courageous heart. I cupped Blake's stubbled face in my hands and faced him squarely. His sister's warning about Kat resounded in my head. *Don't let her manipulate you.*

"Blake, I believe you." My voice was soft but solid. This was a big step forward for me in the trust department. Dr. Williams, my support group leader, would be proud of me.

He blinked his eyes in disbelief. "You do?"

"I do. Are you okay?"

"I feel like fucking crap. Like I have a major hangover. Everything's so hazy."

My poor baby. I wrapped my arms around him and drew him close to me. He held me against him, my head resting on his heart. The heart that belonged to me.

"I think the bitch must have gotten me drunk, but I seriously don't remember what drink I ordered. Or how many."

"Did you blackout?"

"I must have. But I've never done that before."

I digested Blake's words and his condition. He had some form of amnesia. In my rape support group, there were a couple of girls who unknowingly had been drugged at a bar and then date raped. When they woke up naked in a strange bed or in a dark alley, their rapist was long gone, and they had no memory of what had happened.

I had a hunch. Fucking Kat had drugged him and virtually raped him. What a sick chick! I was going to prove it and have my revenge.

"Come on, baby. Let me give you a bath. And then we're going to your doctor."

"I don't need to go to a doctor. I just need to rest and be with you."

"Baby, I want to make sure you're all right. And I have a

theory I want to prove. It's going to take a test."

Reluctantly, Blake agreed. I helped him off with his clothes and then led him to the bathtub.

Chapter 9

Blake

I felt fucking violated by the fucking bitch. Dirty, used, and abused even though I couldn't remember a goddamn thing. The thought of Kat having her mouth any place on my body, let alone my dick, sickened me. I only belonged to one woman. My tiger who was kneeling by the tub and washing away the vague memories of last night. How could I let myself drink my way to submission and oblivion? Hadn't I learned my lesson? I leaned my head against the tub and squeezed my eyes closed, soaking in the guilty pleasure of the tender touch of the woman I loved. And could have lost.

"How do you feel?" asked Jennifer, helping me out of the tub. She draped a large fluffy towel around me.

"Fucked up."

The bath had helped only a little. Waves of nausea still rolled in my chest; my head was spinning, and I was experiencing coordination problems. Even buttoning my jeans was a challenge. Jen helped me get re-dressed and insisted on driving me to our family doctor's office in Beverly Hills. God bless her. I was seriously in no condition to drive.

I tried to think straight. How was I going to handle this mess? Pointing the finger at Kat had all kinds of repercussions—from an unwanted scandal to a rift between my mother and hers. The wedding itself could be jeopardized.

"Jen, I don't want to go through with this," I protested as she pulled her Kia into the parking structure of the medical building where Dr. Klein, an internist, had an office. He had been our family physician for years and had a very close relationship with my parents as well as my sister.

"You have to. For yourself. And for me," she retorted in search of a parking spot. "We need proof that Kat drugged you."

"Drugged me?" My voice rose an octave.

"Yes." She shot the word at me, without giving me a chance to contest it.

"What do I have to do?" I could take a bullet for Jen, but the thought of a long needle being inserted into my flesh freaked me out. I could be such a wuss.

"Not much. Just pee in a little cup."

I inwardly sighed with relief, but the outstanding issues weighed on my chest. "What if it comes back positive?"

"Then we'll know." Her voice was matter-of-fact.

"But what if Dr. Klein starts asking all kinds of questions?"

"You're just going to tell him that you don't remember a thing."

"Are you going to tell Kat's mother?" That would certainly create hell.

"Not if I don't have to. But I'm going to need your help."

My tiger shot me a mischievous smile as she pulled into a parking spot. Somehow, I knew her creative juices were flowing.

Dr. Klein's office was packed, but he was able to squeeze me in with only a short wait. Jen accompanied me to the examining room and made me take a seat on the examining table. She sat down in a close-by armchair.

"Do you want to play nursie?" I asked, my sense of humor trickling back. Perhaps to mask my stress.

"You wish."

Oh, did I. The thought of her in a tight little nurse's uniform giving me a physical—touching me everywhere that needed touching—sent a tiny jolt to my cock. At least, my manhood was intact. Or so I thought. Maybe next Halloween I'd buy her a costume and I could live out my fantasy.

My fantasy came to an abrupt halt when Dr. Klein strode into the small sterile room. A kindly looking man in his mid-fifties, he was holding a clipboard and wearing a stethoscope around his neck.

"Well, hello, Blake. What brings you here today?" He gave me the once-over. "You look a little under the weather. A touch of the flu?"

Jen chimed in. "No, Doctor. He just needs to give you a urine sample, and we need the results back today if possible."

Dr. Klein lifted a brow. "And you may be?"

"Jennifer McCoy. Blake's fiancée. Nice to meet you."

"Nice to meet you too, Jennifer. My wife and I got your lovely wedding invitation. We'll be there."

Jennifer smiled. "Wonderful."

Dr. Klein winked at her. "So did our boy have a little too much sex and get a urinary tract infection?"

"Not exactly, Doctor," I replied. "But I need to have my pee tested for anything unusual."

Doctor Klein's eyes narrowed, creating a deep crease between them. "Blake, are you doing drugs? Cocaine? Ecstasy?"

"No, sir. But I think I may have been drugged."

"That's very serious, Blake. Can you tell me more?"

I remembered Jen's instructions and shook my head. "I don't remember a thing."

With resignation, he took my blood pressure and then listened to my heart. His brows furrowed. "Your heartbeat is erratic and your blood pressure is abnormally low."

Fuck. Maybe I was going to die.

He put the stethoscope to my back and asked me to take a few deep breaths.

"And your breathing is somewhat labored. How do you feel?"

"To be honest, I feel like crap. Sluggish, nauseous, and dizzy."

"Anything else?"

Again, Jen chimed in. "He's having difficulty with his motor skills."

The doctor listened intently. "Like what?"

"Like unbuttoning his jeans."

The doctor shot her a wry look. "I would imagine Mr. Burns is usually very good at that."

Jennifer's face flushed while I let out a small laugh.

"Very well." He ambled over to the sink counter and retrieved a lidded plastic cup sealed in a sanitary wrapper. He handed it to me. "The bathroom is down the hall. I'd like you to fill up the cup at least halfway."

I'd been through this routine for my annual physicals. I had to hold my big cock and aim. The rim of my dick was bigger than that of the cup. This time, I didn't want to do it alone.

"Um, uh, Doctor. Jennifer's right. I'm having a lot of trouble buttoning and unbuttoning my jeans. Can she come with me?"

"I don't see why not. But both of you be sure to wash your hands first. When you're done, just print your name on the label with the marker that's on the shelf, and leave it there. We'll try to get the results back to you in a few hours. There's a urologist I know who owes me a favor."

I jumped off the examining table. "It's pee time."

Jen looked at me sheepishly. "Do I really have to come?"

"Yes. You have to come." I gestured toward the door, my very naughty mind already back in business.

A short minute later, we were huddled in the small, functional bathroom. After we washed our hands, I tore off the cellophane wrapping of the cup and removed the lid.

"Jen, this is going to be a team effort. Unbutton my jeans."

Silently, she did as bid. I'd gone commando. The little rise I'd gotten from my nursie fantasy was long gone. My heavy cock hung low.

"Now baby, grip my dick and aim it into the cup." Her warm hand clamped the lower third. There was a lot more I wanted her to do with it than play fire hydrant, but truthfully, I wasn't sure I could get it up. A terrifying thought sent a shudder through me. Fuck. Did I have permanent damage?

"Am I doing it okay?" Jen asked hesitantly, breaking into my disconcerting thoughts.

"You're doing just great, baby. Here goes."

On the next breath, I shot a stream of pee into the cup. It wasn't quite the same as shooting my load with Jennifer's hand wrapped around my cock, but it felt good. I'd never peed with a girl before. It was strangely sexy. I wanted to reward Jen for believing me. After labeling the cup and sealing it with the lid, I placed it on a shelf with a row of other used cups. Jen commended me.

"Good job, Blake. We should wash up."

I squirted some of the liquid soap onto my palms. Jen followed suit, but while she did, I folded my arms around her tiny waist.

In a rapid heartbeat, I unbuttoned her jeans and slid them down her legs. My small motor skills were improving. I slipped a soaped-up hand under the band of her lacy panties and then lubricated her folds. I watched her lips part and her neck arch back in the mirror above the sink.

"Blake! What are you doing?" she breathed out.

"Thanking you properly for believing me. And for coming here with me."

"Oh!"

I began to caress her slick pussy and soon felt her heat. I had to make this quick. Before Dr. Klein sent someone to check on me. Hastily, I moved my fingers to her clit and circled it vigorously. She bit down on her bottom lip to suppress her sounds though sexy little whimpers lodged in her throat. Her breathing was uneven. Enjoying every minute, I nuzzled the back of her neck.

"Oh, God. You're making me come!"

"That's the plan," I breathed into her ear, rubbing my cock against her backside with the hope I'd get an erection. Fuck.

Nothing. Not even a little twitch. I refocused my energy on Jen, rubbing her nub harder.

"Oh, Blake," she moaned as she bucked against me, her pussy trembling and spilling with her juices.

I planted a chaste kiss on her head and just held her. "Thanks again for *coming,* tiger. I needed you here with me."

"Blake, I'm always going to be there for you."

"The same, baby. The same."

Her dreamy smile met mine in the mirror, and then we headed back to the examination room where we took our former positions. Dr. Klein returned shortly.

"Did you have difficulty urinating, Blake?" he asked. "You were in the bathroom for quite a while."

"No, Doc. Not at all. A little rough at the beginning. I'm not used to peeing in a cup. But once I got it going, no problem." But the truth, there was a problem. A big one. Or should I say a not so big one, depending on how you looked at it and put it into perspective. I couldn't get an erection. I desperately wanted to tell him about it, but I held my tongue.

With a smile, he nodded. "Good. And I must say you're looking a little better than when you first came in. I suggest you go home and rest and keep your jeans buttoned until we have the results of your test. I'll call you as soon as I get them."

I stood up from the examining table and joined Jennifer. Dr. Klein turned to face us.

"And Jennifer, a pleasure to meet you. Congratulations on your engagement. I look forward to the wedding."

Jennifer beamed. "We look forward to seeing you there."

"Ditto." I shook the good doctor's hand and thanked him for seeing me.

Silently, I thanked Jennifer for believing me and not calling the whole thing off. I still didn't know how I was going to handle Kat who was out to sabotage us. Or the new, potentially life-changing problem I faced, thanks to her.

I fucking loved my tiger.

And fucking hated that bitch.

Chapter 10

Jennifer

I wanted Blake to rest. Doctor's orders. It was Saturday, hence no need for either of us to go into the office. So I made him put on his pajamas and tucked him into bed. Then, I heated up the leftover matzo ball soup I'd made and frozen a few weeks ago. He said he wasn't hungry, but I forced him to eat it. In fact, I fed it to him, lovingly blowing on each tablespoon before putting it to his lips. Blake, it seemed, was always taking care of me. The role reversal felt so good. I loved taking care of my man. *That* man who loved me so. He told me he felt a little better after finishing the bowl of the nourishing broth. I smiled. Blake's grandma was right: matzo ball soup was Jewish penicillin as much as it was an aphrodisiac. Blake, however, was in no condition for a romp.

I joined him in bed, snuggling close to him. I flipped on the TV to get our minds off the results of the urine test. In the middle of a *SpongeBob* episode, Blake's cell phone rang. It was Dr. Klein. I asked Blake to put the phone on speaker mode. My heartbeat sped up with anticipation.

"Blake, we got back the results of the urine sample," began Dr. Klein.

"And..." Blake sounded anxious. I clasped his hand.

"Everything is normal except…" The doctor paused. "The lab found a high level of Rohypnol."

"What's that?"

"It's the brand name for flunitrazepam, a drug that is commonly used in drug-facilitated sexual assaults. Otherwise known as the date-rape drug."

There was silence on Blake's end. His lips tightened into a grim, angry line. I knew what he was feeling. I was feeling it too. A maelstrom of rage and abuse.

The doctor continued. "Blake, this is very serious. It's considered a crime. Do you have any recollection of who did this to you?"

Blake drew in a sharp breath. "Doctor, like I told you before, I don't. I went to a club, the one I belong to, and had a cocktail at the bar. Someone must have slipped it into my drink."

I gave his hand a little squeeze, letting him know he'd handled the inquiry perfectly. The doctor responded.

"Well, Blake, I still think you should report it. And let me tell you, you're very lucky. The high dose of Rohypnol mixed with alcohol could have killed you."

A shiver ran through me from my head to my toes. The thought of Kat taking Blake away from me forever was unfathomable. I squeezed his hand tighter, never wanting to let go of him.

Maintaining his composure, Blake told Dr. Klein he would think about it and then took another deep breath. "One thing, Doctor. I hope you'll share none of this with my parents or sister."

"Of course not, Blake. Doctor-patient privilege."

"Thanks."

"Of course. One last question, how do you feel?"

"Better but still queasy."

"That's normal. I want you to rest and drink plenty of fluids. By tonight, the drug should be out of your system."

"I will." Blake paused, placing his free hand on the duvet close to his cock. It had been very still today. A look of uncertainty washed over his face. "Doc, will this flu-nit-shit-whatever drug have any long-term effects on my uh...um...equipment?"

I heard the good doctor chuckle. "No, Blake. You should be absolutely fine."

Blake blew out a breath of relief. Inwardly, I did the same.

With that, the two exchanged good-byes and Blake ended the call. He hastily tossed his phone onto the bed and then turned to look at me. His look of relief had turned to rage.

"The fucking bitch!"

I gently cradled his embittered face in my hands, turning it toward me. "Baby, the good news is you're going to be okay."

Taking me in his arms, Blake thanked me again for trusting him and for making him take the test. But he was still mad as hell. What was most infuriating him was that he didn't know what do next. He explained all the ramifications of taking Kat down. Exposing her. Moreover, Kat most likely still had all the photos on her phone and could use them to spin more evil.

He slammed his fist against the bed. "Fucking, fucking bitch."

Thank God, for the cushy memory foam mattress (we'd never bought a springy one) because on any other surface, Blake would have likely broken some bones with the force of his fist. I lifted the hand to my lips and tenderly kissed the back of it.

"Fucking, fucking bitch," he muttered again.

"No, baby, *fuck* the bitch." My father had always preached, "Don't get mad. Get even."

I told Blake my idea without giving away too many details. And that I needed his help. "I trusted you, baby. Now, you must trust me."

"I do, tiger."

After a sweet kiss, he did as I asked and made two calls. Yes! Things were working out.

Sucking in air through his nose, he set the phone down on the bed and asked me to face him. His large hands took hold of my shoulders. He looked anxious.

"Jen, there's something I've got to tell you about Kat. About our past that I should have told you before."

My pulse sped up and my eyes fluttered. He hadn't been honest with me?

He took in a shaky breath and on the exhale he simply said, "I got Kat pregnant."

My heart skipped a beat. "You have a child?"

"No, tiger." And then a long tense pause. "She had a miscarriage."

"When did this happen?" Though shocked, I kept my tone even-keeled.

"The summer after high school. We were at some graduation party, and I got drunk. As always, she was all over me. Stupid me succumbed. The fucking condom must have torn from her nails, and I guess she was off birth control."

"Jeez."

"Jen, she wanted to keep the baby so I would marry her. My parents were up in arms. Rightfully, neither of them thought we should do that. We were too young. I wanted nothing to do with her, and believe me, the last fucking thing I wanted was to be a father at the age of eighteen. Her parents, however, wanted us to marry. The recession had hurt them, and they were going through lean times. If Kat married me, they would no longer have to support her extravagant lifestyle, and they could smooch off my parents, who had protected their investments. So, they supported Kat's decision. I was fucked. Afraid of a scandal that would embarrass my family, I lied and told her I'd marry her if she kept my identity under wraps until the baby was born. She went along with it, taunting me each day she would break her promise if she caught me with another girl."

Blake had stunned me in into silence. Wordlessly, I listened on. His voice faltered.

"Six months in and barely showing—her friends thought she'd just gained weight—the bitch went horseback riding." Blake paused, taking a breath. "She went into labor. My sister was discreetly there for her, but the baby was stillborn."

"Oh, Blake!" So, that was what Marcy was hiding. I cupped my petite hand over his large one, still splayed on my shoulder. Raw emotion poured through my veins as he went on.

"It was a boy. We had a proper Jewish burial for him and had to name him. Gabriel...after an angel."

The angel of revelation.

"Just our families attended." Blake's voice softened, and he closed his eyes for a long moment as if he were going back in time.

"Jen, I'll never forget that day and that tiny shoebox-sized coffin being lowered into the earth. My little mistake. As our rabbi recited the *Kaddish,* the prayer for the dead, it began to drizzle, and the anger I had toward Kat turned inward. I hated myself and grieved for the little boy I didn't want or would never know. With each shovel of the earth, I grew numb. Kat didn't shed a tear. At the end of the service, she spat in my face and called me an asshole."

He bowed his head. "She was right. I was an asshole. A stupid fucking asshole."

"Blake, look at me." Slowly, he lifted his eyes. "You're *not* an asshole."

My heart was cracking. This story explained so much of Blake. His fear of relationships. And his baby-phobia. My mind flashed back to the lunch we had last year with Jaime and how uncomfortable he initially was with his twins. And then to his uncomfortable reaction to my pregnancy test. The story wasn't over.

"After the burial, Kat had a breakdown. Maybe from a hormone imbalance, depression, or guilt. Or a combination of all three. She tried to commit suicide and her parents institutionalized her. A year later, she was released, and the first thing she did was show up at my UCLA dorm and tell me how much she loved me. One night, she even managed to break in, and I found her naked in my bed. I had to get a restraining order. Fortunately, she went to live abroad but returned to LA last fall. Jen, to make a long story short, she hasn't stopped stalking me. The girl is sick. Poison. I just wish I'd told all of this to you sooner."

"Why didn't you?" My voice was tender, my eyes compassionate.

"I wanted to. She stalked me in Vegas and threatened to tell you herself."

My blood simmered. Did she hit on him?

"I wanted to tell you the minute I came back, but I couldn't with the way you were feeling. Then, the day you went to see Marcy, she fucking assaulted me again at Saks. I thought she'd gotten to you when I couldn't reach you. That's why I flew to Boise. But when I found out about your dad, I just couldn't bring myself to tell you. I didn't need to lay this heavy shit on you and upset you more."

I held his face in my hands and gazed lovingly into his remorseful eyes. He had made the right decisions.

"And then I was going to tell you last night at dinner. And the psycho bitch fucked me over again." His eyes burnt into mine. "Can you forgive me, tiger?"

"There's nothing to forgive, my love. It wasn't your fault. It was a nightmare you had no control over. We just can't hide things from each other."

Silently, he nodded in my palms, and I acknowledged him with a smile on my lips and in my eyes.

"Blake, baby, I love you so much. Do you believe me?"

He drew me tight against him, and the hot, passionate kiss he planted on my lips was all I needed.

Fraught with emotion, I lay in bed with Blake until he dozed off. Quietly, I slipped away and booted up my computer. It was time to take the sick bitch down. For all the pain she'd caused me. And for all she'd caused my Blake. I typed away.

To: Katrina Moore
From: Jennifer McCoy
Subject: Meeting/URGENT

Dear Kat~

I am writing you with tears in my eyes. I am completely devastated by the photos you sent me of you and Blake.

You were absolutely right. Blake is still into you. How could I have been so blind? And so foolish for trusting him with my heart and my life?

I have no choice but to end our engagement and call off the wedding. I've already given him back his ring. With all due respect for his family, I would very much like to meet with you discreetly tomorrow to discuss how we can best break the news to all involved. I am temporarily staying at a bungalow at The Beverly Hills Hotel, which, at least, Blake had the decency to put me up in. I would appreciate if you could meet me there.

I never thought I would thank you, but I owe you my deepest gratitude. Though sadness fills every crevice of my being, it is better to know now where I stand with Blake than to have had my heart broken by him after our union. I can only hope he does not do the same to you.

With my sincerest appreciation~ Jennifer

I reread my e-mail. I loved writing every single word. With a wicked smile, I hit send. Just like I thought…I instantly got a response.

To: Jennifer McCoy
From Katrina Moore
Subject: Meeting/URGENT

Dear Jennifer—
My heart bleeds for you. What Blake did is appalling and I am partly accountable. In all fairness, I tried to warn you. His feelings for me are strong and real. In fact, he just called me and informed me about your breakup. He can't wait to get back together with me. He ended the call by saying that I was his first and only true love.

Yes, I agree we should meet tomorrow. Let's make it 3 p.m. I'll come directly to your bungalow and we'll strategize an exit plan. Thank you for trusting me.

Yours truly—Katrina

Perfection! I confirmed the meeting. A fiendish grin whipped across my face. My newest production, *Fuck the Bitch*, was underway. It was now time to recruit my co-producer and co-stars. Grabbing my cell phone, I made two calls, one right after the other.

Lights! Camera! Action! Everything was in place. Tomorrow could not come fast enough.

Blake had made arrangements for the bungalow—the same one my parents had stayed at during their visit. It was permanently leased by Conquest Broadcasting and used for visiting dignitaries, investors, and out-of-town producers, directors, and stars. Luck was on our side—it was vacant.

I headed over to The Beverly Hills Hotel at lunchtime, leaving my car with the valet. The pink stucco bungalow, located in a very secluded area of the property, couldn't have been more perfect—consisting of an elegantly appointed living room, bedroom, and kitchenette. Soon afterward, my partner in crime, Libby, showed up. She was beaming with excitement.

"You're a fucking genius, girl," she exclaimed, tossing her canvas bag onto the plush Hollywood Regency-styled couch.

"Hope it works," I replied. "Pussy and her girlfriend should be here any minute."

Pussy was Pussy Amour, the co-star of SIN-TV's highly rated prime time show, *Private Dick*. She had recently created a stir in the porn world after revealing she was gay. To the industry's surprise, the fact she was a lesbian only helped the show's ratings. Pussy had some very special talents as did her girlfriend whose name was Swell.

Libby and I were drinking some Diet Cokes when the doorbell rang. I leapt up from the couch to open the door. Sure enough, it was my expected guests.

Pussy, who I'd gotten to know from various conventions, gave me a big hug. I introduced her to Libby and she introduced us to Swell.

Both women were wearing tight-ass jeans, mile-high platforms, and tanks that clung to their planet-sized boobs. Each was a carrying a small overnight bag though they were returning to Vegas in the evening. Bearing a striking resemblance to Pink with their short spiked platinum hair, they could practically be sisters except Swell had piercings all over as well as sleeves of colorful tattoos along her arms.

"Thanks for coming," I said, ushering them into the main room.

"Anything for you and Blake," responded Pussy. "Are you ready to take the bitch down?"

I drew in a gulp of air. "Yes, but I'm nervous."

"There's nothing to be worried about, honey." She shot her companion a flirtatious wink. "Come on, Swell, baby. Let's get ready and set things up."

Taking their bags with them, they ambled arm in arm to the bedroom. Five minutes later they re-appeared.

"Holy shit!" exclaimed Libby, her jaw as wide opened as mine.

Both women were clad in matching black leather bustiers, fishnets, and stilettos. Tattoos were everywhere on Swell's body. Pussy had one, too, of a sex kitten by her shoulder.

"I'm so ready for the Pussy-Kat show," purred the porn star. She let out a ferocious meow and mock-swiped her claws.

I went over the plan with them. Everyone knew what to do. At close to three o'clock, Pussy and Libby flattened themselves against the wall on either side of the bungalow entrance. Swell was in the bedroom. At exactly three, the doorbell rang. My heartbeat sped up. Showtime!

Wasting no time, I swung open the door halfway. Standing before me was Kat, dressed to kill in a tight-fitting designer silk dress that accentuated her D-cup boobs.

"Hi, Kat," I said in my most despondent voice, even adding

in a sniffle. "Let me take your bag."

With a smug smile, she handed me her monstrous purse and stepped inside the bungalow.

"Where would you like—"

Before she could finish her question, Pussy and Libby ambushed her. Pussy seized her arms while Libby grabbed her stiletto-clad feet by the ankles.

"What the fuck?" she shrieked. "What are you doing to me?" Writhing and kicking, she continued to rant as Pussy and Libby hauled her into the bedroom.

"Thanks for coming, Kat," I said brightly, trailing behind them, her handbag slung over my arm.

In no time, we were in the bedroom, and Kat was flat on her back on the bed. Libby and I pinned her down while Pussy and Swell worked together to fasten the pink leather restraints on her wrists and ankles.

"You can't do this to me!" she growled, the restraints quickly in place. "I'll have you arrested."

"I don't think so," I said nonchalantly as I fished through her roomy bag in search of her cell phone. I found it shortly in the zipper compartment.

"Smile!" I aimed the phone at her and snapped a photo.

She made of face of utter disgust.

I tsk-tsked and shook my head with mock-disdain. "No selfies for you today."

"Shut up and undo me!" she spat back at me.

"What do you think, girls? Does she look pretty in pink?" asked Pussy.

"Very!" Libby, Swell, and I responded in unison.

"Who are you?" Kat hissed, her green eyes flaring at Pussy.

"Someone you're never going to forget. And this is my girlfriend, Swell."

After a succulent kiss, Swell rolled her pierced tongue around her lips and in her husky voice said, "Hi, babe."

"Oh my fucking God," Kat cried out, heaving on the bed and trying desperately to free herself from the restraints that were attached to the brass headboard and footboard.

Pussy snickered. "What do you say, girls? Should we find out how pink the bitch's pussy is?"

"I'd say it's showtime." I handed Libby the phone.

"Lights, camera, action!" shouted Libby, adjusting the phone's camera setting to video while Swell reached for a large pair of scissors on the night table. Starting at the hemline, she began slicing Kat's dress apart, inch by silky inch.

"What the fuck are you doing?" shrieked Kat. "This is a two-thousand dollar Armani!"

"Well, now, bitch, it's two-thousand-dollar rag." Swell grinned wickedly as she tossed the scissors aside and simply tore apart the rest of the dress with her bare hands. The hiss of the shredding fabric was like music to my ears. In a few harsh breaths, Kat was stripped down to her matching black bra and thong.

Kat's raging eyes met mine. "What's this all about, Jennifer? Is this just some form of revenge for Blake dumping your sorry ass for me?"

Poker-faced, I slipped my hand into my pocket, and in slow motion, I lowered Blake's magnificent snowflake diamond ring onto my ring finger as she watched with wide-eyed confusion. A giddy smile lit my face.

"News flash, Kat. Blake and I never broke up."

"I don't fucking believe you," she snorted. "He told me this morning it was over between the two of you and that he loves *me*."

I rolled my eyes. "Actually, his exact words were: 'Kat, you've always been the one. I love you so fucking much. My cock can't wait to ravish you.'"

Kat's mouth fell open. She looked as if she'd been struck by lightning. She had put two and two together.

My eyes narrowed with fury. "You fucking drugged Blake and made it look like he was seducing you. I bet the evidence is still right here on your phone."

"Give me back my phone, you cunt!"

I smirked. "Can't. My friend Libby needs to use it."

She fired a dirty look at my bestie. Libby aimed the phone at her and said, "Smile."

Kat made a face, her stunning features scrunching with rage.

Click.

"Are we done now?" she grunted.

Crawling onto the bed, Pussy chimed in. "Actually, we haven't yet begun."

In one swift move, she tore off Kat's scanty lace thong while Swell ripped apart her front closure bra and slid it down her arms. A look of terror washed over Kat's face. Her implants quivered. God, they were big!

"What are you going to do to me?" asked Kat, her voice trembling.

Pussy flicked her tongue just above Kat's hairless triangle. "Nothing. Ask me what it's going to look like I'm do-ing...*Everything!*"

"No!" shrieked Kat, frantically trying to bolt from the bed.

It was futile. Pussy spread Kat's long, toned legs farther apart. Holding down her thighs, she buried her head deep between them. I watched while Libby filmed everything on the bitch's cell phone. Though Pussy wasn't actually licking Kat or doing anything else, she pretended she was. Pussy, the porn star, was just being a great actress.

Kat continued to scream, her body jerking and arching, and her face contorting. Pussy lifted her head and smiled for the camera and then buried her head again between Kat's thighs. Soon her partner got into the act, climbing onto the bed and pretending to be going down Kat's enormous fake boobs. Of course, her mouth never touched down on them, but her moves were effective. Though neither woman in any way performing any kind of sexual act, Kat was writhing and whimpering. Libby, bless her heart, was filming everything from every angle. I swear I wouldn't be surprised if she left her research job at Conquest and moved into production. She was clearly enjoying every moment.

A tortured expression washed over Kat's face that could easily be interpreted as tortured pleasure. Ecstasy. I kept my eyes glued on her as Pussy whispered something in her ear.

"Yes!" shrieked Kat. The perfect response to Pussy's inaudible scripted line: "Do you want me to stop?"

Sweat beads clustered on Kat's face and chest as Pussy repositioned herself between her spread-eagled legs. Her ass in the air, the porn star buried her head back into Kat's center, and as she bopped it up and down, she hummed. It looked like she was going down on Kat and bringing her to the edge. What an actress! Libby was still capturing everything, shooting the scene from all the right angles. Just like a pro!

"Please!" cried Kat. "Please, please, please." It just couldn't be more perfect. Kat sounded as if she was begging to come.

After one more "please," Pussy pulled away and Kat let out a giant sigh of relief. Her body went slack.

Yes, yes, yes! With a wag of a finger, I signaled to Libby to stop shooting. We had what we needed. My production classes at USC had really paid off.

"Hope it was as good for you as it was for me," purred Pussy as she climbed off the bed.

Fury flickered in Kat's eyes. "Fuck you. Let me go!"

Pussy smiled smugly. "Not yet."

"My turn," chimed in Swell, her voice as deep as a man's.

Terror washed over Kat's face.

With a wink, Pussy said, "Come on, ladies. Let's go play gin rummy. Hope you know how."

"Gin," I shouted ten minutes later, seated cross-legged around a coffee table in the anteroom. And at that moment, I heard Kat cry out, "stop it," repeatedly. I hoped Swell, who I didn't know before today, wasn't hurting her. Or violating our agreement and sexually assaulting her. As I flipped over my cards, I asked Pussy if she thought everything was all right.

"Chill, honey. Don't you worry. Swell is an artist."

I wanted to believe her. We played several rounds of rummy, and I was thrilled to learn that both Pussy and Swell were coming to the wedding. Before we could re-shuffle the deck yet again, Swell strutted into the room. She greeted us with a wicked twisted grin.

"Everything went smoothly. The slut has something to

remember today by. Come see."

Leaving the deck of cards on the table, the three of us followed Swell back to the bedroom. Still bound to the bed, Kat was now blindfolded and screaming. "What the fuck did you to do me, you fucking bull dyke?"

I moved in closer and my eyes popped. At the same time, Libby and I burst into mad laughter. We were laughing so hard we were crying.

"What the fuck are you laughing about? Take off this goddamn blindfold, you bitches."

Swell did as bid. "Oh my fucking god," shrieked Kat upon making eye contact with her chest.

"Some of my finest work ever," boasted Swell.

Inked across Kat's breastbone was one word. Of course, I should have known. With all her tattoos, Pussy's girlfriend Swell was a tattoo artist.

"I was going to ink "BITCH," but this is so much better."

BUTCH. I was laughing so hard I wet my pants.

Kat couldn't stop shrieking. Libby raised Kat's cell phone to take a photo.

"Stop it!" wailed Kat.

Too late. *CLICK.*

"Lib, make sure you e-mail me everything."

My bestie gave me a thumbs up. After my laughter died down, my eyes clashed with Kat's.

"What the fuck do you want?" she seethed.

"It's simple. I want you to leave the country by tomorrow and not come back until Blake and I are married."

"Is that a threat?" Venom poured from her mouth.

"No, it's an ultimatum. If I don't have proof, I'm going to

send the footage and photos to your mother. And post it on YouTube and all over Instagram."

"You wouldn't!"

"I would."

Libby chimed in. "And it would be perfect for the new show Blake's developing—*America's Sexiest Home Videos.*

Kat's mouth dropped open, forming a perfect O.

I shot her a wry smile. Oh, and by the way, if one word of your past with Blake leaks out—Which. I. Know. All. About.—you can count on the same."

Kitty-Kat was too shocked to say a word. Her wide-open mouth remained frozen.

Grinning, Libby handed me Kat's cell phone and I slipped it into a pocket. The four of us pivoted toward the door.

"You're leaving me here?" Kat called out in a panic.

"I'll call security shortly. Enjoy your stay at The Beverly Hills Hotel."

With that, my production staff and I said adieu to my shrieking and cursing nemesis and headed to the Polo Lounge to celebrate a job well done. Our own little wrap party. We couldn't stop laughing.

Two hours and two bottles of champagne later, an e-mail dinged on my phone. It was from Kat, who must have made her way home. No message. Only an attachment. A round-trip ticket to Rio in her name. The date of return was not till January. A triumphant smile lit my face as I put my cell phone away. Fingers crossed Blake and I wouldn't be honeymooning there.

A waiter came by, and I took care of the bill.

Fuck the Bitch was a fait accompli.

Chapter 11

Jennifer

When I told Blake the story of how I took Kat down, he doubled over with laughter. Then, recovered from his drugging, he gave me an epic fucking that for sure belonged in *The Guinness Book of World Records*. I had so many orgasms I lost count.

We couldn't be happier that Kat was out of the picture. But things were no less stressful. In fact, they were more stressful. With the wedding only a month away, Enid was in panic mode. In addition to losing Kat, Jeffrey, the receptionist quit on her. Little did she know he was starting up his own event planning business and had stolen her list of "preferred" vendors. I knew this from Chaz, who now was dating Jeffrey. It was hot and heavy and I was so happy for him.

I spoke to my mom every day. Dad was doing great. Except he'd become a little bit of a *kvetch,* complaining constantly about how slowly my mother drove. She begged Blake and me to go to Boise for Thanksgiving, but as much I wanted to, I couldn't. In addition to catching up on my crazy workload (which I was frantically trying to wrap up before the wedding), there were so many last minute wedding details to attend to, including meeting with Blake's rabbi...a wedding cake taste-testing...a meeting with the bandleader to go over our playlist...applying for a marriage license...and going for Monique Hervé's final dress fitting as well as Chaz's first one. Last not but least, there were also all those thank you notes to write. The wedding gifts kept pouring in. The final headcount was at 1150!

On the Saturday after Thanksgiving, which we celebrated at Blake's parents' house, I was going to meet Chaz downtown for my first dress fitting. I couldn't wait to see what he'd designed. He knew the vintage look I wanted but had been very secretive, wanting to surprise me when it was close to finalized. At the crack of dawn, I got a call. With Blake still sound asleep, I reached for my cell phone on the nightstand. It was Chaz.

"Jenny-Poo, it's gone," he said before I could even say hi. His voice sounded frantic.

I bolted upright to a sitting position. "Chaz, what are you talking about?"

"Your dress. There was a fire in the studio last night. Everything was destroyed."

"Oh my God!" I said the three words so loudly I woke up Blake.

"Baby, what's going on?" he asked groggily.

"Chaz, sweetie, hold on." I turned to Blake and told him the news. He was almost as devastated as I was. I returned my attention to Chaz.

"Chaz, where are you?"

"I'm here at the studio. You wouldn't believe what it looks like."

"I'll be there in twenty minutes." Chaz, who had always

been there for me, needed my moral support. Though Blake insisted on going downtown with me, I told him to stay put. In five minutes, I was dressed and out the door.

Libby and Jeffrey were already at Chaz's studio. Or should I say former studio. We stood in a line like four zombies taking in the damage. It was worse than I'd imagined. In addition to the smut-covered walls and charred bolts of fabric, the fire department had gutted and flooded the loft-like space to put out the fire. The studio was a shell of what it had been with puddles of water everywhere along with exposed wires and beams. And it was still smoking.

"Do they know what caused the fire?" A dark thought crossed my suspicious mind. Did Enid or Monique possibly set it? I wouldn't put it past those two wicked women to do something so evil. Or did Kat have something to do with it from wherever she was to get back at me? That psychopath was capable of anything.

Chaz twisted his lips. "The fire department determined it was definitely due to an electrical short. The wiring in this old building is not up to code."

"That's awful," I murmured, relieved that none of those horrid women had anything to do with it. But it didn't make things any better.

My stinging eyes gravitated to a blackened mannequin in the corner. On it were charred remnants of tulle and lace. The dress was burnt beyond recognition. My heart sunk. My fairy-tale gown had gone up in smoke. It belonged in a morgue.

Chaz followed my gaze. "Oh, Jenny-Poo. It was so beyond."

"Maybe you can make another one," chirped Libby, the optimist, before I could utter a word.

Chaz's shoulders slumped. "I wish, but not a fat chance in hell. I have to find a temporary studio, deal with the insurance company, and then replace all the samples for my upcoming Spring line. Plus, it would take over a month to get the imported fabrics I used. Oh, my Jenny-Poo, I'm so sorry."

Masking my disappointment, I wrapped my arm around Chaz's deflated shoulders. "Chaz, shit happens. The most important thing is you're okay."

Jeffrey clasped my despondent friend's hand. "Honey, I'm going to be there for you. Maybe, I'll do a small fundraiser and invite your top clients and our friends to get things going."

"Count me in." I smiled for the first time, grateful that Chaz finally had a significant other in his life who genuinely loved him. If I ever had to spearhead an event, I knew who was going to be my coordinator.

"And wedding girl, if that bitch Enid gives you any grief, you let me know. I've got plenty of dirt on her and her slutty cohort Monique."

"Oooh, like what?" cooed Chaz, instantly cheered up by juicy gossip.

"They give each other pussy."

My eyes almost popped out of their sockets. "No way. They're gay?"

"Way. Gayer than eight guys blowing nine guys. Enid's husband doesn't know she's a lesbo."

Over breakfast which I treated everyone to, Jeffrey shared

more titillating tidbits about Enid and Monique. Enid was a screamer and used a whip. Why should that surprise me? And Monique liked it in her bony butt. We were shrieking and howling at everything Jeffrey revealed—from their feather fetish to their lesbian video fetish. Wow! If I ever had the need to send Enid the video I shot of her daughter she might actually get off on it. I couldn't wait to tell Blake.

December was here in no time. Things for the wedding were falling into place. The wedding rehearsal—and dinner following at The Bel Air Hotel—were all set up for the night before the monumental event. To my delight, Mrs. Cho's adorable little daughters were going to be my flower girls and walk down the aisle with Marcy's twin sons, the ring bearers. Mom and Dad were flying in that morning. And true to his word, Dad would be walking me down the aisle albeit with a cane.

Gloria Zander gave me a surprise bridal shower. Jeffrey, whose client list was growing rapidly, helped her plan it. Held at Shutters, a chic beachside hotel in Santa Monica, Libby was there along with some of my friends from USC and my rape support group. And guess who else was there—Grandma!— though Blake's mother couldn't make it as she was being honored at some long-standing luncheon for her philanthropic accomplishments. To my delight, Vera Nichols, Blake's sassy Vegas manager, also attended as well as Pussy and Swell. And so did Mrs. Cho. The only person whose presence I sorely missed was my mom; she was afraid to leave Dad alone though he'd insisted she fly out. Libby, God bless her, Skyped her in, so she virtually attended. By the end of the lovely afternoon champagne tea, we were all buzzed, and as Grandma rightly said, "Bubala, you have enough sexy *shmexy* undies for Blakela to tear off to last a lifetime." I was going to start that night.

Later that week, I had my final fitting for Monique's wedding dress. I'd resigned myself to being the mermaid bride, not the princess bride. Knowing Monique and Enid were secretly having an affair, I could barely keep a straight face as the former made more alterations to my dress. The dress wasn't perfect, but I hoped my wedding would be. Soon, I'd be floating down the aisle. With all the ups and downs I'd been through, my special day couldn't get here soon enough.

The dress had to be taken in. I'd lost some weight from stress. I'd read on some bridal blog this was common, but Blake was worried about me. He felt between the wedding and my work, I was taking on more than I could chew. He was right, but that's just the way I was. I couldn't wait for our honeymoon—which Blake had planned all on his own. He was mum on the destination. I couldn't suck—or fuck—it out of him. All I knew was it some place neither of us had ever been.

There was one other problem—Bradley. Ever since that restaurant incident, he'd e-mailed me constantly. I refused to open his e-mails and simply put them in my trash file and then deleted them permanently. I wanted nothing to do with him, and I never wanted to see him again. I didn't tell Blake about the e-mails. For all intents and purposes, Bradley Wick, DDS, was dead to me.

On the Tuesday of the week before my wedding, I had my last support group meeting of the year. I wasn't feeling well.

All day long, I'd been experiencing cramping. For sure, stress. Blake didn't want me to go. Not only because of my rundown state, but because there had been a recent chain of gang-driven crimes in the Venice Beach neighborhood where we met. But I insisted. We were going to have a small Christmas party with a gift exchange. Plus, I wanted to thank Dr. Williams for her kindness as well as hug my friends who'd shared and learned to face their fears like me. Blake wasn't thrilled, to put things mildly. He still had to learn I was a big girl and could take care of myself. And he couldn't always control me.

The meeting lasted about an hour. Instead of our normal routine of taking turns to talk about our rape-related issues, we feasted on eggnog and snacks we'd each brought along and shared what we were doing over the holidays. Dr. Williams and my sweet fellow rape victims had been invited to the wedding and were all looking forward to attending. Before leaving, Dr. Williams and I exchanged a hug. She'd helped me so much— especially with my trust issues. I was grateful Blake had urged me to join the group after the Springer attack.

The mid December air was chilly, especially for LA. Wearing only a lightweight wool sweater, I hugged myself as I walked quickly to my car which was parked a few blocks away. The poorly lit streets were dark and desolate. Nearby sirens sounded in my ears. And then I heard footsteps. So I thought. I anxiously looked over my shoulder. No one. My weary, distrustful mind was playing tricks on me. Paranoia was a recurring feeling among rape victims. We feared being followed and thought it could happen again. Holding my car keys, I picked up my pace until I reached my vehicle. Before I could unlock the door, a harsh voice called out my name.

Startled, I flipped around and accidentally dropped my keys. I bent down to retrieve them, but another hand got to them first.

Chapter 12

Blake

As much as I loved my tiger, she still knew how to piss me off. She could be as stubborn as a mule. I didn't want her to go to her rape support group. She was overworked and rundown. Plus, knowing there had been a bunch of gang-related incidents in the seedy Venice Beach neighborhood where they met bugged the shit out of me. If something happened to my tiger, I'd just about die. I'd almost lost her once; I couldn't lose her again. It wouldn't have killed her not to go, but it would kill me if something bad happened to her. I was as protective of her as I was possessive.

Despite my protestations, she insisted on going and told me to take a chill pill. There was nothing I could do to stop her—except tie her up and hold her down—which, in retrospect, I should have done. My cock twitched at the image of her all tied up in ropes. It made me horny as hell. Later when she got home, I was going to live out this fantasy and give her a fucking she wouldn't forget.

She'd left the office early to head over to her group, which met weekly at seven p.m. At 7:30, I packed up my briefcase and headed to my car. Once settled inside, I flipped on the radio. Breaking news. The body of a badly beaten young woman had been discovered in Venice, close to Jennifer's support group center. Her wallet had been stolen and her identity was still unknown. Police and paramedics had rushed to the scene of the crime and were still there. My heart leapt into my throat. I yanked my stick shift into first gear and peeled out of the parking lot.

Fuck. Fuck. FUCK.

Chapter 13
Jennifer

Crouching, my unexpected companion and I were face to face. His nostrils flared. My pulse sounded in my ears.

"Bradley, what are you doing here? And what do you want?"

One word: "You." His fetid breath assaulted me. Shit. He was uncharacteristically drunk.

I tensed but tried to remain calm and thought I could reason with him. But before I could get my lips to move, he shoved me against the car. My head banged against the frame, and in a painful breath, his slimy lips were all over mine and his hands were groping my breasts. The words "Stop it" stayed lodged in my throat as I tried to fight him off. Tearing at his thinning hair. Pushing him away. He bit my lip with his monstrous teeth and I could taste blood in my mouth. *His balls! Go for his balls!* But before I could reach for them, he grabbed my wrists tightly.

"Fuck you, Jennifer," he hissed.

"No. Fuck you, you bastard." Another voice. A voice I recognized.

In a split second, Bradley was off me. Dangling by his collar in the hands of the man I loved. Blake! My hero!

Burning with rage, Blake set Bradley on his feet, spun him around, and—POW!—punched him hard in the face. Wincing, Bradley staggered against the car. Blood poured from his nose. Wiping my own bloody lip, I crawled away and stood up. My heart pounded as I watched Blake punch him again. Bradley moaned loudly and put his small hand to his bloody face.

Blake lifted his hand once more, his fingers balled into a tight fist. Bradley turned his head away and cowered.

"Man, don't hit me again!" My despicable ex was practically sobbing.

A sudden rush of fear surged inside me. Blake was capable of murder. He had killed for me once and he could do it again. As much as I despised Bradley, I couldn't let that happen.

"Please, Blake," I pleaded. "Leave him alone! He's had enough."

Without acknowledging me, Blake held Bradley fastened in his fiery gaze. My heart galloped and my throat clenched. To my relief, he lowered his fist and then slapped both hands on Bradley's shoulders, shoving him against my car door. Bradley's blood-stained lips quivered.

"Let me go," he whimpered.

Blake's lips snarled. "Don't you *ever* mess with my girl. She's mine now. You fuck with her, you fuck with me."

Bradley trembled.

"Trust me. You'll be asking Santa for your two front teeth."

Bradley parted his lips as if wanted to say something. Blake stopped him.

"And if I ever see you touch her, I'll cut off your little dick. You'll be sucking thumbkin."

I watched as Blake kicked him square in the balls. Groping

his groin, Bradley groaned and crumpled to the ground. Blake spat at him.

"Now get the hell out of here, Dickwick. I never want to see you again."

I watched as Bradley crawled away.

Blake's rage didn't die down. With pounding steps, he moved my way. I gazed up at him. His razor-sharp eyes pierced me as he held me fiercely in his gaze.

"What the fuck was he doing here?"

"Oh, Blake! He must have followed me. He's been stalking me online."

"Screw 'Oh Blake.'" A rage that frightened me swept over Blake's face. "Why the hell didn't you tell me?"

I shriveled against the hood of the car. "You've been away. Busy. Preoccupied." I stuttered every word.

"Fuck you, Jennifer."

I shuddered at his angry words.

"You didn't listen to me. I had a bad feeling about tonight. I told you I didn't want you to come here, but you did."

"But—"

He cut me off. "Fuck 'but.' You need to be punished."

He'd punished me once before. But it was playful. I'd screwed up pancakes and he'd fucked me on the kitchen floor, dousing me with maple syrup. But this was different. There was an intensity to him now I'd never known before. It both frightened and excited me.

He flipped me around so I was bent over the hood. My hands splayed on the cold metal. The headlights pressed against my middle. My head was bowed down, but I could still see his enraged reflection in the windshield. "Blake, what are you going to do to me?"

"I'm going to fuck some sense into you."

A retribution fuck. I was strangely aroused. "Fuck you, Blake."

"Fuck you, tiger," he growled, shoving down my skirt along with my panties in one swift swoop and then spreading my legs apart.

His giant cock needed no warm-up. And apparently, my pussy wasn't going to get one either. With a loud carnal grunt, he thrust his thick length into me. And began to ram me. This was fucking with no mercy. I winced. He slapped my ass. I winced again. Hot, salty tears sprinkled my cheeks. He pounded harder, digging his nails into my hips. I rocked into him, oddly enjoying every erotic minute.

"Blake, why are you doing this to me?"

"Because. *Thrust.* I. *Thrust.* Love. *Thrust.* You."

"Don't you have a better way of expressing yourself?" I blissfully wept the words.

In response to my question, an arm wrapped around my waist and I could feel his fingertips trail down to my soaking wet center. He began to rub my clit fervently while he continued to pummel me. Shrieks escaped from my lungs as an orgasm spiraled inside me, taking every cell with it. But before I could climax, he pulled his hand away, leaving my hot bundle of nerves bereft.

"Blake, please," I pleaded. "I need to come."

"I need an apology."

"Anything." I was desperate.

"Say you're sorry."

"Sorry."

"And that you'll never disobey me."

"Never." *Nonsense.*

"Good." To my relief, his hand returned to my clit, and he circled away. My orgasm resumed as if there had never been an intermission. It was coming at me at full force. Crashing through me. "Oh, Blake," I screamed out as his own powerful climax met mine. A head-on collision. No pun intended.

"Tiger," he groaned, pulling me back against him as his hot release coated my thighs.

I felt him pull out and then he flipped me around. A mixture of madness and passion flickered in his half-mast blue eyes. They held me prisoner as he cradled my face in his large hands. Tenderness replaced the fury.

"Are you okay?" His voice was soft.

I nodded. His unblinking eyes bore into me.

"Tiger, I almost lost you once. I can't lose you again. If you die, I die. You own my heart."

My lips quivered at his powerful words. Lifting one of my hands, he slipped it under his suit jacket and held it against his heart. I could feel it beating against my palm. I gazed up at his beautiful face. "Blake, one more promise. I'm never going to leave you."

"Thank you, baby. I needed to hear that." He held me close to him as if never wanting to let me go.

Chapter 14

Blake

We headed home in one car. Mine. I told Jen to leave hers in Venice. She protested, but I told her I'd have someone from the office pick it up in the morning. And if one of the local gangs vandalized or jacked it, I didn't give a shit. I'd buy her a new car. And it wasn't going to be another Kia.

We drove in silence. Her hand stayed clutched on my hand gripping the shift. Sam Smith's "Stay with Me" played on the radio. The words of this soulful singer's song resonated deep inside me. How close I had come to losing my tiger. One time after another. I didn't want to think about it. I just knew I couldn't live without her.

When we got to our condo, I valeted the car and led her through the lobby, my arm wrapped around her shoulders. We were almost one.

Once inside the apartment, I drew a hot bath. The rope fantasy I'd had earlier in the day had gone down the drain. It just didn't make sense now. Right now, I just needed to hold my tiger. Let her know she was mine. Make up for punishing her. And rid myself of guilt. I felt bad about my angry fuck, yet she'd seemed turned on, not offended.

After peeling off her clothes, which I intended to burn since

Dickwick had touched them, I helped her into the tub. My tub was luxurious. Big enough to let six foot three me stretch out, and it had a Jacuzzi. Truthfully, due to our hectic work schedules, Jen and I hadn't enjoyed it much. Mostly, we took showers together.

I watched as she sunk into the breast-deep water. Her sigh was like a symphony to my ears. Turning on the Jacuzzi, I shrugged off my clothes and joined her, settling behind her. She was in my arms, her slender body and head resting against my chest and shoulders. The water gurgled around us, the bubbling jets caressing and massaging. We were in a zone.

I grabbed a large sponge, squirted some liquid soap on it, and then began to wash her everywhere. Dickwick needed to be erased.

"I'm sorry about tonight," I breathed against her delicate neck as I washed the back of it and her shoulders. "Did I hurt you?"

She arched against me, splaying her hands on my thighs under the water.

"No, Blake. You can never hurt me."

I pondered her soft words. They were true. I wasn't capable of hurting my tiger. My burning desire to protect her and fear of losing her ruled me. I'd never thought about the consequences of my actions with any woman. She made me feel things—emotions—I'd never experienced. And sometimes go to extremes. Kill for her if I had to. I wanted to be her superhero forever.

Silently, I continued to sponge her. She hummed into the percussion of the bubbles. As I soaped her tender tits, her chest rose and fell against me. My cock rose beneath her. Her half-wet ponytail tickled me. Impulsively, I pulled it loose from its elastic band and it free fell, cascading over her shoulders like a velvet cape. The silkiness grazed my chest.

Keeping one hand cupped on her pert rosebud-tipped tit, I reached for the tube of shampoo. The only one she used. Gloria's Secret Very Cherry Vanilla. I squeezed a few dollops onto her hair and, with both hands, began massaging it into her scalp until there was a rich lather. The erotic squishy sound and intoxicating scent aroused me, my cock and heart swelling with love and lust, one physically, the other emotionally. I had to have her. Not fuck her. But make love to her. She was thinking the same thing.

"Oh, Blake," she said dreamily. "Take me. Make love to me."

Gently, I lifted her hips onto my erection. She lowered herself onto my thick, aching length, taking me all the way. God, she felt good. So fucking good. I squeezed my eyes shut and let her know with a moan. On the next heated breath, I was gliding in and out of her, my mouth showering her with kisses everywhere it could, my hands working her slick clit, the water bubbling with love. We came passionately together.

Oh baby, stay with me. You're all I need.

Chapter 15
Jennifer

Time flew by. The weekend of our wedding was here before I knew it.

On Friday, December nineteenth, the day of the rehearsal, the familiar ring of my cell phone jolted me out of my sleep. I hadn't slept well at all. The last minute wedding details had vexed me, and both my mind and my stomach were aflutter. I was wound up as tight as a ball of yarn but could unravel at any minute. Moreover, I was sure I was getting my damn period. I'd been cramping on and off all week and the littlest thing made me cry.

The smell of fresh coffee wafted in the air. Blake was already up and out of bed, for sure in the kitchen. I glanced at the clock on my nightstand. It was seven a.m. The phone rang again and I stretched my arm to reach for it. With half-closed eyes, I registered who was calling. It was my mom. Of course, I had told her to call me when they were about to take off. My parents would be here in two hours. In plenty of time for the rehearsal and dinner tonight. I'd wanted them to come out earlier in the week, but unfortunately, Dad couldn't forego his final, much-needed therapy sessions—especially since he was bent on walking me down the aisle.

My mother's teary-eyed voice sounded before I could even say hi. "Jennifer, honey, I have terrible news."

My heart leapt into my throat and I bolted upright. An inner panic button went off. Had something happened to my father? "Is Dad okay?" I choked out.

"Honey, he's fine. But our flight has been canceled."

"Mom, what do you mean?" My words were rushed and pitchy.

"It's blizzarding."

"Oh my God. What about a later flight?"

"I'm not sure." My mother's voice wavered. "According to airport officials, the storm is expected to get worse."

Tears pricked my eyes, and I could feel a knot in the pit of my stomach. How could this be happening? As a tear escaped, Blake, in just his pajama bottoms, strode into the room, holding two steaming mugs of coffee. He caught a glimpse of me and rushed to my side.

"Jen, what's the matter?" He sat down on the edge of the bed, handing me one of the mugs. It shook in my hand.

"Mom, hold on." Setting the mug on the nightstand, I told Blake what was going on.

Tilting his head back, he huffed a breath. "Jeez. Just what we don't need." My eyes stayed riveted on him as he scooted across the mattress to retrieve his cell phone on the other night table.

"Blake, what are you doing?" I snapped, my nerves getting to me.

"I'm going to see if we can send my father's private plane or the company jet to get them."

Oh, my Blake! I relayed this news to my mom as I listened

intently with my other ear to the conversation Blake was having with someone who must be from the Conquest travel department. His eyebrows were knitted as he went back and forth with them.

"Fuck." He flung the phone on the bed. My heart sunk deeper. I knew it was not good. His eyes met mine.

"Jen, they're closing the airport. No planes are allowed to depart or land."

Shit. It was even worse than I thought. With a lump in my throat, I shared the bad news with my mom. Tearfully, she told me she was going to ask Father Murphy, who was with them, to pray. As I was about to say good-bye, my dad got on the phone. Tears of my own were now streaming down my cheeks.

"Hi, Dad," I sniffled as Blake massaged my shoulders.

"Jennifer Leigh McCoy, you stop crying right now. Your mother and I may not be there tonight for the rehearsal, but we will be there tomorrow for your wedding. I said I was going to walk my little girl down the aisle, and I never break my promises."

No, he never had broken a promise in all my life. I wiped my eyes. With a final sniffle and an ounce of optimism, I told my darling dad I believed him and how much I loved him. My love for him, like for Blake, was immeasurable.

Blake went into the office for a few hours while I took the day off. I still had a million details to attend to, plus Enid had insisted I get my hair, nails, and makeup done for tonight's events. And a facial. Soon after Blake departed, I canceled all my appointments. The day was gloomy—for the first time in a long time, gray and overcast. Mirroring exactly how I felt. Mom and Dad had gone back home, and all my googling made me feel worse. The blizzard could last up to twenty-four hours. And it was spreading across the Northwest. Despite my father's promise, the reality that my parents might miss my wedding was eating away at me. And on top of all my worries, I felt like pure crap. More than just tension. Shooting pains stabbed my gut. I was beginning to worry if it was something beyond nerves and the onset of my period. Was I getting sick?

Blake returned mid-afternoon. His sultry voice awoke me; I'd dozed off.

"Jen, it's almost four o'clock. You should start getting ready."

As I fluttered my eyes open and sat up, another one of those sharp pangs dug into me. Clutching my stomach and grimacing, I let out a soft moan, but not soft enough to be unnoticed by Blake. He dashed to my side.

"Are you okay, baby?" His voice was thick with concern.

"Blake, I think I might be coming down with something." It was that time of year the flu was rampant. Many co-workers had come down with it, along with Blake's college roommate, Jake, who was not going to make it to the rehearsal or wedding. Even though I'd had a flu shot, it didn't make me immune.

"Are you sure?" My soon-to-be husband tenderly kissed my forehead. "You don't seem to have a fever."

Well, that was good news. Maybe it *was* just nerves.

"C'mon. Let's take a shower together and get ready."

Maybe a shower was just what I needed.

Wrong. We fucked. I felt worse.

The rehearsal at Blake's parents' house started at six. I was wearing the stunning ivory dress Blake surprised me with in Paris along with my mother's lovely cashmere birthday sweater while Blake was dressed in one of his sexy tapered dark suits. He looked dashing. I, to be honest, still looked—and felt—like crap. Even the makeup I'd applied, including the little extra blush and eye shadow, couldn't camouflage my pallor or glazed eyes.

We got there a little early. Mayhem. Pure mayhem. That's the only way to describe the scene. It was like a movie production. Except crazier and more chaotic. Workers were everywhere, and amidst them was a frazzled Enid, dressed to the nines, heels and all, shouting orders through a megaphone. Hundreds of white folding chairs were being set up in the Bernsteins' vast backyard for tomorrow's ceremony, and a giant tent was in the process of being erected for the reception.

"Goddammit. How hard is it to fill a bowl of water and stick a stupid fish in it?" Enid screamed into a walkie talkie. And then into her ringing cell phone, "What do you mean, you idiot? I asked for Beluga caviar, not Sevruga. Just deliver it, but after tomorrow, you're fired."

"Oh, hello Jennifer," she said in a most condescending tone upon taking note of me. She snubbed Blake, who had his arm wrapped around me. I told her my parents wouldn't be coming to the rehearsal because of a snowstorm.

She rolled her eyes and let out a haughty huff of air. And then she narrowed her eyes at Blake. "Seriously, Blake, this would have never happened if you'd married Katrina."

Though she was a continent away, the mention of her name made my skin prickle. Blake held his own.

"*Seriously*, Enid, you need to get your head examined. You're one sick bitch."

Like mother like daughter. Enid's jaw dropped to the floor and stayed there while Blake ushered me away to mingle with our guests.

Seeing friends and family was a welcomed comfort.

Overlooking the backyard, the elegant, spacious veranda began to fill with all the wedding party participants—from the eight hired blond bimbo bridesmaids from Central Casting to those near and dear to us.

Blake's sister Marcy, upon arriving, gave me a hug and then observed me in true doctorly fashion.

"Jennifer, are you all right? You look very pale."

"Yes. Just a case of pre-wedding nerves," I said as another gut-wrenching pang stabbed me. The good actress I was, I smiled through the pain. Perceptive Libby shot me a concerned look. Her sharp, analytical mind could cut through bullshit like a knife.

Enid's thundering voice intercepted my thoughts. She held her megaphone to her face. "Attention, everyone. The rehearsal is about to begin."

One by one, Enid gave the wedding party their marching orders as if she were General Patton. With Rabbi Silverstein already at the altar, Grandma led off the procession. She was followed by the groomsmen, who proceeded in pairs and included Chaz and Jeffrey, and then by Blake's best man, Jaime. With a squeeze of my hand, Blake was the next to go. His parents flanked him. As he stepped onto the verdant lawn,

Blake looked over his shoulder and blew me a kiss. For a fleeting moment, my gloom lifted. I blew one back at him.

As he disappeared into the ominous night, the bevy of bridesmaids, which included Gloria and Marcy, trailed behind him.

Libby and I were the only ones left. Along with Marcy's twin boys, the ring bearers, and Mrs. Cho's daughters, the flower girls. They had managed to score a snow globe and, huddled on the floor in the corner, were watching the little fish inside it swim around in circles. Squeals and laughter filled the air.

"Children," barked Enid. "Your turn. Chop chop!"

The children ignored her. They were too busy playing.

Scowling, Enid marched over to them. She snatched the snow globe and, to my wide-eyed horror, tossed it across the room. The glass shattered and the fish went flying.

Mrs. Cho's sweet little girls burst into tears.

"Meanie!" cried out one of the twins.

My eyes traveled to the fish flapping madly on the floor by my feet. In my overcharged emotional state, tears seared my eyes. The poor little thing. He was gasping for air. I could feel his pain. At this very moment, I, too, felt like a fish out of water. Helpless. Suffocating. Desperate. I fell to my knees and scooped the tiny orange creature into my palms. In a heartbeat, Libby, wearing one of Chaz's little black dresses, was by my side with a bowl of water. *My Libby! Always there for me!*

"Get up, you ridiculous girls," seethed Enid as I struggled to get the fish into the bowl. He was squirming and jumping in my cupped hands. The captivated children had gathered around us.

Libby's freckles jumped off her face as they did when she was enraged. She cranked her neck and gazed up at Enid.

"Shut up, you bitch!" she barked as I finally managed to get the fish safely into the water. It happily swam about.

The cheering children burst out in laughter. "She said the b-word," singsonged one of the twins.

Enid was livid, but for the first time all day, I was on the brink of laughter. Libby didn't hold back and high-fived one of the twins.

"Move it, you imps," growled Enid, snapping her bony fingers at the children, "or I'm going to replace you with some *professional* children who know how to behave."

One of Mrs. Cho's daughters stuck her tongue out at the bitch while the other flung a handful of seashells at her from the basket she was holding.

"You little brats!" Enid screeched as she broke into a hot flash and began fanning herself. As the flustered wedding planner physically ushered the rambunctious children outside, a clap of thunder resounded.

Shit. Was it going to rain?

Still squatting, Libby gave me a hug. "I love you, Jen. Are you okay?"

I nodded, biting back the urge to tell her the truth.

"Next!" shouted Enid.

"That's me." With an affectionate squeeze of my hand, my maid of honor stood up and filed out the door. *Don't leave me, Lib!*

I was all alone. I should have been happy. Excited. But unbearable sadness devoured me along with agonizing pain.

Mendelssohn's "Bridal March" drifted into my ear. My

cue.

"Go!" screamed Enid with a sweeping wave of her free hand.

Slowly rising to my feet, I slumped toward the door, so missing my father and my mom. As I stepped outside, a bolt of lightning flashed and then midway down my lonely, painful walk down the aisle, the sky opened up. A sudden torrent of rain began to pour. In the near distance, the shrieking members of my wedding procession scurried about, dashing into the reception tent for shelter. I heard Enid scream through her megaphone, "Goddamnit. Will someone get me an umbrella?"

I stood there motionless. Tears mingled with the pounding raindrops. They stung my eyes, my skin, and soaked me soul-deep. Ahead of me, one person stood as still as me, drenched under a canopy of drowning flowers. *That* man who was waiting for me. *That* man who would always be there for me, whatever storm we weathered. Somehow, some way, through the tears, the pain, and all the rain, I made my way into his arms.

Chapter 16
Jennifer

"**B**aby, how do you feel?"

Upon a kiss on my forehead, I peeled my eyes open. One at a time…slowly. Blake came into focus. Consciousness crept through my veins.

This was my day. My special day. But nothing spoke to the moment.

"Like shit," I croaked. I was definitely coming down with a bad flu. I ached all over and last night I'd had the chills. Even Blake's warm body blanketed around me hadn't stopped my teeth from chattering. The rain had only made things worse. Thank goodness, the rehearsal dinner was canceled on account of everyone getting so drenched.

"Fuck," mumbled Blake, grabbing his cell phone. "I'm calling Dr. Klein to find out if there's anything you can take."

I listened as Blake spoke to his family doctor. Pacing, he wanted to know if there was a prescription that would alleviate the symptoms. His mouth twisted as he said in a glum tone, "Okay doctor, I understand. I will."

My heavy-lidded eyes searched his. He shook his head with dismay. "Tiger, there's nothing you can do except take Advil. The doctor said it's likely the new strain of the flu that's becoming an epidemic."

"Blake, I don't want you to kiss me after we say our 'I do's.'"

"Baby, I'd kiss you if you had the fucking plague. And I'll carry you down the aisle if I have to."

To prove it, he crushed his lips on my mine. My cell phone rang. I broke the kiss. My heart jumped. It was my mother. I perked up and sighed with relief. Great news! The blizzard had stopped and the airport had re-opened. They were on a flight. She and Dad along with Father Murphy would be here by early afternoon. I suddenly felt much better.

The day was overcast, but, at least, it had stopped raining. That my parents would be here for my wedding was my ray of sunshine. In slo mo, I threw on some jeans and headed over with Blake to his parents' house at noon. I was carrying a small bag containing white satin heels I'd found at Target and a few bare necessities while Blake had his tux in a garment bag folded over his arm. Despite how crappy I felt, I couldn't wait to see him in it.

Blake's mother, Helen, met us at the front door. Wearing designer workout clothes, she gave us each a double cheek kiss, careful not to muss her still wet manicured nails. Her coral nail polish perfectly matched the gown she would be wearing.

"Children, you must see what Enid has done," she said excitedly, looping her arm through Blake's and leading us to the sprawling backyard. Holding Blake's other hand, I shared the good news that my parents would be in LA shortly.

"Darling, I'm so thrilled they'll be here," responded Helen as we made our way past the pool. "What do you think?"

Speechless, I couldn't believe my eyes. In the free-form pool with its grotto waterfall, synchronized swimmers from the U.S. Olympic team were practicing their routine while caterers were setting up pre-wedding cocktail stations all around it.

"It's going to be so divine," gushed Helen as she ushered us to the grassy ceremony area.

My eyes popped. The humongous yard had been totally transformed, and not for a minute would one think it had been subject to a downpour. All the white folding chairs were set up, and giant conch shells filled with abundant white roses and blue orchids lined the aisle. Ahead of me, workers were frantically replacing flowers and seashells on the canopy under which Blake and I had kissed in the rain last night. They were also setting up the altar.

"Everything looks beautiful, Mom," Blake muttered, squeezing my clammy hand.

"Oh, darling, the best is yet to come. Wait until you see inside the tent!"

Five minutes later, we were in the throes of the most dazzling spectacle I'd ever seen.

"Wow," I murmured as Helen walked us through it. The vast tent was draped with swags of coral silk and pearl-white tulle. Grandiose chandeliers dripping with strings of pearls and crystal starfish dangled from the soaring ceiling. There must have been close to one hundred tables, still be setting up by frantic workers. Tall crystal vases filled with most amazing white flowers, seashells, pearls, and more of those sparkling starfish adorned each one. And at each seat was a snow globe filled with water, sparkles, and a colorful live fish. The décor was simply breathtaking.

"Come take a look-see at the dance floor, children." With unbounded enthusiasm, Helen led the way and beamed. "Honestly, have you ever seen anything like it?"

I couldn't help but gasp. As if Enid hadn't taken the under-the-sea theme to the extreme, the see-through dance floor was an aquarium filled with colorful tropical fish. I actually felt seasick stepping on it. Or maybe it was more of the flu. Swaying on my feet, I gripped Blake's hand tighter as nausea rose to my chest and another shooting pain ripped through me.

"Are you all right, darling?" asked Helen, lifting a brow as far as she could.

Blake responded before I could. "Jen's feeling a little under the weather. She may have the flu."

"Oh, dear."

"Helen, I just need to rest for a bit. I'm sure I'll be okay." I was lying through my teeth. Despite the Advil, I was feeling worse and worse. The stomach pains had intensified and my energy was depleting.

Blake's mother affectionately clasped my hands in hers. "Of course, darling. You can lie down in one of our guestrooms."

"You will do nothing of the sort!" came a shrill voice. Enid. Dressed in a shrimp-pink silk suit, she stampeded our way. She glanced down at her diamond watch. "You're late. You were supposed to be here at 11:30. Hair and makeup have been waiting patiently for you. Both the *In-Style* photographer, who's going to document your bridal journey, and the portrait photographer have been driving me crazy wanting to know where you are. And you've also kept Monique waiting."

Before I could get my mouth to move, an accented voice came through the walkie talkie she was clutching. "*Señora, tenemos un problema. Los peces se están muriendo.* I could actually see steam coming out of Enid's flaring nostrils. "What do you mean the fish are dying? Feed them, you moron, and get someone to go to the fish supply store to buy new ones!"

The image of dead, bloated goldfish floating upside down sickened me further. Suddenly, I just wanted my mom to be with me. And then it hit me. Something was missing. I glared at Enid.

"Enid, where are the place cards my mother shipped?" They weren't on the tables.

She gritted her teeth. "You mean those *quaint* little picture frames with the glued on shells?"

My blood boiled. "Yes."

She snorted. "They'll be on tables at the entrance so our guests will know where they're sitting."

Helen chimed in. "With all due respect for your mother, I insisted we use them. They're really quite charming."

I breathed a sigh of relief and was thankful for Helen's support. I was sure our guests would love them. They were a perfect keepsake. And they would sure last a lot longer than these holed-up, oxygen-deprived goldfish. Maybe a lifetime.

My cell phone rang. I hastily retrieved it from my purse and my spirits brightened. It was my mother. That meant they had landed!

"Mom, you're here?" I said with bated breath.

As her voice filtered into my ears, my heart sunk like the

Titanic. "Oh, no!" This just couldn't be happening. Shell-shocked and shaken, I listlessly slipped the phone back into my bag.

"Baby, what's the matter?" Blake was alarmed.

"It's my parents. Their plane was diverted. They're in Dallas along with Father Murphy. They're on a connecting flight, but it won't be here until nine tonight." I fought hard to hold back tears as the conversation ping-ponged back and forth.

Enid: "Darling, let's worry about that problem later."

Helen: "Enid, Jennifer doesn't feel well and this is serious."

Enid: "Puh-lease."

Blake: "Mom, I'm going back to the house to see if we can send Dad's plane to get them."

Helen: "Sweetheart, that's just what I was thinking. If I recall, Dallas by air is three hours away. That means, potentially we can get the McCoys here by five o'clock with the two hour time difference if there aren't any delays. Blake, I'll head back to the house with you."

Helen turned to me and then did something I so needed. She gave me a warm motherly hug. "Darling, keep your chin up. We'll get your parents and Father Murphy here."

I quirked a small, grateful smile. For the first time since I'd known her, I felt a connection to Blake's mother. She had my back.

"Come, now," hissed Enid, wrenching me away. "Let's get down to business."

A violent spasm rocked my abdomen as she hauled me away.

"Finally!" snapped Monique as I staggered into an opulent guest suite on the main floor of the Bernsteins' palatial mansion. Like the rest of their house, it was filled with expensive antiques and artwork. My dress, on a padded hanger, hung from an ornate tri-fold corner mirror while the starfish headpiece was perched on a nearby velvet chaise. Both were wrapped in protective plastic.

Monique was not alone. Two clone-like assistants flanked her and scuttling about was a hip-looking couple who I assumed was doing my hair and makeup.

"Should I change into the dress?" I asked Enid. My voice was weary when it should have been bubbling with excitement. Besides feeling terribly fluish, I was so stressed over my parents.

Enid rolled her eyes at me again. "Of course not. You need to do hair and makeup first. Go to the guest bathroom where you'll find a robe. Get undressed, but be sure to put on your bridal undergarments. And one more thing...please take off that *hideous* jewelry you're wearing. It doesn't go with your dress."

She was referring to the pink tourmaline pendant necklace and matching earrings Blake had given me. Anger surged inside me. No way. They were staying.

"I'm not taking them off," I said defiantly.

Enid pursed her lips in disgust. "Fine. We'll just photoshop them out for the publicity pictures. Maybe replace them with pearls."

Seething, I bit my tongue as she pointed to the door of the

ensuite bathroom. Five minutes later, I emerged wearing a fluffy terrycloth robe and matching slippers. Beneath the robe, I had on the beautiful lace lingerie and silk stockings Gloria had given me at my bridal shower. Clutching my cell phone, I placed the bag with my shoes by one of the couches. Just as hair and makeup were about to begin, my phone rang. Blake! My heart galloping, I hit answer. YES! Great news! His father's private jet would be leaving soon to pick up my parents and Father Murphy. Enid shot me a dirty look as I let Blake know how much I loved him.

"Monique and I will be back shortly. I'm leaving you in very good hands. Philippe and Irma have done hair and makeup for countless celebrities."

My eyes stayed fixed on Enid and my dress designer as they strolled out of the room. I wondered—were they going to get in a little pussy time somewhere? If only Helen knew. Feeling so much more relaxed now knowing my parents would be here in time for my wedding, I inwardly chuckled at the thought.

Seated in a richly upholstered armchair, I told Philippe I wanted my makeup to be as natural as possible (the way Blake preferred it) while Irma worked on my hair. "Ow," I yelped as she yanked it up into a high ponytail.

"What are you putting on my eyes?" I asked Philippe.

"False eyelashes. Your eyes will photograph so much better."

What? I didn't need false lashes. My lashes were long and thick, one of my best features. I fluttered my heavy lids, getting used to the sensation.

One agonizing hour later, he handed me a large hand-mirror. "You look divine," he cooed.

"So divine," echoed Irma, now done with my updo.

Anxiously, I raised the mirror to my face. Gasp! I didn't recognize myself. My lips were painted lobster red; glittery aqua marine eye shadow coated my lids; my lashes looked like fish fins, and my hairstyle resembled an octopus. This was so not me. I looked like a sea monster!

Before I could utter a word, Enid and Monique came breezing back. Enid's suit jacket was unbuttoned and stray hairs fell onto her face. For sure, they'd had a little romp.

"Marvelous," breathed Enid in her throaty voice as she circled me.

"But—"

Her face tightened. "Remember, Jennifer, there are no buts." She turned to Monique. "*Darling,* what do you think?"

"Positively sublime. She's so going to be the siren bride. Time to get her into her dress."

I watched as Monique gathered the gown and carefully lifted off the plastic. Ten minutes later, with the helping hands of her assistants, I was in it and wearing my white satin heels along with the glittery starfish headpiece.

I glared at my reflection in the three-way mirror. The bride was supposed to look radiant, but I was anything but. My glazed, heavily made-up eyes blinked back tears. Despite the alterations, the ruffly mermaid-style dress still fit all wrong and the butt pad made me look distorted.

I was swimming in my dress.

I was drowning in a sea of sorrow.

I was floundering for words.

Monique screwed up her face. "How dare you lose more

weight! My assistants are going to have to make some last minute alterations."

Enid growled. "I'm going to charge Helen extra for all the unnecessary work and stress you've caused us."

And what about all the stress she'd caused me? I held back treacherous tears as Monique's clones began to pin the *vomiticious* creation down the sides. I so wanted my mom.

Back in my robe, I stumbled to a couch and sat down hunched over. One hand cupped my head, the other my tummy. While Enid excused herself to check on what was going on outside, Monique watched over her assistants as they worked together to stitch down the gown with the portable sewing machine they'd brought along. My cell phone rang. My heart pounding, I slipped it out of the robe pocket. Blake again. More great news! His dad's private plane had landed in Dallas and my parents were on their way. He promised to keep me posted.

"How are you feeling?" he asked, after sharing the good news.

The truth: Like crap. Though my case of nerves had subsided, the shooting pains in my abdomen were coming at me more frequently and sharply. Clutching my stomach, I lied through my teeth and told Blake I was feeling a little better. He didn't need more stress.

"Baby, hang in there. I can't wait to say 'I do'," he breathed into the phone.

"The same. I love you." He returned the words and ended the call as another bolt of pain shot through me. While most brides probably wanted their wedding day to last forever, I couldn't wait for mine to be over. Anxiously, I fiddled with my glittering snowflake diamond ring. The memory of Blake surprising me with it—hidden in a snow globe no less—danced in my head and temporarily took my mind off all my troubles.

A familiar voice cut into the fond memory and widened the small smile on my face. Grandma!

"Bubala, I heard you're coming down *vith* something. Flu *shmu!* I brought you a *bissel* of my chicken soup. Jewish penicillin."

"Enid's going to get mad you're here."

"Enid *shmenid.*" Handing me a steaming bowl of her aromatic soup, she plopped down next to me on the velvet couch. "Eat!" she commanded.

"Thanks, Grandma," I murmured, forcing myself to put a tablespoon of the hot broth to my lips. I blew on it and then sipped the flavorful liquid. You know what? The soup *was* magical. As it coursed through me, I felt a little better. I helped myself to several tablespoons more.

"Mmmm. So good. I'll never make it as good as you."

Grandma flicked her wrist dismissively. "Bubala, you'll learn."

"What the hell are you doing?" Enid. She was back. At the sound of her shrill voice, I almost choked on a mouthful of soup.

"*Vhat* does it look like?" barked Grandma as I coughed.

"Give that to me," hissed Enid, stomping my way. "You're going to totally ruin your lipstick."

"Here you go, you *klafte.*" Before I could blink, Grandma snatched my spoon and scooped up a matzo ball from the half-full bowl. My face lit up as she flung the giant ball at Enid. Whoot! It smacked the bitch in the face. Enid shrieked.

"How dare you!" she cried, wiping the crumbly fragments

off her cheeks. Her eyes were flaring. I couldn't help laughing.

"What are you laughing at?" Enid seethed, gritting her teeth.

Rather than responding, I gave Grandma a hug. I loved this woman. She had *chutzpah!* Balls. Big ones.

Monique sprinted over to Enid. "Darling, are you okay?" she asked, flicking off bits of the dumpling from her lover's chin as if they were deadly insects. The fashion designer shot Grandma a scathing look. "What the hell did you do?"

Grinning wickedly, Grandma scooped up another perfectly formed matzo ball. *"Vould* you like to try *vun* too?"

With a gasp, Monique defensively shielded her face with her hand and turned to Enid. "Come on, darling. Let's get out of here before this dangerous woman does something to me." Wrapping her other arm around Enid, she ushered her out of the room.

"Vhat is it *vith* those two?" Grandma asked after Enid and Monique were gone.

"There's more than meets the eye."

"Oy! They *shtup vun* another?"

"So I hear."

"Vait till I tell Helen!"

Tell Grandma; tell the world. I had a hunch everyone in town would soon know about Enid's dirty little secret. And it could be the talk of the wedding. With mild amusement, I took another sip of soup.

Grandma stood up. "Bubala, feel better. Time for me to get ready for the *vedding.* I've got a hot date." She winked.

Luigi, Blake's seventy-eight-year-old tailor, had recently become Grandma's new friend with benefits. They were adorable together, and Grandma couldn't stop talking about his Italian "salami."

I thanked Grandma for coming to my rescue and gave her another big hug before she marched out of the room. I finished the rest of the soup while Monique's assistants continued working on my gown. Grandma's comic relief and the effects of her magical soup were short-lived. A stately grandfather's clock chimed five times. It was five o'clock. My parents would be landing any minute. I silently prayed they'd be here soon. Unsettling nerves again mixed with painful spasms. I could barely stand up when one of Monique's assistant asked me to take off my robe so she could help me into the altered gown. With effort, I managed. And with even greater effort, I stumbled back over to the tri-fold mirror. Yes, the taken-in dress definitely fit me more snugly, but the area where the skirt fanned out in a cascade of ruffles—it was like having a rope tied around my knees. Oh my God. I could barely take a step in the mermaid gown, which would make dancing at my wedding near impossible, let alone walking down the aisle. As I stared at my frightening bridal self, I felt like crying.

"Is there anything you can do to make it looser around here?" I asked the seamstress, tugging at the impossibly tight area.

She shook her head. "There's not enough fabric or time."

I grimaced. Not because of my disappointment but because of the relentless abdominal pain. It was getting worse. Like a hundred knives jabbing me.

In the mirror, I saw Monique's other assistant coming toward me. She was holding a jeweled creation in her hand.

"This is your bouquet. Ms. Hervé wants you to get used to

holding it."

I eyed the so-called bouquet. It was a sparkling concoction of crystal starfish, pearls, and seashells. Not a fresh, fragrant bloom among them. The assistant handed me the arrangement. Grabbing it with one hand, I wasn't prepared for the weight of it. Seriously, the clunker must have weighed ten pounds. Libby had better catch it because if I missed and hit her in the head, it was going to knock her out. I fucking hated it.

My cell phone rang again. "Could you please hand me my phone," I asked the seamstress. Given how long it would take me to walk back to the couch in the constricting gown, I might miss the call. Fingers crossed, it was Blake letting me know my parents were en route. He'd arranged for a limousine to pick them up at nearby Van Nuys Airport.

"Are they on their way?" I asked Blake while Monique's two assistants took a break.

"Baby, there's a problem."

A problem? My heart hammered madly. "What's going on?"

"There's a Sig-alert."

"What do you mean?"

"A big rig toppled over. The traffic on the 101 is at a total standstill."

Oh my God! How could this be happening? "Blake, when are they going to clear it?"

I could hear Blake inhale and exhale on the other end. "I don't know. To make matters worse, it was a tanker, so there's an oil spillage too."

No, no, no, no. "Blake, is there anything you can do?" My raspy voice was thick with desperation and despair.

Silence.

"Blake, are you there?" My desperation was close to panic.

"Sorry, tiger. I got distracted. How do you feel?"

It was time to tell him the truth. Two words: "Like crap." My voice was watery. I was on the edge.

Blake: "Shit. Gotta go. Guests are showing up by the droves, and I've got to mingle with them. Hang in there, baby. I'll call you if I hear anything. Or come up with something."

"Love you," I mumbled, holding the phone limply in my hand as we ended the call. I immediately speed-dialed my father, eager to talk to him, but my phone went dead. Shit! I'd not kept it charged. And worse, I didn't have my charger with me. In my feverish stupor, I'd left it at Blake's condo. *Shit. Shit. Shit.* I now couldn't receive any updates—from either Blake or my parents.

At an all time low, I did the only thing any bride in this situation would do. Before the tri-fold mirror, I sunk to my knees, not caring if I split open my hideous gown. I couldn't help myself. I started to cry. Scratch that. I started to bawl. Big snotty, tears fell onto the jeweled bouquet as my shoulders heaved. This was my wedding day. I was sick as a dog. My dress was a mess. My parents were inaccessible. For God's sake. Couldn't one little thing go right?

I didn't know how long I'd been sobbing when I felt two warm hands on my shoulders, massaging them gently. Slowly, I lifted my head and gazed into the mirror. Squatting behind me was Blake's mother Helen, dressed to kill in her magnificent one-shoulder coral gown and a dazzling array of diamonds.

"Sweetheart, it's going to be okay. We're not starting the wedding until your parents arrive."

I met her compassionate eyes in the mirror. I looked scarier than ever. My pale skin, now blotchy, was stained with a sea of tears, and squid-like streaks of inky mascara trickled down my cheeks.

I twitched the smallest of smiles. No words. I had no words. And then in the mirror, another figure appeared. Enid.

"It's after six o'clock. Guests are grumbling. Getting drunk on oyster shooters, which, by the way, we're running out of."

Helen cranked her long neck to face her. "Then let them drink water." The sharp tone of her voice was new to me.

Enid's face hardened. Her voice was ice-cold. "Helen, darling, I cannot disappoint our guests. I've never delayed an event. The show must go on."

Helen stood up and squarely faced Enid. "Blake and my husband are perfectly capable of entertaining *our* guests."

That was true. Both were natural-born showmen. Like father like son.

Enid's eyes narrowed. "Helen, I run the show, and I say the show must go on." She snapped her fingers. "It's as simple as that."

Helen's eyes shot back daggers. "Darling, I'm flitting the bill, and I say there's no 'show' until the McCoys get here. My future daughter-in-law is *not* walking down the aisle without her parents." She snapped her fingers. "It's as simple as *that.*"

Wow! I'd never seen Helen like this. She was in total battle-mode. A ninja warrior.

Smoke was shooting out of Enid's nostrils. I could practically smell it. "Helen, you don't seem to understand. I have a reputation to uphold. My events always go off perfectly. Without delays."

Not wasting a second, she put the walkie talkie she was holding to her mouth. "Attention. Please have the guests take their seats. The wedding is about to begin."

Helen, to my astonishment, snatched the device and put it to her mouth.

"Attention. This is Helen Bernstein. Please have the guests take their seats and make an announcement that the wedding is a little delayed." And then with force, she hurled the walkie talkie against one of the painting-lined walls. *Slam!* The little black box fell apart as it hit the floor.

"How dare you?" shrieked Enid.

Helen smiled smugly. "I've always had a good throw. You should know, I'm the designated pitcher at my annual 'Big Sister' charity softball game."

Enid was seething. "This would have never happened if Blake had married Katrina."

"Blake never wanted to marry your skanky daughter. What she did to him was abominable."

"What your son did to *her* was unforgivable. And to our family. We almost went under. Why do you think I became an event planner? Because I wanted a career? Hardly. I needed the fucking money. We were broke. Clayton almost had to sell the house. And we had to fine-dine at Sizzler. Do you honestly think I like working for you? Hardly. You're a fucking rich bitch. Your money keeps me afloat."

"Well, Enid. You'd better think of a new *fucking* career. Because…You're…fired!" My future mother-in-law aimed her thumb and index finger at her like a gun.

Enid gasped, her mouth dropping wide open with shock. And then the unbelievable happened. On the next breath, she lunged at Helen, almost knocking her to the floor. "I hate you, you fucking bitch!" she shrieked.

Catching her balance, Helen yanked at Enid's hair. "It takes one to know one." She yanked again. Enid yelped, "Fuck you!" and retaliated. A giant clump of Enid's ebony hair—holy shit, a ten-inch hair extension!—fell to the floor, followed by a wad of Helen's platinum locks.

Before I could blink, the two women were at each other like two Siamese fighting fish. Hissing. Shrieking. Clawing. Gnawing. My eyes stayed wide as Enid ferociously tore apart the shoulder fabric of Helen's stunning dress. This hiss of the splitting silk sent goose bumps to my skin. Helen retaliated with a kick to her adversary's shin.

"I'm going to deduct the cost of this dress from your bill," hissed Helen, now tearing at Enid's blouse while she bent down to nurse her leg. The pearl buttons popped off and—ping, ping, ping—landed close to my feet. The dueling divas continued with Enid getting the better of poor Helen after punching her hard in the gut. I'd had enough. Adrenaline pumping through my blood despite my horrible pain, I aimed my weighty jeweled bouquet at Enid and flung it like a grenade. It flew through the air and BINGO! It got her smack in the head. With a moan, she spiraled downward onto the floor. With a triumphant smile, Helen gave me a thumbs up. Her expression then contorted into one of utter disgust as she glowered at defeated Enid.

"Get up and get out of here." My soon-to-be mother-in-law's gruff voice was fueled by rage. "And don't you ever step foot on my property again. Security will escort you to the front gate."

Dazed, Enid staggered to her feet. Another voice at the doorway caught my attention. Monique. "Oh my God. My dress!" Her startled eyes darted from Helen to Enid. Panic-driven, she flitted to her disheveled, unsteady partner. "Enid, darling, what's going on here? Are you okay?"

Rubbing the back of her head, recovering Enid pinched her Botoxed face so hard a crease curled between her brows. But before she could say a word, Helen lashed out at her again.

"And you can take your *girlfriend* with you." *Holy cow! Helen already knew.*

Enid turned crimson. Pursing her lips, she breathed loudly in and out from her nose. Her fists clenched so tightly her knuckles turned white. Finally, her mouth parted.

"Monique, darling, we're no longer needed here. Let's go." She hooked her arm into the crook of her lover's elbow. Questions begging answers danced in Monique's eyes, but she held them back. The two women stalked to the door. At the doorway, Enid turned her head and smiled wickedly. She gave Helen the evil eye.

"You and that wannabe daughter-in-law of yours will be sorry." Her icy gaze shifted to me. "Blake will never be yours, you peasant."

Her hurtful words sent a shiver up my spine. At the same time, a sharp pang stabbed my gut. I clenched my stomach and suppressed a wince as Enid and Monique slipped away. Helen took me in her arms. "Don't let her get to you, my dear. You are perfect for Blake. I'm so thrilled you're going to be my daughter-in-law. And you must absolutely promise to be on my softball team. I need a backup pitcher."

"Sure, Helen," I murmured, grateful that this incredible

woman had come to my rescue. Her warm embrace was interrupted by a familiar welcomed voice.

"Honey!"

Mom! I spun around. There they were. My beloved parents. My mother, dressed in a lovely oyster white suit, and my dad in a dapper English-style morning suit. A massive brace encased his right leg, and he was holding a spiffy cane that complemented his suit beautifully. My heart swelled with happiness. Tears of joy flooded my eyes. My mother broke away from my dad and sprinted to me. He limped behind her.

"Oh, Mom, I'm so glad you're here," I said tearfully as she gave me a maternal hug—something I'd been craving for so long. My dad was next. It felt so good to be in his arms. He smiled broadly. "I told you I was going to walk my little girl down the aisle." And here he was. He looked so handsome to me, leg brace and all.

"You look beautiful, Jennie," he said with a proud smile.

No, I don't. But his heartfelt words made me *feel* beautiful. And that was all that mattered.

My mother, with her discerning eyes, studied me. "Honey, are you all right? You look faint." My perceptive mother knew me well.

"I have a little bit of a bug." My alarmist mother immediately put her hand to my forehead. "I'm taking Advil. I'll be okay." Truthfully, now that my parents were here, everything was okay. Nothing could keep me from my wedding day.

"Where's Father Murphy?"

"He's in the backyard conferring with the Bernsteins' rabbi."

I quirked a smile. All was good.

Relaxing, my mother beamed. "Everything looks so beautiful. And guess what! I saw George Clooney and Hillary Clinton!"

My star-struck mom. I loved her so much. As for me, the only stars that mattered at my star-studded wedding were Blake...and my parents. They were here. Here at last!

Helen interjected. "I'm going to leave the three of you alone while I freshen up and change into another gown." She hugged my parents. "I'm so thrilled you made it. I'll meet you shortly along with the others in the wedding party on the veranda. The wedding of the century is about to begin."

Chapter 17

Blake

Thank God, Jennifer's parents arrived safely and just in time. Standing under the shell-encrusted *chuppah* beside my best man, Jaime, and surrounded by members of the wedding party, I faced our thousand-plus guests. So many famous faces. And so many I didn't recognize. My parents' social connections could not be rivaled. Photographers were scattered everywhere, taking photos with their flash cameras. Overhead, helicopters circled the dark gray sky. News crews were trying to get the scoop on the Hollywood wedding of the century. For sure, it would be a featured story on tonight's newscasts, but I sure as hell wasn't going to tune in. Dressed in my tux, I waited anxiously for my bride. I hadn't seen her since early afternoon.

"The Wedding March" began to play. Enid had managed to install an elaborate organ—the kind you saw at Radio City Music Hall—in our backyard along with a state-of-the-art sound system. The music reverberated in my ears. To be honest, that's not the music my tiger had wanted to walk down the aisle. She had hoped to walk down to *our* song: "The First Time Ever I Saw Your Face." But Enid insisted that be our first dance song. The bitch, we'd decided, was just not worth fighting. So we compromised.

My eyes stayed glued on the veranda. Where was she? My heart hammered. Finally, a vision in white appeared on the arm of her dapper father. My tiger. My bride. My wife-to-be. She met my gaze, and a small smile curled on her lips.

The walk to the *chuppah* was a long one. And Jen walked very slowly down the winding path with her still disabled father. One baby step at a time. While Harold was beaming, her smile looked forced, her face pinched. My poor baby! I knew she felt like shit and hoped she'd taken another Advil. And I knew she wasn't thrilled about her wedding gown, but to me it was beautiful. And she was beautiful. Every eye was on her as she made her way down the aisle. Cameras and cell phones flashed.

The minutes felt like hours. As she took hesitant steps, she occasionally turned her head to acknowledge our guests. My eyes never strayed from her, and when she met my gaze, they silently told her everything was going to be all right. And that I loved her. Mind, body, and soul.

Overwhelmed with tingly emotion I'd never felt before, I just wanted her beside me. And actually thought about sweeping her off her feet and carrying her to the altar. I wanted to say our vows like it was yesterday and exchange those two magical words, "I do." We just had to get through tonight. Tomorrow, we would be on our way to the secret honeymoon destination I'd painstakingly arranged. I couldn't wait to be lying on a beach and making glorious love to my new wife on the day I turned thirty.

Chapter 18
Jennifer

Walking down the aisle, I clung to my father's arm as if it were my lifeline. Because at this very moment, it was.

Intense pain chipped away at me. Like an ax to my abdomen. I seriously felt like I was going to die.

Only one other person kept me going—Blake. *That* man who would soon be my husband. My beautiful hero, looking so handsome in his tux under a canopy of seashells and flowers. His smile and his eyes pointed at me.

Dad and I walked slowly down the aisle, each step a small victory. With my constricting gown and his leg brace, we were a perfect match. In my other hand, I held my heavy bouquet, now missing some seashells and beads. And in his, his cane.

As I took tiny steps down the aisle, I tried to acknowledge our guests. I looked left and right and then back at Blake, whose loving gaze gave me the courage to continue.

I was an emotional and physical mess. A mixture of nerves, chills, and pain. My strapless mermaid gown was not suited for the chilly December air. Goose bumps popped along my bare arms and my teeth chattered.

Just walk and breathe. And try to smile, I told myself. *You can do it.* I forced a small smile and took in the sea of people in front of whom we were going to say our vows. But truthfully, I was treading water. Barely staying afloat. I was truly not sure I was going to make it to the altar. My father, God bless him, held me steady. I met Blake's loving gaze once more, and a sudden rush of wet heat puddled between my legs. A rush like I've never felt before.

The walk down the aisle felt like an eternity. But I made it. Dad proudly took his place beside my radiant mom, and Blake took me in his arms. I heard him whisper, "I love you."

"I love you too," I whispered back. We turned to face Rabbi Silverstein and Father Murphy.

The ceremony began. Blake clasped my free hand. His so warm, mine so icy cold. It was difficult to hear what our officiants were saying. Helicopters were hovering overhead, and the chattering of my teeth filled my ears. And then halfway through it, Blake did something so unexpected. He took off his tux jacket and gently placed it over my shoulders. I heard our guests go "ooh." Oh, my Blake! My gallant Blake! But neither his hand nor his jacket could warm me up. Or make the excruciating pain go away.

The alternating words of Rabbi Silverstein and Father Murphy drifted into one ear and out the other. Whatever viral infection I'd contracted was consuming me. Another sharp spasm ripped through my body. Of all days to fall ill! I squeezed Blake's hand and bit down on my bottom lip to suppress a wince. And then another spasm and another. They grew relentless. Managing to hold on to the bouquet, I clutched my belly. A concerned Blake looked my way while our officiates continued the service.

I should have been savoring every word, but they couldn't

come fast enough. We finally said our vows. With the loud chop-chop-chop of the helicopters above and my voice a mere whisper, I could barely hear myself. And Blake's sacred words were likewise washed out.

Lastly…finally…the exchange of our "I do's" and wedding bands. The latter were tied to aqua velvet pillows Marcy's eager twins were holding.

"Do you, Blake Adam Burns, take Jennifer Leigh McCoy to be your lawful wedded wife?" were the words I was longing to hear. But to my surprise, old-fashioned Father Murphy turned to the attendants and thundered, "If anyone here has any objections to this couple getting married, let them speak now or forever hold your peace."

"Yes! I do," a familiar sharp voice shouted out.

Shocked, I pivoted around. Oh my God! It was Kat! Standing up in the back of the crowd in a high-necked white goddess gown. What was she doing here? Her venomous eyes met mine and then another sharp, unbearable pain stabbed me. I clasped my lower abdomen and warm wetness met my hand. I glanced down and gasped. A rapidly expanding crimson pool was seeping through my gown.

I can't really tell you what happened next. Just this.

I heard my mother's panicked voice. "Oh, dear Lord!"

Then Grandma's. *"Oy vey iz mir!"*

And then, as I felt my knees buckle, I heard Blake shout out, "Someone call 911!"

He caught me in his arms and then everything went black.

Chapter 19

Blake

My father always said: "The only thing you can ever expect in life is the unexpected." I just didn't expect this.

I was sitting in the back of a racing ambulance, the siren blaring in my ears. Thank God, my sister Marcy was with me or I think I would have totally lost it. My heart was in my throat and my breathing was shallow. My sister squeezed my hand while my eyes stayed locked on my beautiful unconscious bride. The paramedics had told us she'd lost a lot of blood and was likely still bleeding internally. Hooked up to a portable IV and an oxygen tank, she was wrapped in a heavy blanket, which at least spared me the agony of seeing her blood-soaked wedding gown.

Foreboding thoughts bombarded me. At the top: Was I going to lose my tiger? If Kat had anything to do with this, I was going to have her committed. The image of her smirking at me as I ran past her with my fallen bride in my arms flickered in my head. What the hell was she doing there? I could only surmise she flew back from Rio, and her equally mental, devious mother put her on the guest list. Without a doubt, she was still determined to stop me from marrying Jen. The sick bitch was out for blood, and I wouldn't put it past her to go as far as murder. I shuddered.

"Are you okay, Blake?" My sister's soft words cut into my dark thoughts.

I shook my head. "Marcy, I'm scared shitless." I searched her eyes for a sign that everything would be all right.

"Blake, I'm going to stay with her. We're going to do a CAT scan and go from there. Stay calm."

A KAT scan was more like it. To make sure the psycho hadn't laced my baby's veins with poison. Or stabbed her.

Fifteen agonizing minutes later, we pulled up to a private entrance to Cedars-Sinai Medical Center. We were given special treatment partly because my sister was a respected doctor there, heading up the OB/GYN department, but mostly because my family had donated enough money to have a wing named for them. My breath hitched painfully in my throat as I watched the paramedics transfer my beauty to a gurney in record speed. To my absolute horror, she began to convulse. Her tiny body was bucking up and down.

"What's happening?" I asked, my voice pure panic.

"Shit. She's going into hypovolemic shock," cried out my sister. "Someone lift up her legs. Move it! Move it!"

Nausea rose to my chest. I was so close to vomiting I was afraid to open my mouth to ask what this meant. Whatever the hell it meant, it wasn't good.

Pushing the gurney, the team of paramedics and nurses raced through the automatic doors of the hospital, with Marcy and me holding on to the railings and keeping up with the pace. Everything was happening so fast it was a blur.

We headed down a long corridor toward a set of double

doors. The sign above them read: "MEDICAL PERSONNEL ONLY"

"Blake, you're going to have to stay here," breathed my sister as the hospital team wheeled her through. "There's a waiting room down the hall."

"No fucking way," I blurted.

"Blake, please. It's hospital regulations." Marcy looked at me imploringly.

I felt like bashing a wall, but I fought my urge and gave in.

Marcy squeezed one of my balled-up hands. "Blake, I'll let you know what's going on as soon as I can."

Five minutes later, I was slumped in an armchair in the nearby waiting room. I sunk my head between my hands and rubbed my throbbing temples. My heart was in my stomach, my breathing labored. Shit. What was taking so long? What was wrong with my tiger? Was she going to be okay? The sound of rapid footsteps cut into my mental ramblings. I looked up. Jen's parents and mine. Like me, they were all still dressed in their wedding finery. Jen's mother's eyes were all red and puffy from crying, and her father looked like he'd aged a hundred years. Worry was etched deep in my parents' faces.

"Any word?" asked my father, the most composed among us.

I could hear my jackrabbit pulse hammer in my ears. My lips pinched, I silently shook my head.

"My little girl's going to be okay," murmured Jen's father, but his words were not convincing. Tapping his cane, his arms tightened around Mrs. McCoy's trembling shoulders. She held a hand to her mouth to muffle her sobs.

I loosened my bow tie, and then squeezed my eyes shut,

hoping I could make this nightmare disappear. My sister's voice brought my moment of reprieve to an abrupt end. She was now out of her bridesmaid gown and clad in green scrubs.

"We're taking Jen to surgery," she said solemnly.

I leapt to my feet. "Surgery?"

"Marcy, can you please be more specific?" asked Jen's dad, his voice shaky.

"We found a mass behind her uterus."

Still cupping her mouth, Mrs. McCoy could no longer contain herself. "Oh, dear Lord!" she sobbed. Her husband was quick to put a comforting arm around her while my mother, standing next to her, clasped her other hand.

That ruled out Kat, but confusion mixed with fear. My voice faltered. "But she told me everything was okay after her visit with you."

Marcy pressed her lips thin. "Blake, she was. The ultrasound didn't detect this."

"Fuck." *Fuck, fuck, fuck.*

Marcy continued. "I'm heading up to surgery now."

"Can we see her before she goes?" spluttered Jen's mom through her tears.

"I'm afraid not. She's already in transit. The operation will likely last three hours. I suggest you all get some rest."

Three hours? I wasn't sure if I was going to last that long.

Her eyes soaked, Jennifer's mom asked if there was a chapel in the hospital. She and her husband wanted to go there to pray.

Pray. That's all we could do. I was going there too.

Chapter 20

Blake

"No, no, stop! Please don't hurt me!"

My eyes snapped open. Jen was screaming in her sleep. All hooked up to tubes and monitors, she writhed in her hospital bed, her voice a hoarse whimper.

Alarmed, I bolted from the bedside chair where I'd fallen asleep. I was still in my tux shirt though I'd unbuttoned it and chucked the bow tie. In a frightened heartbeat, I was by her side. She must be having one of her Springer nightmares. I smoothed her damp hair, my fingertips grazing her forehead. Her skin burnt beneath my touch. She was hot. I hoped she didn't have a fever. A sign of infection. Sweat beads laced her pale skin. She looked as if all her blood had been drained from her. My poor tiger. She'd been through so much.

Sunlight streamed into the room. It was morning, so I thought. I was dazed myself. Last night's events whirled around in my head, but clarity quickly filled my mind. My baby had had surgery. The lengthy operation had gone well, my sister said. With no complications. Both my parents and Jen's had anxiously hung out at the hospital until they could see her in recovery. It was going on midnight. Once they saw her resting peacefully, despite all the tubes and monitors she was hooked up to, my sister insisted everyone go home. There was nothing we could do at this point. Jen's tearful mom didn't want to leave, but Harold convinced her it was in everyone's best interest. My parents drove the McCoys to our house where they were staying. Only I stayed behind. I needed to be here for my Jen when she came to. She was transferred to her own private room—a slick suite that looked more like it belonged in a five-star hotel than a hospital. My baby deserved the best. The hospital staff was kind enough to provide me a cot, but I couldn't take my eyes off her. Despite being hooked up to all sorts of gizmos, she looked so peaceful. Like an angel with her long satin curls fanned out across the fluffy pillow. I was mesmerized by her beauty, the rise and fall of her chest, and every soft breath. Leaning over her, I gently traced a finger over her warm silky lips—those lips that had set my heart and soul on fire. I relived that first kiss—a kiss from a spunky, blindfolded girl that had forever changed my life. A kiss that had made me love and need someone more than the air I breathed. Memories of all our good times together danced in my head. Our wedding was not among them.

As I watched her breathe into the wee hours of the morning, the fragility of life hit me like a plane going down. How fast and suddenly it could be taken away. Though she'd pulled through the operation, there was one big unanswered question. I tried to force it to the back of mind, but it weighed on my heart until sleep finally took hold of me.

Her hallucinatory screams catapulted me back to the moment. I was expecting to awaken to my sleeping beauty. Not this. She continued to twist and turn. I caressed her tortured face as she feverishly shook it side to side.

"Jen, Jen, it's me. It's okay. I'm here. Do you hear me?" I tried to sound calm but inside panic gripped me. With my free hand, I pushed the call button for a nurse or doctor.

I continued to say her name, my voice desperate, and stroke her hair. Finally, her eyes fluttered opened and met mine. Oh, those beautiful green orbs! I was so happy to see them. She calmed, but a mixture of terror and confusion was still etched deep on her face.

"Blake," she whispered, her voice a mere rasp. "Where am I? What happened?"

It was so good to hear her voice as faint as it was. It took all I had not to shed a tear. I tenderly kissed her warm forehead, my lips on fire from the mere touch of her flesh. I gazed at her lovingly and reverently. Her bewildered eyes stayed fixed on mine.

"Tiger, you're at Cedars. You were hemorrhaging. You had to have an operation."

"Surgery?" Fear flickered in her eyes.

I nodded.

"What did they do?" Her voice was so small.

My heart was splintering. Should I tell her? My father always said the truth is the best medicine. I swallowed hard.

"Jen, baby, you had a partial hysterectomy."

Her eyes blinked several times. "Meaning what?"

I chewed my lip. I fucking didn't want to tell her. "Meaning they found a mass on your uterus and had to remove part of it along with one of your ovaries."

Silence. I was expecting tears, but none materialized.

"Does that mean I can't have babies?"

My lips pressed together in a thin dismal line. "I don't

know." While I knew how much my tiger wanted to give me a den full of little cubs, I'd always love her whether we had children or not. And that wasn't what was eating at my heart. She read my anxious face.

"Do I have cancer?" Her tiny voice was stoic. Oh, my brave tiger.

My heart was shredding. I was so close to shedding tears. "I don't know. They're doing a biopsy. The results should be back in the afternoon."

"Okay," she murmured.

No, it was so not fucking okay. What had I done wrong to deserve this fate? It shouldn't have been her. My angel. No way.

Sparing me from saying another word, a nurse walked into the room. Petite, she looked Filipino and was wearing a cheery pink smock.

"Ah!" she said brightly. "You're awake, Ms. McCoy."

Ms. McCoy. My heart stuttered. Damn it. She was supposed to be Mrs. Burns this morning. And I was supposed to be fucking her brains out on our honeymoon though right now that didn't matter. My tiger was alive. And that's all that counted.

Without wasting a second, the nurse, whose name was Wanda, plunged one of those high-tech thermometers into her ear, took her pulse, and checked her charts. I held my breath.

"She has a slight fever; nothing to be alarmed about. All her other vitals seem normal."

I blew out a sharp breath of relief. Now, if only her biopsy came back normal. I silently prayed to God.

"I'd like to sponge her down," said the sweet nurse, cranking up her bed so my tiger was in a semi-sitting position. Her locks of hair curled like ribbons along the pillow.

"May I do that?" I implored while she ambled to the bathroom.

"I don't see why not," she replied, a slight chuckle in her accented voice.

She returned from the lavatory with a wet washcloth in her hand. She handed it to me. "Here you go," she said with a smile. "Just be careful around her incision. I'll be back soon with something for Ms. McCoy to eat."

I thanked the sweet nurse and began to wash my tiger, beginning with her face. Gently, I traced the warm wet cloth around it. She closed her eyes.

"Are you okay, baby?"

She replied with a weak nod.

"Do you hurt?"

"Just a little. But I feel so weak and nauseous."

The pain meds were doing their job, but I was concerned about her queasiness.

"You lost a lot of blood. Marcy had to give you a transfusion."

As I made my way down her slender arms, she blinked open her eyes. "Marcy?"

"Yeah. My sister was the surgeon. She's the best there is. She saved your life."

A small smile curled on her lips. The first since she'd regained consciousness. "Blake, I need to thank her."

I smiled back at her. "I'm sure she'll be here shortly."

I lowered her thin blanket down to her ankles. She looked so thin. So frail. Gingerly, I lifted her hospital gown, and for the first time, I saw where the incision was. A large thick bandage covered the area—just below her abdomen. My tiger's beautiful breasts quivered. She managed to take a peek.

"Guess I won't be wearing a bikini again."

I laughed. Only my tiger could make me do that when I wanted to fucking cry.

"I hear one-pieces are 'in' this year. And truthfully, tiger, I'd rather see you wearing nothing."

She squeezed my free hand. "Oh, Blake. I love you so much." And then the floodgates broke loose. Tears streamed down her cheeks.

"Baby, what's the matter?" Panic gripped me by my balls.

"Oh, Blake, what if I have cancer? I don't want to leave you."

I dabbed her tears away with the cloth. "Stop it, baby. You're a tiger. You're going to get through this." I paused. "*We're* going to get through this, do you understand?"

Thank fucking God, I had some acting skills. On the outside, I stayed calm, but inside I was cracking. I felt so fucking powerless. I was *that* man who was supposed to protect her and save her from the evils of the world, but this time, her superhero couldn't save her from the uncontrollable and unknown.

She nodded, the tears still falling. And then she smiled again, this time, a real smile, and held my gaze in hers. With her hand, she traced the outline of my jaw.

"Happy Birthday, Blake."

Balls. I'd totally forgotten it was my thirtieth birthday. And then I remembered what I'd wanted. It was plain and simple. I'd wanted to wake up to my wife. Start the next decade of my life with the girl I loved with my heart, my body, and my soul.

Damn it, I was going to make that happen. So, my bride

was wearing a hospital gown instead of a wedding gown, but right now that was the most beautiful dress in the world. I lowered my lips to hers and let her know how much I loved her. Weak as she was, she didn't resist. She cradled my head between her hands, her hot tears warming my face. Warming every part of me. Today, Jennifer McCoy was going to become Jennifer Burns.

Chapter 21

Jennifer

C alamity Jen.

That's what Libby often called me. Aptly.

My wedding had been the biggest calamity of my life. A disaster. I'd totally fucked it up. Let down my future husband. His parents. My parents. And over a thousand guests.

"I'm sorry I screwed everything up," I sniffled as I forced myself to break away from Blake's passionate kiss.

Blake gently brushed away my tears. "Stop it, tiger. It's not your fault."

"But all those people...all that money your parents spent..."

"Fuck the money, baby. My parents won't miss it. And except for our families and close friends, those people mean nothing to me. Or to us."

The bubbly nurse, who'd returned, made me drink some water. Blake held the cup as I sipped it through a straw. The cool liquid felt good against my parched palate and raw throat. Then another cheerful hospital attendant pranced into the room with a breakfast tray. A light meal of scrambled eggs, toast, and juice.

"Eat," Blake ordered, sitting on the edge of my bed.

With my fatigue, nausea, and the results of the biopsy weighing on my heart, I had no appetite, but I took a few bites to make Blake happy. I'd much rather be holding his hand than a fork.

My eyes grew heavy. Blake ruffled my hair and gave me a light kiss on my forehead. "Baby, rest. I'm not going anywhere." A faint smile spread on my lips as I closed my eyes.

I don't know how long I'd been out when my eyes blinked open. Blake was still there seated beside me. But standing beside him was a tall, lanky long-haired young man with warm twinkly eyes who bore a striking resemblance to Jesus. He was clad in a long white robe with a notched high collar and holding a pamphlet in one hand. A priest? Nurse Wanda was in the room too. My blood ran cold and my heart beat as fast as a hummingbird's wings. Something was wrong. Terribly wrong. *Cancer.* Was he here to read me my last rites?

"Blake, are we saying goodbye?" I stammered.

That dazzling mischievous smile I loved so much lit up his face. "No, baby, we're saying our vows."

My heart continued to beat in a frenzy while he introduced us. Reverend Dooby was a newly ordained Universal Life Church minister. We were all God's children. A shocking but beautiful reality swept over me like a warm summer shower. We were getting married.

In my drugged-out haze, the reverend's laid-back voice drifted in my ears like a magic carpet. It was some New Age ceremony with words like love, peace, and harmony abounding. Blake held my hand, his eyes never leaving me.

The reverend came to the end of his pamphlet. "Do you, Blake Burns, take this beautiful babe to be your wife?"

"I do." Blake smiled.

"And do you, Jennifer McCoy, take this handsome dude to be your husband?"

"I do," I whispered, my eyes watering. So much for Shakespeare.

Reverend Dooby closed his pamphlet. "Yo, bro, it's ring time."

My eyes stayed glued on Blake as he dipped a hand into a side pocket of his tuxedo pants. To my utter surprise, two SpongeBob Band-Aids appeared. He looked at me sheepishly.

"Sorry, baby. Borrowed these from the children's ward. Marcy's twins still have our rings so they'll have to do for now."

Oh my Blake! My smiling lips quivered as he handed me one. Then, he gently lifted my left hand, which fortunately wasn't hooked up to IVs. A tear rolled down my cheek as he wrapped the Band-Aid around my ring finger just above my magnificent engagement ring. The brilliant snowflake diamond sparkled in the ray of sunshine that beamed through the curtains.

It was my turn. My hands trembling, I copied his actions and wrapped the other Band-Aid around his left fourth finger. With a cheek to cheek grin, he admired my handiwork.

Reverend Dooby's voice echoed in my ears. "I now pronounce you husband and wife."

We were married! Blake gently drew me close to him. His mouth pressed on mine in a passionate embrace I wanted never to end. Our tongues danced and our bodies melted into one. We had just vowed to spend the rest of our lives together...to cherish each other until death do us part. I felt no pain as my fear succumbed to everlasting love.

The sobs of Nurse Wanda brought me back to the moment. "I'm sorry. I always cry at weddings. But this one is so special." Her tears were contagious. I was crying too.

Breaking the eternal kiss, I held my new husband's breath-taking face in my hands.

His eyes bore into mine "Mrs. Burns, thank you for the best birthday present ever."

"Oh, Blake, how can I ever top it?"

"By asking me the same question next year."

Chapter 22

Blake

The McCoys showed up a couple of hours after our nuptials. Nurse Wanda was back in the room, taking Jen's temperature.

"Good news, Mrs. Burns, your temperature is back to normal."

Mrs. Burns. Man, I loved those two words. And hoped I'd be hearing them for the rest of my life. Jen's prognosis was still gnawing away at me. My stomach was twisted in a knot.

Jen smiled sheepishly at her parents. "Mom, Dad...Blake and I have something to tell you." She shot me a look asking for a go-ahead. I nodded. Mrs. McCoy bit her lip, expecting bad news. My tiger continued.

"Um...uh...we got married this morning." She proudly held up her hand to show off her marriage "band"-Aid. I proudly did the same.

A warm smile spread across Harold's face while his wife exploded into tears.

Jen furrowed her brows. "Oh, Mom. Are you mad at me?"

Jen's mother reached into her small handbag for a lacy hankie. Dabbing at her tears, she rushed to Jen's bed and hugged her. "Oh, honey, your dad and I are so happy for the both of you. We love you so much."

A dazzling smile flashed on Jen's face. "I love you both so much too."

Mr. McCoy shook my hand. "Welcome to the family, son."

About an hour later, Libby and Chaz showed up while her parents were grabbing a bite to eat at the hospital cafeteria. Thrilled to hear about our marriage, they brightened Jen's spirits and kept her distracted. Especially Chaz, who made Jen laugh so hard it hurt. While waiting at the head of the long valet line for his car after the wedding fiasco, Kat had cut in front of him. He did what he'd always wanted to do. He slapped the rude psycho bitch. Way to go, my man!

Feeling a little stronger, Jen told us about the catfight between my mother and Kat's. Man, I would have given my left foot to see my mother kick Enid's ass. And score one for my tiger for almost knocking the bitch out. Despite my gloom, I laughed *my* ass off with Jen's best friends. I had a newfound respect for my mother, the warrior.

Libby and Chaz spent a half hour with us. Shortly after they left, the McCoys returned to the room, and my parents and Grandma showed up. Jen and I shared the news about our marriage with my family. They were thrilled, especially Grandma who exclaimed, *"Zei gezunt.* So *vhen* are you going to make me some beautiful grandchildren?"

My heart skittered. *From her lips to God's ears.*

My mother pecked my cheek. "Congratulations, darling. And happy birthday. I brought along the perfect cake to celebrate."

Only my mother would think about my birthday at a time like this. Before I could say another word, in walked two burly hospital attendants, wheeling in our twenty-layer ocean-themed wedding cake—complete with multi-colored macaroon shellfish dotting the pearl-white frosting. For sure, thirty candles were lit among the many layers. I mentally rolled my eyes. But I had to love her.

"Following Meg's excellent suggestion, we took the rest of the reception food to a homeless shelter. But we decided to keep the cake. Whatever's not eaten, we'll give to the hospital staff."

My mother and Jen's exchanged warm smiles. My mother meant well. She cared about people. She cared about me.

"Now, darling boy, make a wish and blow out the candles."

"Candles *shmandles.* Such a *vaste* of time," growled Grandma as I prepared to do the honors.

There was only one wish to make. You know it. Drawing in a deep breath, I blew out the candles. All thirty with my pursed mouth and puffed out cheek*s.*

Together, Jen and I sliced the first piece of cake, my strong hand cupping her limp one. My birthday cake was our wedding cake and vice versa. In wedding tradition, we fed each other a mouthful and moaned.

I thought about my wish. *Oh baby, stay with me.*

The minutes crawled by. Every hour felt like an eternity. Jen dozed on and off while we anxiously awaited the biopsy report. I was on pins and needles. Every fifteen minutes, I texted my sister who texted back with the same two words: *No news.* Let me tell you, patience was not one of my virtues.

Finally at five p.m., a little after Jen awoke from a nap, Marcy ambled into the room. It now resembled a florist's shop with all the beautiful fragrant flowers sent over by friends of my parents. Clad in a white lab coat, she was holding a clipboard with some papers attached to it. I couldn't read her expression—it was a total poker face. My stomach clenched. She glanced down at the charts.

"I'm afraid..."

Oh, fuck. God, no! My racing heart was about to beat out of my chest.

"...Jennifer is going to be stuck with my brother for a very long time."

It took me a second to deconstruct her words. And when I heard her utter the magic word "benign," I swear my cock did a happy dance.

In my haze of over-the-top happiness, I could hear Jen's mother weeping, "Thank you, good Lord. Thank you."

I rushed to my tiger's side. I took her into my arms. "Did you hear that, baby? You're going to be okay."

Her glistening eyes searched mine. "Blake, why are you crying?"

Balls. Blake A-for-Alpha Burns was an emotional car wreck. I'd held back tears of sorrow, but I couldn't hold back tears of joy.

She kissed away my tears. Whoever said real men don't cry needed to have their fucking head examined.

Chapter 23

Blake

My tiger was released from the hospital on Christmas Day. It was the best Christmas present I could have gotten. While she was frail, she was home and on the road to recovery. And we were husband and wife. We were now wearing our matching platinum wedding bands. Marcy had brought them to the hospital. They were both inscribed with one word: "Forever."

"Merry Christmas, Mr. and Mrs. Burns," said the cheerful doorman as I helped my slow-moving but radiant wife into our building. "Surprised to see you back from your honeymoon so soon."

"A little change in plans," I replied. Jen giggled.

When I got to my apartment, I unlocked the door and then swept my tiger into my arms.

Jen gazed up at me. "What are you doing, Blake? You know, I can walk."

I rolled my eyes at her and kicked the door open. "Jeez, tiger. Tradition. I'm carrying you across the threshold."

A big smile flashed on her wan face, and she smacked a kiss on my lips. "Oh, Blake, you're such a romantic. But please don't make me laugh because it hurts!"

Jen's eyes lit up when I carried her into the living room. I'd managed to score a Christmas tree at the last minute at a lot not far from Cedars. A last minute deal that nobody wanted, it was smallish and kind of scruffy like an undernourished rescue dog. When I spotted it, I knew it was mine. Just like my Jen, it was a survivor and needed TLC. Jen's mom, God bless her, rushed to Rite-Aid and scored some bulbs and decorations at fifty percent off. The tree, I must say, was shining brightly just like my tiger.

"Oh, Blake!" she exclaimed as I set her down on the couch. "You got me a Christmas tree?"

"No. I got *us* one. Merry Christmas, Mrs. Burns."

"The same, Mr. Burns."

I lowered myself onto the couch next to her. She snuggled against me, folding her legs over mine and resting her head on my shoulder. Her knees grazed my cock. I inhaled the intoxicating cherry-vanilla scent of her hair and then kissed her scalp lightly. It felt so good to cuddle her.

"Baby, I'm sorry I don't have a Christmas present for you." The truth: we were supposed to be on our honeymoon, and I was going to surprise her with something special. I still hadn't shared that destination with her, nor was I planning to.

Lifting her head, she cradled my face in her hands. "Wrong. I have you, baby. The best Christmas present a girl could ever hope for."

Impulsively, I pulled her face to mine. I crushed my lips against hers and wasted no time making the kiss hotter and deeper. Maybe she couldn't fuck, but she sure could kiss.

Jen's parents came over for dinner as did mine. So did Grandma and Marcy, minus her twins. My nephews stayed at home with their nanny, preferring to play with the boxload of 3D Nintendo games I'd bought them for Chanukah.

Jen's mom made her traditional Irish stew, and Grandma brought over a pot of her matzo ball soup. My tiger ate voraciously, and it pleased me. Her healthy appetite signaled she was getting better.

Respecting Jennifer's fragile state of health, our guests didn't linger. After I cleaned up with everyone's help, Jen and I curled up on the couch and watched a Netflix movie. *Frozen.* The very flick we'd seen last Christmas day when I'd showed up at her house in Boise and surprised her. She loved this movie. And just like before, she cried her eyes out. It so fucking turned me on. And it gave me an idea. I had to admit. Sometimes, I was a fucking genius. No pun intended.

We welcomed the New Year in together with what we decided would be an annual tradition—we boiled two lobsters. Jen named hers Kat, and I named mine Enid. Over champagne, we toasted to our new life together.

Jen recovered slowly but steadily. As much as she wanted to get back to work, I made her stay home an extra week just to play it safe. And when she finally did go into the office, we drove there together as Jen was not permitted to drive for the rest of the month.

The hardest part was that we couldn't fuck—specifically, I couldn't sink my cock into her pussy or her ass. We had to get the okay from Marcy that she was fully healed internally and that might take up to two months. That's not to say that my cock didn't get any action. We got creative and I fucked her every other way I knew how. And lucky for Jen, her clit was not off bounds. Nor were sex toys if they were used externally. By the time what we hoped would be Jen's final visit to my sister, she was jokingly complaining that her jaw was strained, her fingers calloused, and that her cleavage and her armpits, my substitute pockets of paradise, were chafed. She'd also had to replace the batteries of all our sex toys. And she was positive her healthy weight gain could be attributed to all the high caloric cum she'd swallowed. I actually believed her.

On Friday, February the thirteenth, the day before Valentine's Day, I insisted on accompanying Jen to her morning appointment with Marcy. Hopefully, it would be her last. Jen caved in but made me sit in the waiting room. I was the sole male in a sea of women, several very attractive, and felt a little conspicuous when I caught their eyes on me. I gave them a little wave and told them I was here with my wife. God, I loved saying that word. They responded in unison with a disappointed chorus of "Ohs" and went back to their cell phones and magazines. I took out my iPhone, but while I answered some e-mails, my mind wandered.

It was strange to think of my sister examining my wife. Exploring parts that were meant only for me. In my mind's eye, I pictured Jen in those stirrups, legs spread wide, her perfectly preened pink pussy in full view. My cock flexed. I had the burning urge to bust through the door and fuck her on the examining room table. But the thought of my sister watching quickly put that fantasy to rest though I was still horny as hell. Fingers crossed Jen would be cleared to have real sex. It had been way too long—in fact, the longest my cock had gone without pussy in my entire adult life. Twenty long minutes later, the receptionist broke into my wet dreams and told me my sister wanted to see me in her office. My heart accelerating, I leapt up from my chair.

Jennifer was already seated in Marcy's office when I came flying in. A smile sparkled on her face. Marcy, seated behind her desk, lifted her recently acquired reading glasses onto her head.

"Hi, babe. How'd it go?" I asked, taking the chair right next to Jen's and sounding on edge.

"Great news."

Marcy took over. "Yes, Jennifer has healed beautifully. The two of you can resume sexual intercourse immediately."

Immediately? Like could I fuck Jennifer over Marcy's desk right here and now? "Seriously?" I asked incredulously.

Jen squeezed my hand. "Really, baby."

My cock jumped with joy, but at the same time, a cocktail of apprehension and anxiety seeped through my veins. While I'd counted down the days to sink my cock into my tiger, unsettling questions hammered my brain. Could I hurt her? Tear her apart? Make her bleed? "Will there be any complications?" I asked Marcy, thinking maybe we should do it in one of her examining rooms for the first time just in case. Again, that image of fucking my wife in those stirrups flashed in my mind.

Jen answered my question. "Marcy says you can do it as

hard as you want."

Nodding, my sister smiled at me sheepishly. My cock was doing a happy dance.

"Yes!" I said with a victorious air punch. The two of us were taking the day off from work. Boss's orders.

And then if I couldn't be flying higher, Marcy shared one other bit of good news.

Let me rephrase. It was the best fucking news I'd heard all year.

Holy crap! I was ready to pass out the cigars.

And then I did something I should have done a long time ago. Before Jen's smiling eyes, I hugged my sister.

I drove home like a mad man. Skimming red lights and exceeding the speed limit.

"Blake, what the hell are you doing?" shouted Jen, her ponytail whipping across her face. "You're going to get us killed."

"Getting us home."

Ten short minutes later, I zipped into my condo driveway and brought my Porsche to a screeching halt. I literally jumped over my passenger door and yanked Jennifer out. Grasping her hand, I raced past the wide-eyed doorman to the elevator. A press of a button and a ping. The elevator doors parted, and in one swift move, I hauled her into the car and shoved her against a wall. My body pressed against hers in a heated fit of desire and need.

"Blake, I can't breathe," Jen panted out as the elevator

doors closed.

"In a few minutes, you won't be walking either," I panted back, gnawing her everywhere and rubbing my already stiff cock against her belly. I slid my hand into the waistband of her jeans and glided my fingers between her legs.

"Jeez, Jen. You're so fucking hot and wet," I breathed against her neck as I maneuvered my middle finger into her entrance. Fuck, she felt good. She fisted my hair and moaned.

"You okay, babe?" I asked, still anxious.

"Yes," she breathed out. "Blake, I don't think we're moving."

She was right. I slammed the palm of my free hand against my floor button and the elevator ascended. I pumped my finger up and down Jen's tunnel. It was dripping wet. Intact.

"Blake, are you going to fuck me in the elevator?"

"I may have to." Dry humping her while I finger fucked her was setting my cock on fire.

Fortunately, the elevator reached our floor with no stops.

Two desperate minutes later, we were stripped to the bone and I was on top of her. My throbbing cock was rock-hard and so fucking ready, but I wanted to taste-test her first—warm her up for me. I spread her legs and then raised myself so I was kneeling between them. Not wasting a second, I went down on her, inhaling the sweet smell of her sex. After flicking and licking her slick folds, I powered my tongue deep inside her. A loud moan escaped her throat.

"Oh God, Blake. So good," she cried out, arching up against my hungry mouth.

So good. Just the words I wanted to hear. I began to fuck her with my tongue, driving in and out of her without abandon.

She bucked wildly against my face, her moans turning into melodic whimpers. The fact that she was so sexually responsive was sending me over the moon and making my swelling cock ache with desire. I moved one hand to her clit and rubbed it vigorously. Jen's whimpering morphed into screams as she headed toward orgasm. Her fingernails clawed my skin. The pain mixed with the pleasure I was giving her and was driving me crazy with lust.

A heartbeat later, she succumbed and juddered around my tongue while my taste buds melted in her delicious juices.

Letting her ride out her orgasm, I withdrew my tongue and lifted my head to get a look at her. Still breathing heavily, she looked good and fucked. Now, it was my turn. My cock was ready for its grand entrance, but I had to admit I was suffering from stage fright. The questions I'd pondered in my sister's office whirled around again in my head. I was still afraid of hurting her with my monstrous cock. And new insecurities surfaced. Could I still fill her to the hilt? Would she feel me? Would she come for me around my cock like the tiger she was?

I repositioned us so that I was hovering over her on the balls of my feet, my hands anchored by her head and holding me up. Her legs were now bent and raised like a happy baby, her ankles hooked around my neck. Somehow, that stirrup fantasy lurked in my head. My anxious cock was lined up with her pussy.

"Baby, I want you to insert my cock into your pussy." I wasn't taking any chances. Despite my sister's assurances, I feared I would rip my tiger apart with a forceful thrust and my size.

My eyes stayed on her beautiful, impassioned face as she

fisted my big cock, her fingers barely able to meet. It twitched with anticipation upon feeling the crown at her entrance. The build-up of being back inside her had my blood racing.

"Baby, take your sweet time," I moaned as she slid my cock, inch by thick inch, into her warm wet chasm. Oh, God yes! She was doing it—taking me to the hilt. I let out a hiss when my cock hit her womb.

"Blake, do I feel okay?" Worry was etched on her face.

"Oh, fuck, yes, baby. Better than ever."

A smile of relief curled on her lips as she clenched her muscles around my pulsing shaft. My brave tiger hadn't told me she was as anxious as me. Up until now, neither of us knew if the surgery had any physical impact on her.

"Am I hurting you?" I asked nervously as I slowly withdrew.

"Oh Blake, you feel amazing. I've missed you so much."

"The same, baby." Relief crashed through me. It felt so fucking good to be home. I thrust my cock back into her, ready to ravish her. But I controlled my strokes, starting off slowly, and then gradually picked up my pace. A look of rapture washed over her face.

"Faster, harder, Blake! I'm not going to break."

In no time, I was pounding into her, ruthlessly and relentlessly. You'd think my cock would have no stamina after two months with no pussy, but let me tell you, Mr. Burns was blessed with muscle memory. There are fucks. And there are epic fucks. We were heading toward the latter. My cock was in overdrive, and every magic spot was within striking distance.

She clutched my biceps to give her more leverage and rocked her hips into mine with each powerful thrust. I'd almost forgotten how fucking fantastic it felt to fuck her. She was so tight, so wet, so hot. And so mine.

"Don't stop," she panted out.

"Don't worry, baby. Not a chance in hell." I wasn't going to stop hammering her until the elderly, hard-of-hearing couple next door was calling security.

Our eyes never lost contact. Her face flushed with lust as my cock continued to plunder her sweet pussy. I grunted and growled. She howled. There was something so urgent and savage about this position that brought out our inner animals. My insatiable tiger was back, and my cock was back where it belonged with feral ferocity.

I had newfound respect for the men who served our country. Especially those stationed on ships in the middle of nowhere or twenty thousand leagues under the sea in submarines. I mean, how the fuck did they do it? Months away from loved ones and no pussy. They all deserved medals of honor for their courage and bravery. I was about to get a medal of my own. I'd never lasted this long. Deep inside, I never wanted her to let me go.

And then unexpectedly, she began to sob, "Oh God, oh God," and my fears bounced back into my head.

"Tell me you're okay, baby." Borderline panic.

She nodded feverishly. "Yes, yes, yes! Oh, Blake, I'm about to come!"

My balls retracted as she began to convulse around my pulsating cock. On the roar of my name, I slammed into her one more time and my own massive orgasm assaulted me. I'm talking nuclear. My whole body jerked as my hot release showered her magnificent pussy. Our half-mast eyes stayed locked in a haze of passion.

While my cum spilled into her, my heart filled with a deep love for the woman who was my wife. For the woman who would one day be the mother of our children. I crushed my mouth on her parted lips.

After a few luscious minutes, I withdrew from her. I rolled onto my back and shifted her so her head was resting on my chest. She was still sobbing.

"Why are you crying, baby?" I asked, brushing away her hot tears.

"Oh, Blake. That was so amazing, but I was so afraid. Afraid we wouldn't have what we had."

I caressed the top of her head. "Baby, I was a little freaked out too." Am I fucking kidding? I was scared shitless. "But what we have now is greater than what we had before. That was the best fuck I've ever had."

My words didn't stop the tears, but they did put a bright smile on her face. I drew her tight against me. We stayed in that position for several long, blissful minutes, neither of us saying another word. Jen finally broke the soulful silence. Her tears had subsided.

"Blake, we should shower and head into the office," whispered my diligent and so talented wife.

"No, Mrs. Burns, we're going to work from home today."

And trust me, we had our work cut out for us.

And a lot of catching up to do.

We fucked all day. All night. And all through the next.

The. Best. Valentine's. Day. Ever.

Chapter 24

Jennifer

I sobbed out my orgasm. Loud, heaving sobs that to the unknowing ear might have been construed as the sounds of someone grieving a lost loved one.

They were just the opposite. The sobs of ecstasy. Of someone who was spilling with love and pleasure so intense, it couldn't be measured.

Oh, my Blake. He had made glorious love to me. Fucked me with such care and reverence. Letting me put his cock inside me with my trembling fingers. Waiting until he knew I could take him to the limit before he started to thrust. And those first strokes were so tender and slow. Like he was caressing my pussy. And then he took me as if he owned me because he did. As my orgasm took over, like the waves of a tsunami taking everything in its wake, every worry I'd had washed out to sea. My eyes had stayed locked on his impassioned, glistening face as he'd watch me come and simultaneously grunted out his own climax of cataclysmic proportions.

And then we'd talked. Shared our insecurities and fears. Blake's honesty and vulnerability struck a deep chord in my heart. Yes, we both didn't really know what to expect and we'd avoided the touchy topic, but I had an idea. Unbeknownst to him, I'd done a lot of research online about what sex was like after a hysterectomy. Some said it was better, but most women complained about pain and the loss of sensation. Since I'd had only a partial hysterectomy, I was hoping I'd be in the former group, but there was no guarantee or way of finding out beforehand. When Marcy gave me the clearance that it was okay to have sex, I should have done a happy dance. Instead, I was a nervous wreck. I just didn't let Blake know that.

Blake held me close to him, his heart beating like a love song in my ear. The silence that followed transported me to another place. I felt not only a physical and emotional connection to him but also a spiritual one that couldn't be put into words. We'd at last consummated our marriage. He belonged to me and I belonged to him. We'd put the needs of the other before our own. He didn't just make me a better person. He made me the best person I could be. Tears of pure bliss streamed down my face. We were husband and wife.

The days and months that followed flew by and were the happiest of my life. Blake and I settled into a routine of work hard, play hard, and fuck hard.

We saw his family a lot. Every Shabbat, we went to his parents' house and one Friday night, his grandma came over and helped me do it at our place. I was taking a course at the local synagogue on Jewish holidays and customs and was even contemplating studying Hebrew. Whether I'd convert or not was still up in the air, but these endeavors made me closer to

Blake and his family.

We socialized a lot, too, though we were trying to cut back on the number of galas and premiers Blake got invited to. Yes, we ran into his former hook-ups more times than we wished, but I was quickly gaining self-confidence as Mrs. Blake Burns. We even ran into Kitty-Kat, who gave me predatory stares but stayed far away from us, knowing what I damn well could and would do to her. I kept her phone with the *Fuck the Bitch* footage in a safety deposit box. And had a spare copy.

We went out often with Gloria and Jaime. And sometimes along with their adorable twins who were now walking and talking. It was so cute the way they called us Jen-Jen and Bwake. Blake and I talked a lot about having kids of our own though we both knew that journey was not going to be a typical or easy one.

We also socialized quite frequently with Blake's sister Marcy and her twins. She'd saved my life and I was forever beholden to her. The little monsters were not monsters at all— just two rambunctious little boys who enjoyed watching cartoons and playing board games as much as I did; they loved SpongeBob, but still couldn't beat me at Junior Scrabble. To my utter delight, Blake had grown much closer to his sister and his nephews, and we were both there for her when she had to contend with her ex. The wedding present she had promised us was beyond our belief. No price tag could be put on it.

I was still attending my weekly support group for rape victims. Blake's wonderful mom was organizing a benefit in the Fall that would raise a ton of money and help us expand our reach out program as well as move to safer headquarters. Jeffrey, her new event planner, was overseeing it. That was one gala Blake and I wouldn't miss.

And once a week, I got together with my best friend Libby for a girls' night out. She'd flown to France and broken up with her longtime boyfriend Everett. Though saddened, she was handling it pretty well. Blake had a friend he wanted to fix her up with, but right now, she just wanted to be single and concentrate on her career.

The only people I missed seeing regularly were my parents. They'd come to visit me one more time while I was recuperating from my surgery, but once I'd fully recovered, we Skyped and then they embarked on their dream trip—sailing to Europe on the Queen Mary. They e-mailed me daily and sent me many postcards from their month-long travels abroad. Dad's leg had completely healed, and they were having the time of their lives. I couldn't be happier for them. I told Blake that if our schedules allowed, I wanted us to visit them in Boise sometime in the summer.

Work was amazing; I loved my job. My block of telenovelas based on bestselling erotic romances was a huge success; the ratings had gone through the roof—skyrocketed—and had even exceeded analysts' expectations. At the May Upfront in New York, Blake and I announced that MY-SIN TV was being spun off into a 24/7 cable channel. The audience of advertisers and affiliates exploded with excitement. In addition to airing more telenovelas, we were expanding the block with reality programming and talk shows targeted at women. Leading it off in the morning was one of the programs I'd proudly developed. Rather than telling the audience about it, Blake and I had decided to give them a sneak peek. The curtain rose behind us, and there was Grandma and her erotic book club heatedly arguing about who was the sexiest book boyfriend—among them, Christian Grey, Jesse Ward, and Lucien Knight. "*Oy!* That Lucien!" quipped Grandma. "Trust me, any Viking *shmiking* who can get his *shmekel* up in the *vinter* in *Norvay* is every *vomen's vet* dream." The audience burst into laughter. And so did Blake and I. He squeezed my hand, and then when the lights went dark, he kissed me. There was no doubt in my mind that Grandma's new show, *The Sexy Shmexy Book Club*, was going to be a big hit. And at the young age of eighty-six, she was going to be a huge star.

One Saturday morning in July after a delicious wake-up fuck, Blake told me to start packing my bags.

"Are we going away for the weekend?" I asked him, seated cross-legged on our bed and still bared to him. He was always still full of surprises.

"No." A wicked smile curled on his kissable lips.

I shot him a puzzled look. I could tell from the expression on his face he was up to something. "Can you, at least, give me a hint?"

He affectionately tugged my ponytail. "Does the word 'honeymoon' mean anything to you?"

Oh my God! My heart skipped a beat. We'd never taken one. The secret destination he'd teased me with had never materialized after my surgery. Work had gotten in the way. Excitement mixed with panic.

"But, Blake, I haven't cleared my schedule. I've got so much going on."

"Don't worry. Mrs. Cho and I took care of it. We canceled most of your meetings, and whatever there's left to do, Myles and Mrs. Cho can handle."

My heart began to race with excitement. "Blake, where are we going?"

He winked. "Not telling. It's still a surprise."

All I knew it was somewhere neither of us had ever been. My mind spun with possibilities.

"What should I bring along?"

He smirked. "Except for your passport, as little as possible. You won't be needing much."

A rush of hot tingles clustered between my legs. My eyes widened. Now, he really had me curious and excited.

"When are we leaving?"

"At noon. On my dad's private plane."

"Oh my God!" Teetering between elation and panic (the former winning), I flung my arms around him and kissed him fiercely. Our tongues danced passionately together.

He playfully tweaked my nipples and then slid a hand across my still heated wet cleft.

"Now, baby, I'm going to show you some of the activities our destination has to offer."

In a short hot breath, he was again fucking me senseless. I was so looking forward to our trip.

Chapter 25

Blake

We'd been two hours in the air, and it was time for my first surprise. To keep the surprise a surprise, I'd forced Jen to wear a blindfold. She'd reluctantly gone along with my demand.

"Blake, it feels like we're descending. Are we landing?"

I wished she could see my fiendish grin. "We have to make a little stop." *Just wait.*

"Why can't I take this blindfold off? I want to see where we are. Mexico?"

Impulsively, the little sneak reached for her face. I grabbed both her petite hands by their wrists in my large one.

"Uh, uh, uh, tiger. You're forcing me to do something I wasn't sure I wanted to do, but now I have to."

She turned her head toward me, her little scrunched up nose peeking out from the blindfold. Fuck, she was cute.

"Like what, Blake?"

Without saying a word, I dug my free hand into the seat pocket where I'd stored my backup accessory. Then, in one smooth move, I pinned her hands behind her and snapped the metal devices around her slender wrists. The clink was like music to my ears.

"Blake! You've handcuffed me." She futilely tried to tear her hands apart, stretching the chain to its maximum pull. I stifled laughter.

"Baby, if you don't behave, I've got some ropes close by to bind those defiant little hands."

She grunted in frustration. I was enjoying every minute, and she was turning me on. While the plane descended, something ascended. It was time for Jen to make a little visit to *my* cockpit.

Writhing, she continued to tug at the cuffs to no avail. She let out a loud sigh. "Okay, Blake, if you promise to take these off me, I'll do anything you want."

Jeez. She was making it so easy peasy. With swiftness, I zipped down my fly. Out sprung big ole Mr. Burns, who was thoroughly enjoying the ride. I think by the expression on her face she knew what I wanted.

"Deal. Go down on me, tiger." Before she could utter a word, I shoved her head to my cock. In a heartbeat, her warm mouth was covering my wide crown.

"Suck on me, tiger. Suck on me hard. I want to come hard and fast." She nodded as I urged her mouth to descend, pressing on her scalp with the palm of my hand. She didn't need any more flight instruction from me; my tiger knew exactly what to do. Exactly how I liked it. I hissed and arched my spine as she slid her mouth down my rigid shaft, her tongue blazing a trail. My head pressed hard again the headrest. Holy shit. She was taking me to the hilt.

"Jesus, baby. That feels so fucking good." I could feel my mega-sized dick fill the hollows of her cheeks and the tip touch the base of her throat. Without prompting, she quickly returned to the crown, and then began bopping her head up and down my enormous erection with the ferocity and velocity of the tiger she was. My greedy cocky couldn't be happier. My balls were tightening and heat coiled through my groin. Just as the plane touched down, I came with a massive explosion of hot cum in her mouth. I yanked up her head by her ponytail and crashed my lips onto hers, rewarding her with a fierce, savage kiss. She moaned into my mouth as I tasted myself on her tongue.

"Baby, we've landed," I breathed, breaking the kiss. Holy fuck. What a landing! My cock was still flying high.

She ran the tip of her talented tongue around her lush lips, licking off the remains of my release.

"Blake. *Ahem.* The handcuffs..."

"Right." I lived by my father's words: a deal is a deal. Except there was one little problem. I couldn't find the fucking key.

Shitballs. This wasn't part of the plan. It was time for our next activity and this was so not going to look good.

Chapter 26

Jennifer

B lake was not a happy camper nor was I. He was driving like a maniac. A Chevy pickup no less. He'd asked Mrs. Cho to have someone pick us up when we landed, but somehow that had gotten lost in translation and instead she'd rented him a pickup truck. As mad as I was at him, I'd do anything to see my metrosexual hubby behind the wheel of this vehicle. *That* man in a pickup was like Batman in an RV.

"We need to find a Walmart," he grumbled.

"Why?" I gritted. I was still blindfolded and handcuffed, and I had no clue where we were except I knew it wasn't some romantic island. I waited impatiently for his response.

"So, I can buy a chainsaw and saw off your handcuffs."

Gah! The thought of Blake with a chainsaw sent a shiver down my spine. My life could be over. Mr. Born with a Silver Spoon in his Mouth was not exactly what I'd call handy. The only power tools he had any experience with were his tongue, his hands, and his cock.

"What about a locksmith?" My voice was urgent. "I'm sure one could make a key to unlock these damn things."

"That's a good idea, tiger."

"Why don't you take off my blindfold so I can keep my

eyes peeled for one? And where the hell are we anyway?"

"That's not happening. And I'm not telling."

Two minutes later, Blake swerved off the road with a screech. My neck jerked painfully. I think I had whiplash. Horns were blasting at us from all directions.

"What the fuck are you doing, Blake? You're going to get us killed!"

"There's a Walmart straight ahead of us," he replied brightly.

Ten minutes later, Blake was leading me through the bustling mega-store. He had his fingers curled around my neck since holding one of my pinned back, cuffed hands was not an option. I could barely move my fingers. The fucking handcuffs were cutting off my circulation. Oh, was he going to pay for this. Big time!

I could only imagine what people thought as I stumbled through the store, trying to keep up with Blake's pace. Maybe they thought he was a bounty hunter who'd captured his prey. Or an undercover cop who was carting away a shoplifter. Well, at least with the blindfold, I couldn't see their bewildered expressions.

"Slow down," I yelled.

Without slowing down, Blake asked, "Where do you think we can find a locksmith? I've never been to a Walmart before."

Of course not. Mr. Beverly Hills had lived a life of privilege. The only department store he'd ever stepped foot in besides Saks was Neiman Marcus. Needless Markup as Libby and I often called it.

"The hardware department," I seethed.

"This store is so fucking big. That could be a mile away."

"Ask. Some. One."

Twenty long minutes later, because everyone Blake asked gave us different directions, we were back outside in the parking lot where a locksmith was stationed.

"Can you make us a key that will unlock these cuffs?" Blake asked him.

Standing with my back to the locksmith, I felt him take my hands in his and examine the cuffs.

"Sure, but it's going to take two hours."

Blake's voice grew louder by an octave and desperate. "What! We have to be somewhere important in a half hour."

Where the heck were we going? I was more curious than ever.

Blake continued. "Do you have a Plan B? I don't care what it fucking costs."

The locksmith stretched my hands apart as far as they would go. He then splayed them on the counter. "Keep your fingers spread and don't move an inch."

BANG! My heart hammered. BANG again! Suddenly, my hands were free from one another. I massaged my wrists, not happy the cuffs were still circling them.

"Blake, how are we going to get these off?"

"We'll figure it out later. For now, think of them as jewelry."

Jewelry, my ass.

"How much do I owe you?" Blake asked my liberator.

"Forget it. It's on the house. Just tell me, was the sex good?"

"Yeah. It was fucking amazing."

Grimacing, I let Blake whisk me away. "How could you

say that?"

"Lighten up, baby. You know you loved it."

Damn it, he was right.

We were back in the Chevy. I wasn't talking to Blake. Fuming, I kept my cuffed hands folded tightly across my chest. I'd had enough of this ruse. Blake's shenanigans. A short fifteen minutes later, we turned off the freeway and began winding down some city streets. At what must be a red light, I finally broke my silence.

"Now, where are we going?"

"You'll see in five minutes."

Sure enough, five minutes later Blake parked the truck and helped me out of it.

"Watch your step." His arm around my shoulders, he ushered me up the curb.

"Can't I take this damn blindfold off?" I asked, inhaling the intoxicating scent of roses and honeysuckle evocative of my childhood. Maybe he was taking me to some romantic garden. Several unsteady steps later, I found myself crossing a threshold. A mélange of delectable aromas instantly wafted up my nose.

"Blake, where are we?" In a quick heartbeat, the blindfold slipped off, and in a stunned blink, I knew. I was home!

"SURPRISE!" shouted out the people nearest and dearest to me, all dressed in Sunday finery. My parents, Blake's parents, Gloria and Jaime Zander with their twins, Libby, Marcy and her twins, Vera and Steve Nichols and their son

Joshua, Mrs. Cho and her family, my therapist, Dr. Williams, and, last but not least, Grandma with Luigi the tailor. Also gathered in the hallway were Father Murphy and some of my parents' closest friends. The people I'd grown up with. My jaw dropped to the floor. I was simply aghast.

"Blake, is this some kind of surprise party? My birthday's not till October."

He smacked a kiss on my cheek "No, baby. It's a surprise wedding."

A wedding? "But—"

My mother, looking positively stunning in a damask silk suit that matched the color of her gray-blue eyes, broke out of the crowd and gave me hug before I could say another word.

"Come on, honey. Let's get you ready."

"But, Mom, I have nothing appropriate to wear."

Beaming, she took my hand. "Excuse us, everyone. But the mother of the bride has to get her little girl ready." I shot a glance at my handsome, smiling father who winked back at me. Then, I let Mom lead me to the stairwell with my head turned, my eyes never losing contact with Blake's. A cocky, triumphant smile lit his face. Oh, my Blake! *That* man who never stopped surprising me. His love filled the room.

A few breathless moments later, I stepped foot into my bedroom. And yet another shocking surprise.

Chaz! "Darling, just say yes to the dress."

He was holding up the most beautiful gown I'd ever seen. I gasped, clapping a hand to my wide-open mouth.

"Do you like it, Jenny-Poo?"

"Oh my God, Chaz. It's gorgeous." Tears were brimming in my eyes as I beheld his breathtaking creation. It was the dress I'd always dreamed of. A sleeveless, ivory confection with layers of tulle and lace, tiny scattered pearls, and a sweetheart neckline. I knew in my heart every stitch was made with love. Oh, my sweet Chaz!

I broke away from my mom and ran up to hug him. Tears were now free-falling down my face.

"Darling, you're going to crush the dress. Come on, let's get you dressed."

To my utter delight, my best friend Libby joined us, and a half hour later, the magnificent dress cinched my narrow waist and grazed the carpeted floor. It fit me to a tee. Beneath the gown, I was wearing delicate lace lingerie and thigh-high silk stockings from Paris. All courtesy of Gloria. And a pair of ivory satin heels with sparkly snowflake shoe clips, courtesy of Libby.

"Mom, was this your idea?" I asked as she and Libby fluffed the dress.

"No, my darling. It was all Blake's."

My heart melted.

"I just helped him orchestrate it. And I must tell you, dear, his mother was a saint and helped so much. She's an amazing woman."

I smiled. I was so happy Helen and Mom were bonding. That was important to me. And since the Hollywood wedding debacle, she'd grown closer to me and relinquished control over Blake's social life. I had a lot to learn from her.

Chaz broke into my thoughts. "Jenny-Poo, we're not done yet." My eyes followed him as he pranced over to my closet and opened it. Hanging from the hook was an exquisite long lace veil. I recognized it immediately. It was the one Blake's grandma had worn in that photo I'd once admired.

"Grandma insisted you wear it," my mother said brightly as Chaz adjusted it over my head. It trailed along the carpet.

"Oh, Jen, you look like a princess," gushed Libby, who once again was going to be my maid of honor. "Take a look at yourself."

Grabbing my hand, she led me to a full-length standing mirror in the corner of my small room.

I let out a little gasp as I stared at my reflection. My mother stood behind me and I could see her eyes watering in the glass.

"Oh, my little girl."

I spun around and gave her another hug. "Oh, Mom. I love you so much."

And then, I hugged Libby and Chaz again.

"No tears!" chastised Chaz. "They'll ruin your complexion."

"One last thing, darling," said my mother, dipping her hand into the pocket of her suit jacket.

"What's that?" I asked, eyeing a scrap of blue lace that looked very old.

"Something borrowed. Something blue. It's the garter I wore when I married your father. It belonged to your late grandmother."

My Irish grandmother, Maeve. A woman I'd heard much about but had sadly never met. I was close to losing it as I lifted my gown. My mother held it up as I slid the treasured heirloom up my silk-clad leg. Her eyes wandered to my wrists.

"Honey, I meant to ask you, what are those unusual bracelets you're wearing?"

I glanced at the shiny cuffs as I continued to inch the garter up my leg.

On one, the words "My tiger" were engraved; on the other, "You. Are. Mine."

I replied to my mom. "Oh, just some jewelry Blake wanted me to wear for our nuptials."

My Blake! At this moment, there was no happier or luckier girl in the world than me.

Chapter 27

Blake

I'll never forget the expression on my tiger's face as she stepped into her backyard on the arm of her proud, beaming father. She stopped dead in her tracks and her jaw dropped to the snow-covered ground.

That's right...snow in July. With the help of my mother and her new party planner, Jeffrey, I had magically transformed the McCoys' backyard into a winter wonderland. A snow machine was making snow and a fine layer dusted the lawn. While Jen was getting ready, I'd helped my nephews and Vera's son, Josh, finish building the snowman. He looked just like the snowman Jen and I had built that first Christmas together. We were getting married under a *chuppah* covered with snow white flowers on the very spot where we'd created our snow angel. Mr. Snowman, wearing a black bowtie and tall hat, was sharing the best man spotlight with my bud, Jaime, who stood next to Libby, Jen's maid of honor. Seats had been arranged for our guests, who I'd flown in on the Conquest Broadcasting jet, and there was also a white baby grand piano. Sitting at it was Roberta Flack herself—yes, I'd flown her in—playing and singing our song.

As the songstress tenderly sang "The First Time Ever I Saw

Your Face," my cock flexed and my heart melted as I beheld my beautiful bride, her eyes glistening with joyous tears. The earth moved beneath my feet as she slowly approached me, her gaze never leaving mine. I was giving her the wedding she always wanted. The wedding she deserved. The wedding we would remember forever.

Mr. Peace, Love, and Happiness was officiating. Yup, Reverend Dooby. Under a slightly overcast sky, I took my tiger in my arms, and we exchanged our vows. To put each other's needs before our own and to never stop loving each other in good times or bad times. She recited a sonnet while I recited a poem I'd composed. With snowflakes dancing all around us, I lifted her veil and tugged her head back by her ponytail. I held that pretty face in my gaze for a long hot beat and then kissed her the way I had the first time. That very first time I'd seen her face and my life had changed forever. As my mouth consumed hers in a passionate, all-consuming kiss, the sun broke through the clouds. Our snow angel was watching.

Chapter 28
Jennifer

That man.

As I stood on the balcony of the private villa Blake had rented and watched the sun set into the cerulean Tahitian sea, I couldn't stop reliving my wedding. They say the third time's a charm, but I would marry *that* man again and again. The beautiful memories whirled around in my head as the soft sound of the surf resounded in my ears.

Blake had given me the wedding every girl dreamed of. A celebration of love shared by the special people in our lives. I recited the Shakespearean sonnet and he composed a poem. Just for me. Okay, so he stole the first line from another Blake—"Tiger, tiger, burning bright"—but the rest of it was totally original. And so, so moving. The words were still dancing in my head. He compared me to a star and told me he loved me close up and from afar. And then he said I gave him direction and guiding light. "Until death do us part. My heart is yours; yours mine whatever our plight." He would totally always love me.

And then we said our "I do's" and he kissed me deeply, passionately. Just like that very first kiss that had started it all. When I danced in his arms to Roberta Flack's soulful rendition of "For the First Time in Forever" from my favorite movie, *Frozen*, my heart swelled with happiness, and then I danced in the arms of my dad to the singer's moving rendition of "The Wind Beneath My Wings." Yes, my other forever hero. I melted in his arms too.

Both my dad and Blake's gave awesome speeches that brought laughter as well as tears. And heartfelt, often hilarious toasts abounded. Everyone had an outrageous story to tell about Blake. My man was a very naughty boy. And I loved him all the more for it. One, in particular, tickled my heart. Jaime's. He ended it by toasting me: "To the woman who taught Blake Burns that his cock is connected to his heart." Everyone roared with laughter while a blushing Blake kissed me again.

I got a little drunk and sang "Roar" to Blake while Roberta belted the piano. Soon after, Libby caught my bouquet of fresh flowers picked right from our backyard, and Chaz caught my garter. But there was going to be another wedding before theirs. Over champagne and my mom's delicious homemade buttercream wedding cake, Grandma made a toast to her Blakela and Bubala *shtupping* in good health forever and then an announcement. She and Luigi were stopping off in Vegas on their way back to LA and getting married *shmarried*. Cheers erupted! YAY for Grandma!

After Grandma's announcement, Blake stole me away from the festivities, and we fucked our brains out in my childhood bedroom; the dress stayed put, and under the layers of tulle and lace, I came a multitude of glorious times.

Soon afterward, we reboarded the private plane. Though no longer blindfolded, I still had no idea where we were going. Blake still refused to tell me. And it was dark. Yet had it been daylight, I still wouldn't know because I didn't spend much time gazing out the window. My face was either buried between Blake's thighs or hovering over a chair cushion while he rammed into me from behind. And in between fucking our brains out, I slept dreamily in his arms in an in-flight bed made for royalty.

I returned to the moment. As the South Seas sun disappeared into the ocean like a ball of fire, a warm breath tickled my neck and a sultry voice swept me out of my delicious memories. Blake. My husband.

"Merry Christmas, baby."

I felt something hard and cold drape around my neck. I looked down and gasped. Circling my throat was a strand of lustrous beads that hung down past my breasts. They were iridescent green—almost the color of my eyes—and had a pavé diamond clasp. I spun around. Leaning against the balcony, I soaked in my breathtaking man. Shirtless, he was wearing a pair of white sweats that hung sexily low on his hips and skimmed his perfect pelvic V. The tropical breeze ruffled his tousled hair and that dazzling smile lit his gorgeous sun-kissed face. I cupped my palms over his broad sculpted shoulders and searched his ocean-blue eyes.

"Blake, Christmas is not for another five months. What is this?" Whatever this exquisite necklace was, it was mega-expensive.

He adjusted the strand. "They're Tahitian peacock green pearls—the rarest of all. I was going to give them to you last Christmas but—"

His voice trailed off, but before he could say another word, I crushed my lips against his. "Oh Blake, they're so beautiful. I love you so much," I gushed after breaking away.

With a yank of a string, he pulled off my bikini top. My breasts quivered under his lustful gaze. Grasping the rope of pearls, he began to slowly circle them around my nipples. At the erotic, cold touch of them, my buds hardened, and a hot rush of tingles blossomed in my core. Goose bumps spread across my flesh while wetness pooled between my legs.

"I want a proper thank you, *Mrs.* Burns," he purred, now squeezing together my breasts with the strand. My eyes shot down. A big bulge dominated his sweats. Obviously, the pearls were multi-functional. My new piece of jewelry was his new toy.

As his mouth melted into mine, I slid down his sweats and then my bikini bottom. Fisting his wondrous cock, I glided it inside me.

"That's better." He winked as he began to pound me.

By the following morning, his cock had been many places. And so had my pearls.

Mrs. Burns had a lot to look forward to. Our honeymoon had just begun.

Epilogue

Blake

Christmas, Five Years Later

"**M**erry Christmas, tiger," I said brightly after planting a loud wake-up kiss on my wife's warm lips. My gaze stayed on her as she fluttered opened her eyelids. She looked like an angel, her mouth parted slightly, her porcelain skin flawless, her lustrous hair fanned out like wings, and her eyes dreamy.

She smiled. "Merry Christmas, baby."

After five years of marriage, Jen had not converted to Judaism. But she had taken some courses at our family synagogue and was even studying Hebrew so she could read the prayers with me. And she'd become, thanks to Grandma's mentoring, a wonderful Jewish cook—even able to make a Chanukah brisket as good as hers. The arrangement we had worked for both of us, and best of all, we celebrated all the holidays we'd each grown up with. I had to admit Christmas was my favorite.

Jen sat up slowly. Her still sleepy eyes glanced down at my hand. "What's that you're holding?"

A fiendish grin spread across my face. "It's one of your Christmas presents," I replied, handing her the small gift-wrapped box. A sparkling green bow topped the shiny red paper.

Carefully, she plucked off the bow and then tore off the wrapping. Excitement danced in her eyes as she beheld the black velvet box beneath.

"Come on, open it," I urged. I couldn't wait to see the expression on her face. This was a good one. God's former gift to women was a genius when it came to giving gifts. Call me the gift that keeps on giving.

"Okay," she murmured, snapping open the lid. Her eyes grew wide as she stared at the iridescent pink ring.

"Is this a piece of jewelry?" she asked, her tone perplexed. She lifted the ring out of the box and put it on her middle finger. I must say it went very nicely with the pink tourmaline heart-pendant necklace I'd given her our very first Christmas together. Except it was a little big. Okay very big. That's because it was made for something super big. My cock.

I slipped the ring off her finger. "Baby, it's a toy for you. A piece of jewelry for *me*. A cock ring."

Her brows shot up. "A cock ring?"

Despite my giving her a battery-operated sex toy every Christmas (my little tradition), she was still so naïve it was adorable. I couldn't help but laugh. "Yeah, it's going to make me bigger and more powerful."

"But, Blake, you don't need to be any bigger or more powerful."

"Trust me, baby, every man can use a little extra something. And you're just going to love the attached vibrating heart bullet."

I'd done a lot of research looking for the perfect battery-operated accessory. Trust me, I was not the one-size-fits-all type of guy. The cock ring I'd finally found was made of a soft, stretchy material. It could expand as I expanded. Nice—totally worth the exorbitant price unless it was false advertising. I shoved the duvet down and there he was—Mr. Burns—commando and at attention, ready for playtime in our favorite playground. I'd woken up, as usual, with a mighty boner.

"Put the ring on me, tiger."

Wordlessly, she took the ring from me and slipped it over my enormous erection. Her innocent green eyes met mine, begging for further instruction.

"Now slide it down to the base."

Responsively, she edged it down with her deft fingers until it was right where I wanted it. It felt good—not too loose, not too tight. I flicked on the vibrator. The soft buzz sounded in my ears as I sat back on my elbows and flexed my knees.

"Sit on me, baby, facing the mirror." In my extensive research, I'd learned that reverse cowgirl was the ideal position for maximizing the benefits of this little toy. It happened to be one of our favorite positions. And this magical toy was only going to make it better.

Guiding my cock into her, she did as bid. I had a bird's eye view of her sweet ass and the beautiful curve of her back. Man, that delicious pair of dimples where the two met was so damn sexy. They fucking turned me on.

I began to thrust in and out of her, picking up speed with each long, hard stroke. I could feel my cock getting bigger, as if that was possible, swelling to epic proportions. A super-erection! My breathing grew shallow and I was working up a sweat. My buzzing cock was making me buzz everywhere. Jen reached her hands back and placed them firmly on my hipbones to hold on. This was one hell of a ride.

"Oh, Blake," she cried out, throwing her head back. "This is amazing."

Watching the two of us fuck in the mirror, I couldn't agree more. Besides being so hot and wet, she was taking my cock to the hilt. I felt the tip pounding her womb with each powerful thrust—for sure hitting her magic spot—while the vibrating bullet attachment stimulated her clit. I always went many rounds, but my, I meant *her,* new toy was sustaining my erection beyond belief. Holy shit! This toy was the bomb. Seriously, I'd give it ten stars on Amazon if I could. As my tiger began to whimper on the brink of an epic orgasm, a loud knock-knock-knock sounded at the door. *Shit.*

"Mommy, Daddy! Wakey up! I wanna see if Santa came and left me *pwesents."*

The other love of my life. Our adorable three-and-a-half-year-old...Leo. My heart melted at the sound of his sweet little raspy voice.

"Coming, sweetie pie," shouted Jennifer. "And so is Daddy." Oh, fuck were we. On the next hard thrust, she convulsed all around me while I exploded like a stick of dynamite. Playtime was over. Time to *unbig* myself. Next activity. I couldn't wait to open presents under our Christmas tree. To see my little man's expression as he unwrapped his, and that of my tiger when she saw what I had in store for her. *Ho! Ho! Ho!*

Our majestic Christmas tree sat in the bay window of our large living room. Almost ceiling high, it was decorated with many of the ornaments Jennifer had collected as a child. We'd picked out the tree together with Leo and had decorated it over cookies and hot chocolate. Leo loved helping hang the ornaments as much as he loved helping light our Chanukah candles.

Right after Leo—named after my grandpa, Leonard—was born, I sold my Wilshire Corridor condo and found our dream house right on the beautiful, coveted street across from the Santa Monica Stairs where Jen and I worked out every weekend. While it was hardly the size of my parents' palatial estate (something neither Jen nor I wanted), it was stately and spacious and reminded Jennifer of some of the large houses in Boise she'd grown up around. There was a big grassy back-yard, a gated pool, and a guest house where Jen's parents stayed whenever they visited. Which was often. In fact, they were occupying it right now. Barely dawn, I was sure they'd be here later in the morning to share our Christmas festivities. Most Christmases, we traveled to Boise and Sun Valley, but this time, we needed to stay close to home. Just in case...So, Jen's parents, never wanting to miss a Christmas with their beloved grandson, came to LA.

"Oh boy, Daddy! Looky at what Santa got me!" Leo squealed as he tore apart a huge box wrapped with whimsical snowman paper and a big bow. He could barely hold the package in his little hands. "Combat Wombats!"

"Wow!" I winked. "You must have been a really good boy." Yours truly, Santa, had cleaned out the entire section of these bestselling toys. I'd bought him everything from action figures to the motorized Wombatmobile, which he could actually sit in and drive down the street.

Leo smiled broadly, his two cute dimples bracketing his mouth just like mine. "Will you play with me, Daddy?"

God, I loved that last word. And the way he said it. *DAD-dee*. And I loved being *that* man. I told him for sure after breakfast. Leo gleefully opened the rest of his presents—okay, I was spoiling the kid, but what the hell—and then Jennifer and I exchanged ours. She handed me mine first. It was monstrous and quite heavy. I carefully tore apart the exquisite metallic wrapping. At the sight of what was beneath, my eyes grew wide and my heart smiled. It was a framed oil portrait of Leo and me. I fucking loved it.

"Tiger, I love it," I said, forcing myself not to say the f-word in front of Leo. I smacked my lips against hers. Leo was too busy playing with his new toys to notice.

Jen smiled warmly and brushed her hand through my hair. "I want you to hang it in your new office."

That was a great idea. At the age of thirty-five, I was now the head of Conquest Broadcasting. I'd inherited my retired father's expansive top floor office suite and had more wall space than I knew what do with. I knew exactly where I was going to hang it. Right by the entrance so I could look at it all day. I gently set the painting down on the antique rug. Now, it was my turn to give Jen her present. I handed her a small Christmassy shopping bag to which I'd attached a large SpongeBob "Merry Christmas" balloon.

"I know it doesn't look like much." My voice trailed off as she took the bag from me and removed a bright red eight by ten envelope. My eyes stayed fixed on her as she unfastened it and slipped out a single sheet of paper. Her green eyes widened and her jaw dropped to the floor as she read the announcement. The paper shook in her trembling hands.

"Oh my God, Blake. You bought back Peanuts?"

Peanuts was the children's network she'd hoped to work at when she was first hired by my father, but he'd sold it just before she came on board. Jen had always dreamed of working in children's programming but was forced to work for the porn channel I headed up. SIN-TV. What a fine job she had done. With passion and perseverance, she'd created a mega-successful women's erotica channel, MY SIN-TV. But now, it was time for her to move on. And to have a family-friendly career. I'd closed the top secret deal only yesterday. Peanuts was officially now once again part of the Conquest Broadcasting media family. And it was going to be part of our little family too.

I held Jen's stunned face in my gaze. "And, tiger, you're going to run it. Get used to your new title: President, Peanuts TV."

She gasped. A hand flew to her gaping mouth. Finally, she found her voice. A stammer. "B-but, who's going to run MY SIN-TV?"

"Don't worry about it, baby. I'm promoting Myles." Myles Harding was my gay head of programming for SIN-TV, but I'd learned he'd been dying to work for our women's counterpart. It was all going to work out perfectly. My tiger was finally going to have the chance to live out her dream and create her very own SpongeBob. And a lineup of programs that would make me proud—and our children elated. She was going to be *our* superhero. With my thumb, I tilted up her chin.

"Do you like your present, tiger?"

A huge smile adorned her face. "Oh, Blake, it's the best Christmas gift ever." She flung her arms around me and crushed her lips against mine. Our tongues danced joyously, and I became lost in our passionate embrace. A little voice broke us apart.

"Mommy, I'm *hungwee.*"

Jen flushed with embarrassment and excused herself to make breakfast.

While she toiled in the kitchen, Leo and I retreated to the adjacent family room where we cuddled together on the comfy over-stuffed couch. With Leo snug on my lap, I picked up the remote and clicked on the big screen TV facing us. Wouldn't you know it...the SpongeBob Christmas episode was on—the very one I'd watched with Jen at her parents' house—our fateful first Christmas together. Leo loved SpongeBob as much as Jen and I did. As was our ritual, the two of us sang the silly opening credits song together at the top of our lungs, shouting out SpongeBob SquarePants each time it was mentioned.

The episode began, and Leo instantly broke out into a cluster of giggles at one of SpongeBob's hilariously endearing antics. His sweet laughter was contagious. Ruffling my little man's unruly dark hair, I joined him.

My little cub. He was the spitting image of me. Except he had Jen's incredible long-lashed green eyes. Every time I looked into them, I recalled the first time I set my eyes on Jen's—the day I interviewed her for a job at SIN-TV. And how they'd mesmerized me and reduced me to a spluttering mess.

Grandma had said, "Blakela, you're gonna get *vun* just like you." She was right, and she was wrong.

I was a holy terror as a child. But not, my Leo. I knew every parent boasted their kid's the best kid in the world. But let me tell you, mine was. He'd been the perfect baby. Slept the night and was all smiles. And now he was the sweetest, smartest toddler in the world. Already potty trained. Number one in his pre-school. And definitely, the most popular kid too. Little girls fawned all over him. This kid was born a player. On the playground, he was already breaking lots of shovels *and* hearts. I was going to have to teach him a thing or two about love when he got older.

Leo was the perfect name for him. Born in July, he was definitely a lion. He ruled the playground; he ruled our lives. He roared when he cried; he roared when he laughed. His middle name was Ness, which meant miracle in Hebrew and indeed, he was. A gift from God. Following Jen's hysterectomy, Marcy had told us since Jen had been spared an ovary, she could still produce quality eggs. The problem was she couldn't carry a child. Marcy turned us on to one of her colleagues—a top fertility doctor. And simultaneously introduced us to a very special surrogate who wanted to carry our child. On the very first attempt, one of my little swimmers fertilized one of Jen's eggs via IVF—in vitro fertilization. The embryo was transferred to our surrogate and nine months later, we were a family.

Halfway through the cartoon, the tantalizing aroma of pancakes and sausage drifted in the air. I was famished.

Just as the episode wrapped up, Jen called out, "Guys, breakfast is ready."

I set my little man on the floor. "C'mon, I'll race you to the kitchen."

Leo's eyes lit up. It was another one of our rituals. I always let him win. I was raising him—or should I say, we were raising him to be a winner just the way my parents raised me. And instilling in him the value of going after what you want in life. So far, that was a lot of toys, cookies, and goodnight stories.

"Mommy, I beat Daddy again," boasted Leo as he energetically ran into the large kitchen on his little pajama-clad legs.

A big smile beamed on Jen's animated face as I feigned exhaustion with pants. What an actor I was! The one thing I never had to act out was climaxing with my tiger. Fortunately, Leo's room was far away enough from ours so my tiger could still roar my name. And man, did she.

With breakfast already on the table, Jen swept Leo into her arms and smothered him with kisses. "That's awesome, my sweetness."

I eyed them proudly. Happiness filled every crevice of my body. I always knew my Jen would make a great mother and she was. And soon, there would be another cub to add to our den.

Joining them at the kitchen table, I couldn't wait to dig into breakfast. I was ravenous. I reached for the bottle of maple syrup on the lazy Susan, and as I doused my sausage with it, my eyes met Jen's. Ever since that breakfast over five years ago at Jaime and Gloria's beach house, maple syrup made me horny as hell. It had the same effect on Jen. We read each other's eyes. Yup, she was thinking what I was thinking. Right after breakfast, we'd have our live-in nanny take Leo for a ride in his new Wombatmobile down the street while we fucked our brains out and sent each other orbiting.

As Jen poured coffee from the French press into my mug,

her cell phone, charging on the counter, rang. Her signature ringtone—the melody of Roberta Flack's "The First Time Ever I Saw Your Face"—played. Setting the glass vestibule down, she leapt up from her seat and sprinted to the phone. My gaze stayed riveted on her great ass and taut legs that had become shapelier and more muscular from doing the Santa Monica Stairs with me regularly. Her ponytail bounced with her sprite gait.

Putting the phone to her ear, her eyes grew as wide as saucers. "Oh my God," I overheard her say. "I'll be right there." She ended the call.

"Baby, what's going on?"

"Marcy's at Cedars."

"Holy shit!" *Fuck.* I didn't mean to curse in front of my son. I just couldn't help it.

"I'm heading over. Get there as soon as you can."

Not bothering to change out of her sweats, Jen grabbed her car keys. She brushed by the table, giving Leo and me each a big kiss, and dashed out the door.

It was time to break out another expensive box of Cuban cigars.

Jennifer

Libby wasn't supposed to give birth for another two weeks. Her water had broken early, and when I arrived at Cedars, she was already in the delivery room. Marcy was hovering over her, in green scrubs and a facemask, similar to the ones I was forced to put on. A team of nurses surrounded them.

Libby was plopped up against a mountain of pillows, clad in a pink hospital gown, her knees bent and splayed.

"Lib!" I shouted out, running up to her side.

My bestie smiled faintly and managed to wave to me.

"Breathe," Marcy commanded.

"How's she doing?" I asked Blake's sister, my voice laden with worry.

"Great."

Libby blew out short, sharp breaths. Pants.

I squeezed her hand. Her fiery red curls were matted to her sweat-laced face.

"Push," ordered Marcy.

"Fuck," grunted Libby as she did as asked. Her freckled face turned as red as her hair.

"Are you in pain?" My voice was shaky.

Breathing as instructed, she shook her head. Her extended belly rose up and down.

Libby was giving birth to our second child.

Yes, my best friend in the world, now happily married to a great guy and the mother of twins (another story!), had offered to be our surrogate after I told her Marcy, our first surrogate, felt our chances for a successful pregnancy would be better with a younger woman.

Choosing not to remarry though she was contently involved with an older, respected doctor, Marcy was now close to forty-five. She was the best sister-in-law in the world. That day in her office two months after my surgery, she gave Blake and me a priceless wedding present. The gift of life. *A family.* As I watched Libby labor, I flashed back to that moment and then to the epic birth of Leo. After a long struggle, he came out roaring like a lion.

A shriek from Libby pierced the air and cut into my thoughts. My already frenetic heartbeat sped up.

"One more push!" urged Marcy.

My unblinking eyes stayed glued on my best friend as she grunted a loud breath, tears streaming down her scrunched up face, and then they widened as a tiny dark-haired head emerged between her bent legs. I bit down hard on my bottom lip as she continued to grunt and push out the tiny life form with Marcy's gloved hands gently guiding it into the world.

The next thing I knew, the unmistakable wails of a newborn were filling my ears.

With a heavy sigh of relief, Libby fell back against the pillows. I hugged her.

"Lib, you did it!"

"We did it!" Libby beamed, her voice strong for a woman who'd just given birth.

Oh, my Lib! *Always there for me!* My eyes shifted to Marcy.

Smiling beneath her mask, she cradled the tiny baby in her arms while two of the nurses cleaned her up and then swaddled her in a soft pink blanket.

"Congratulations!" they said in unison as they transferred her into my arms.

Breathless and wordless, I gazed down at our little girl. Our miracle. Our beautiful miracle. I couldn't wait for Blake to meet her.

Blake

It took all I had not to drive like a madman. Thank fucking God, the streets were empty. A rarity for LA but typical for Christmas Day. Jen's father was seated beside me in the Range Rover (our family car), and in the backseat, Leo was strapped into his car seat with Mrs. McCoy planted on the adjacent cream leather seat. My heart was in my throat and beating a mile a minute. "Santa Claus is Coming to Town" was blasting on the radio, and Leo was singing along in his adorable pitch-perfect voice. Oh, yeah, Santa had come. That's for sure. But I just didn't expect *this* present today of all days. The plans we had for later were scrapped—to see an animated movie and then go to Chinatown with my parents, Grandma, and Luigi. I tried calling Jen. No answer. Clenching the steering wheel and my teeth, I could hear my palpitating heart in my ear and feel it beat in my throat. Libby was way early and I was fucking freaking.

Arriving at Cedars, I left the car with the VIP valet, and with Leo riding me piggyback, I dashed into the hospital. The McCoys trailed close behind us, fit enough to keep up with me.

"Daddy, why we go to the hospital?" Leo breathed into my ear. "I no fall down."

Besides being born here, he'd been to Cedars once before—the emergency room—when he'd fallen off our backyard jungle gym and cut open his chin. My poor little man needed three stitches. While he was as brave as the lion he was, yours truly, Mr. Cowardly, almost needed smelling salts to get through the ordeal.

"Why, Daddy?" my son asked again.

"It's a surprise," I said breathlessly. *And it better be a good one.*

"Tell me, Daddy, what it is," Leo begged.

Before I could respond, my cell phone rang. My breath hitched as I picked it up on the first ring. Jen!

Thank you, Jesus. Now, I just had to find Room 3020.

Jennifer

"Oh honey, she looks just like you!" said my teary-eyed mother, who was gathered around me along with my elated father, Blake, and Leo. I was seated in a comfortable armchair, our newborn in my arms. Libby, believe it or not, had already rebounded from the record-fast delivery and was taking a stroll through the maternity ward to give us some alone time with the new addition to our family.

"An Irish beauty!" chimed in my proud dad.

I glanced down at her. Indeed, she was with her milky skin, a tuft of ebony hair, and long-lashed blue-green eyes. Just fed, her rosebud lips pursed with contentment. I gently kissed the top of her silky scalp and inhaled her intoxicating newborn scent. Lifting my head, my eyes met Blake's glistening blue orbs. Standing motionless, he was a cross between a zombie and a god.

"Here, Blake. Hold her." I stood up and carefully transferred our little bundle of love into his strong manly arms.

"Hi, princess," he said softly, the awed expression on his face melting my heart.

Never taking his eyes off her, he slowly lowered himself to the armchair. Leo was eye-level with the baby.

"Say hi to your sister, Maeve, my little man."

Maeve. Blake and I had chosen that name together. An homage to my late grandmother, it meant "the cause of great joy" and indeed, she was. The best Christmas present ever.

Staring at his sister, Leo asked, "Where did she come from, Daddy? Don't babies come from mommies' tummies?"

A smile lit Blake's lips. "She's magic. Just like you."

Puzzled, adorable Leo cocked his head. "Me abracadabra?"

Blake chuckled. "One day when you're a big boy, I'll teach you the trick."

Leo reciprocated with a big dimpled smile and then unexpectedly, he kissed our newborn on her forehead. My beaming parents hovered over them.

I quickly snapped a photo with my iPhone. And then I blinked my eyes like the shutter of a camera lens and took a mental snapshot of this magnificent moment that would stay in my mind forever. The album of life.

Overwhelmed with emotion, I continued to gaze at Blake—*that* man with whom I'd shared this incredible journey. Life, I'd learned, is not a fait accompli. A simple dare can change the course of everything...take you down a miraculous road you thought you'd never travel. A road to happiness and true love.

As Blake lovingly held our little girl with our precious little boy beside him, my heart exploded. My body tingled from my head to my toes. And tears welled up in my eyes. Blake had given me more than happiness. He'd given *me* joy. An emotion so powerful it couldn't be put into words.

I looked forward to the next leg of our journey. To raising our children and growing old together. In my heart, I knew Leo would one day grow up to be *that* special man to a wonderful woman and our little princess would find her own *that* man to love and protect her. Like I had with Blake Burns.

My husband. My lover. The father of our children. My hero.

Oh, how I love *that* man.

THE END

…well, almost…

A LETTER FROM BLAKE

Hey there, all you beautiful and sexy readers~

Come on. You know me by now. There's no way I was going to let my tiger get the last word in as much as I love her. I am, after all, that good-looking guy on the cover, the one who inspired this story.

I just want to thank you for sharing our adventure. It was some rollercoaster ride, huh? A couple of times we almost fell off. And no way could I have saved her. But there's something mightier than a superhero. Another four-letter F-word. *Fate.* They say fate's a bitch, but I'm glad she is because Jen and I ended up together.

My sister told me Jen's made me a better person. She's right. My tiger has. Remember that guy at the beginning who thought with his cock? Well, I've got to admit I still do, but like my pal, Jaime Zander, said at our wedding, I learned my cock is connected to my heart. My cock has an appetite but my heart hungers too. I fuck hard. I love harder.

It's sometimes hard to believe the player you once knew is now the family guy. Man, if I'd only known what it's like to hold a newborn in my arms, I would have had kids a lot sooner, but I had to wait for the right woman. Jen will tell you I went to heaven and back. And the first time my little cubs smiled at me, my heart melted like an M&M in my mouth.

Just like my father, I'm damn good at my new job though I'll confess Mr. Gift Who Keeps Giving spoils those two beautiful kids. I'm also a little over protective. Okay, so I'm over the top in that department. Being a parent brings out the superhero in me. Trust me, God help the man who lays hands on my princess—even worse, who lays her. He'd better have a safe place to hide.

Yup, Jen turned me into a man I can be proud of. A loving, loyal husband, father, friend, and lover. And she turned me into a poet too. I've come a long way since copying Hallmark cards and writing those dumbass limericks. Okay, so my poetry isn't going to win a Pulitzer, but I've got to say it's pretty darn good.

They say the third time's a charm. And it is. After our third wedding, we got our happily every after. We still have our little ups and downs—what marriage doesn't?—but it's perfectly imperfect. I will love Jen for richer, for poorer (fat chance), in sickness and in health until death do us part. My tiger's stuck with me forever. I will always be *that* man.

Thank you for rooting for us. Putting up with us. (Yeah, I know you wanted to slap us more than a couple of times.) And sharing our story. **I T**otally **A**nd **A**lways **L**ove **Y**ou!

I.T.A.L.Y.~ xo Blake

P.S. And our story's not over! Be prepared to laugh, cry and swoon all over again!

A NOTE FROM NELLE

My Belles~

Thank you so much for reading THAT MAN: THE WED-
DING STORY. If you loved it, I hope you will write a review.
It doesn't matter how long or short it is. It would mean so
much to me as reviews help others find my books.

I can't wait to bring you THAT MAN 6: THE ANNIVER-
SARY STORY. In case you missed the earlier preview, check
it out on my website:

nellelamour.com/that-man-6

Other books that feature scorchin' hot Blake Burns and his
tiger include my UNFORGETTABLE Series (also available as
a Box Set) and my romantic comedy standalone, BABY
DADDY. Check them out these hot and hilarious romantic
comedies on my website!

UNFORGETTABLE
nellelamour.com/unforgettable-series
BABY DADDY
nellelamour.com/baby-daddy

If you want to read a sampling of my books, please check out
my romance compilation.

NAUGHTY NELLE
nellelamour.com/naughty-nelle

I hope to bring you more books soon. Both REMEMBER ME, a steamy, suspenseful romance ripped from the headlines, and my "mystery book," a brand new standalone romantic comedy, will be published in Fall 2018. Please follow me on social media to learn about my releases, sales, and giveaways!

MWAH! ~ Nelle ♥

ACKNOWLEDGMENTS

As I wrote the two little words, "The End," tears filled my eyes. What a journey this has been! I have so many people to thank.

Deep breath! This is going to be long and I hope don't forget anyone.

Usually, I thank them last, but this time they're going first. My family. Thank you for putting up with me while I wrote and edited this epic story over the past year. My sweet girls, I'm sorry for all the crappy meals, the number of times I growled, "Leave me alone," and all the times I told you to Uber home. A special shout out goes to my husband—my very own *that* man who picked up much of the mommy slack while I slaved at my computer. By the way, he's convinced he's Blake. I say wishful thinking, or should I say I wish. Regardless, thank you, babe, for your love and support—and for admittedly giving me some of my best Blake lines.

My second heartfelt round of thanks goes to my amazing beta readers. Across the series, they include in alphabetical order: Kelly Butterfield, Michelle Coddington, Amber Lynn Escalera, Kashunna Fly, Kellie Fox, Alma Garcia, Tracy "Sunshine" Graver, Gloria Herrera, Wanda Kather, Cindy Meyer, Kim Pinard Newsome, Jen Oreto, Sheena Reid, Jasmine Roman, Jenn Moshe, Karen Silverstein, and Jeanette Sinfield. I'm blessed to have the best betas in the whole wide world. You are all so smart, funny, and insightful, and didn't hold back for better or for worse. You have become more than betas; you have become my friends.

Arianne Richmonde and Adriane Leigh, my two best writer friends (my BWFs) also deserve big hugs. Thank you for reading *THAT MAN* and for all your great suggestions. Most of all, thank you for keeping me sane and getting me through the many times I thought I could never write another word or finish. Trust me, only fellow authors understand the formidable challenge of writing a book, let alone a five-part series. I don't know what I would have done without my besties, who listened to my rants as well as shared many laughs and glasses of wine.

Many of you may remember that *THAT MAN 1* first appeared in *Love and Laughter,* a romantic comedy anthology. I want to thank Zirconia Publishing and all the wonderful, hardworking authors who participated in that anthology and worked painstakingly together to make it a *USA Today* bestseller. These amazing ladies and a gent include Abi Aiken, Harper Ashe, Dez Burke, Adriana Hunter, Arianne Richmonde, Aubrey Rose, Marian Tee, and Terry Towers. Love to you all.

The success of the *THAT MAN* series can also be attributed to the many hardworking bloggers who embraced Blake Burns and wrote wonderful reviews that helped spread the word. A special thanks to Mary Tatar of Love Between the Sheets Promotions who spearheaded my blog tours as well as wrote some of my favorite reviews. There are so many bloggers to thank, but I want to single out a few who have been with me throughout my writing career and who have gone out of their way to put *THAT MAN* in front of readers. They include in no particular order: Jen Oreto/*Book Avenue Reviews,* Becky

Barney/*The Fairest of All,* Ellen Widom/*The Book Bellas,* Selene Cabadas/*Sassy Girl Reviews,* Gloria Herrera/*As You Like it Reviews,* Desirae Shie/*Books, Chocolate, and Lipgloss,* Jennifer Noe/*The Book Blog,* Mags Pereira and Jewelz Fowler/*SMI Book Club,* Lynn Booth/*Chasing Orion's Rouge Odyssey,* Sheeba Ellison/*Bedtime Reviews,* Lorraine Masterson/*Rusty's Reading,* Gillian Gybras/*A is for Alpha B is for Books,* Cindy Meyer and Deborah Presley /*The Book Enthusiast,* Jennifer McCoy/*SubClub Books,* Lisa Pantano Kane and Jennifer Skewes/ *Three Chicks and Their Books,* and Nicole Scott/*My Book Filled Life.* I also want to thank the wonderful Kylie McDermott and George Turney/*Give me Book Promotions* for hosting the Cover Release and Release Blitz for both the THAT MAN TRILOGY (Boxed Set) and *THAT MAN: WEDDING STORY (*Boxed Set).

In addition to being one of my favorite bloggers, Gloria Herrera is also my incredible assistant. She is responsible for all those amazing graphics you see on Facebook and does so many other things for me. She keeps me organized and sane, and makes me laugh with her wicked sense of humor. If it it weren't for her, I seriously don't know how I'd find the time to write. She deserves more than a thanks...a hug! I adore her!

I would be remiss not to thank one other entity—the amazing newsletter, *Book Bub.* I feel so blessed that you chose *THAT MAN 1* as one of your "Free Books of the Day." Thanks to that promotion, the story of Blake and his tiger touched the hearts of countless readers and made *THAT MAN* an international bestseller.

The team that ultimately brings my books to fruition merits a big shout out. Thank you, Paul Salvette/BB eBooks for flawlessly formatting both my e-books and paperbacks and putting up with all my crazy revisions; Arijana Karcic /Cover It! Designs for all the glorious covers. and Karen Lawson for proofing my manuscripts and for making me laugh with your snarky comments. A big kiss goes to Robert Reider, my gorgeous cover model, and to his delightful mother Klara, who reached out to me and has become a lovely friend.

Almost last but not least, I want to thank all my readers who have embraced *THAT MAN* and fallen in love, like me, with Blake Burns. Had it not been for your support and encouragement, I wouldn't have written Blake and Jen's wedding story or yet another continuation, *THAT MAN* 6: *The Anniversary Story*. A special shout-out goes to those who have written heartfelt reviews, sent me heartwarming emails, and commented or PM'd me on Facebook. Your kind, often beautiful words always brighten my day and make me persevere. My love to all of you; you are the reason I write.

Finally, I want to thank my father-in-law, aka "Mr. I. Wackit," and my open-minded mom for believing in me and being proud of me. And thank you, Daddy, too, for always being there for me. So much of your *menschiness* inspired Blake. I miss you and will always love you. *Sniff*

Okay. I did it! I hope I got everyone!

To all my Belles, thank you again from the bottom of my heart for your love and support. It means the world to me. While you await my next book, enjoy Grandma's famous matzo ball soup. The recipe follows!

MWAH! ~ Nelle ♥

BE SURE TO SIGN UP FOR MY NEWSLETTER
Newsletter: nellelamour.com/newsletter

GRANDMA'S FAMOUS MATZO BALL SOUP
(Serves 6)

Bubalas, trust me, the *vay* to a man's heart—and his *shmekel*—is through his stomach. Make him my delicious matzo ball soup and you'll be *shtupping* for hours. *Zei gezunt!* Enjoy!

INGREDIENTS

CHICKEN STOCK

- 1 4-5-lb chicken (preferably Kosher), cut into 8 pieces
- 1 pound chicken wings, necks, and/or backs
- 2 large yellow onions, unpeeled, quartered
- 6 celery stalks, cut into 1" pieces
- 4 large carrots, peeled, cut into 1" pieces
- 1 large parsnip, peeled, cut into 1" pieces
- 1 large shallot, quartered
- 1 head of garlic, halved crosswise
- 6 sprigs flat-leaf parsley
- 1 tablespoon black peppercorns

MATZO BALLS

- 3 large eggs, beaten
- 3/4 cup matzo meal
- 1/4 cup schmaltz (chicken fat), melted
- 3 tablespoons club soda (my secret ingredient for fluffy, melt-in-you mouth balls)
- 1 1/4 teaspoon kosher salt

GARNISH

- 2 small carrots, peeled
- Pinch of kosher salt
- 2 tablespoons coarsely chopped fresh dill
- Coarsely ground fresh black pepper

PREPARATION

CHICKEN STOCK

- Bring all ingredients and 12 cups cold water to a boil in a very large (at least 12-qt.) stockpot. Reduce heat to medium-low and simmer until chicken breasts are cooked through and tender, about 20 minutes.

- Transfer breasts to a plate (remaining chicken parts are strictly for stock). Let breasts cool slightly, then remove meat and return bones to stock. Shred meat. Let cool, tightly wrap, and chill.

- Continue to simmer stock, skimming surface occasionally, until reduced by one-third, about 2 hours. Strain chicken stock through a fine-mesh sieve into a large saucepan (or airtight container, if not using right away); discard solids. You should have about 8 cups.

- **DON'T** *VAIT!* **DO AHEAD**: Stock can be made 2 days ahead. Let cool; cover and chill. Keep reserved chicken meat chilled.

MATZO BALL MIXTURE

- Mix beaten eggs, matzo meal, schmaltz, club soda, and salt in a medium bowl (mixture *vill* resemble *vet* sand; it *vill* firm up as it rests). Cover and chill at least 2 hours.

- **DO AHEAD**: Mixture can be made 1 day ahead. Keep chilled.

ASSEMBLY

- Bring chicken stock to a boil in a large saucepan. Add carrots; season *vith* salt.—Reduce heat and simmer until carrots are tender, 5–7 minutes. Remove from heat, add reserved breast meat, and cover. Set soup aside.

- *Meanvhile,* bring a large pot of *vell*-salted water to a boil. Scoop out 2-tablespoon-size portions matzo ball mixture and, using *vet* hands, gently roll into balls. (I LOVE ROLLING THE BALLS!)

- Add matzo balls to *vater* and reduce heat so *vater* is at a gentle simmer (too much bouncing around *vill* break them up). Cover pot and cook matzo balls until cooked through and starting to sink, 20–25 minutes. (DON'T LET THEM SINK ALL THE *VAY*. SINKERS ARE STINKERS!)

- **DO AHEAD**: Using a slotted spoon, transfer matzo balls to bowls. Ladle soup over, top *vith* dill, and season *vith* pepper. And enjoy!

ES GEZUNTERHEYT!

ABOUT THE AUTHOR

Nelle L'Amour is a *New York Times* and *USA Today* bestselling author who lives in Los Angeles with her Prince Charming-ish husband, twin princesses, and a bevy of royal pain-in-the-butt pets. A former executive in the entertainment industry with a prestigious Humanitas Prize for promoting human dignity and freedom to her credit, she gave up playing with Barbies a long time ago, but still enjoys playing with toys with her husband. While she writes in her PJs, she loves to get dressed up and pretend she's Hollywood royalty. Her steamy stories feature characters that will make you laugh, cry, and swoon and stay in your heart forever.

To learn about her new releases, sales, and giveaways, please sign up for her newsletter and follow her on social media. Nelle loves to hear from her readers.

Check out her cool website:
www.nellelamour.com

Sign up for her fun newsletter:
nellelamour.com/newsletter

Join her FB Reader Group: Nelle's Belles:
facebook.com/groups/1943750875863015

Follow her on Bookbub:
bookbub.com/authors/nelle-l-amour

Join her Facebook Fan Page
facebook.com/NelleLamourAuthor

Follow her on Twitter:
twitter.com/nellelamour

Email her at:
nellelamour@gmail.com

Follow her on Amazon:
amazon.com/Nelle-LAmour/e/B00ATHR0LQ

BOOKS BY NELLE L'AMOUR

Unforgettable
Unforgettable Book 1
Unforgettable Book 2
Unforgettable Book 3

Alpha Billionaire Duet
TRAINWRECK 1
TRAINWRECK 2

A Standalone Romantic Comedy
Baby Daddy

An OTT Insta-love Standalone
The Big O

THAT MAN Series
THAT MAN 1
THAT MAN 2
THAT MAN 3
THAT MAN 4
THAT MAN 5
THAT MAN 6

Gloria
Gloria's Secret
Gloria's Revenge
Gloria's Forever

An Erotic Love Story
Undying Love
Endless Love

Writing as E.L. Sarnoff
DEWITCHED: The Untold Story of the Evil Queen
UNHITCHED: The Untold Story of the Evil Queen 2

Boxed Sets
THAT MAN TRILOGY
THAT MAN: THE WEDDING STORY
Unforgettable: The Complete Series
Gloria's Secret: The Trilogy
Seduced by the Park Avenue Billionaire
Naughty Nelle

Made in the USA
Columbia, SC
03 January 2023

75433768R00221